RUNNING FOR LOVE

THE FOR LOVE SERIES BOOK 2

AMY LONG

FULLMETAL**WORLDWIDE**

FULL METAL WORLDWIDE

ALSO BY AMY LONG

To the man who saw how great we would be together before
I did.
Thank you for running after me.

RUNNING FOR LOVE

THE FOR LOVE SERIES BOOK 2

CHAPTER ONE

DANA

"So, how are you settling in?"

The words are out of Liv's mouth as soon as we sit down for lunch. It's been a few years since we lived in the same city but now that I'm in the D.C. area too we'll be able to make lunch a regular thing, even if I have to picnic in her classroom to do it.

"If you mean, are all the boxes unpacked, then I'm settling in well. There's just a few left in the garage, but it's mostly done. If you mean at my job, I'm settling ok. I hate being the new girl, everyone already has their cliques, and you have to figure out which one you want to be a part of and if they'll have you. It's like high school all over again."

"Tell me about it. Middle school faculty is the same way." Liv says candidly. "But of course, once people found out I'm married to a Senator, they all wanted to be my friend."

"Bless your heart," I reply with sarcasm and an eye roll.

"Shut up." Liv laughs, throwing her napkin at me. "Well, now that you're settled, you need to meet people. Reed and I have friends over every Sunday for dinner, I told you about it before. It's an informal thing, and I want you to come."

"Oh, how the tables have turned. Not that long ago I was saying the same thing to you." I remind her.

"I know. When I moved to Dallas, you forced me to get out of the house and meet people. And because of that, because of you, I met Reed. I want to return the favor."

I did do that and look how happy they are. Really, I told her she needed to meet a man, and that's exactly what happened. Sometimes, I'm brilliant.

"Who all will be there?"

"It's the same group of people every week as long as they're in town. They've become like a second family to us. It's a few of our neighbors, Dave, with whoever he's seeing at the moment," Liv rolls her eyes, "and a few people Reed and Dave know from work."

"Other senators?" I ask warily. Being friendly with a senator who happens to be married to my best friend is one thing but hanging out with a group of senators every weekend seems a little daunting.

"No, no other senators. Just regular people. You do know senators are regular people too, right?"

"Of course I do. I know Reed." Who I still get a little nervous around. Probably because the man is too handsome for his own good. I swear if he was a model, he would be on the cover of every men's magazine.

"Hello, Sweetheart." Speak of the devil.

Reed Langford, US Senator and Liv's husband, slides out the chair next to Liv and sits. She beams at him, leaning in for a kiss he happily supplies and for a tiny little second, I'm jealous.

The chair next to me scraps across the linoleum floor before a body drops into it and settles up to the table beside me. A navy jacket covered arm rests next to mine on the table and I'm studying the masculine hand attached when a voice draws my attention.

"Since they're a little busy, let me introduce myself."

My brain starts processing him frame by frame. His tanned hand and long fingers. Silver watch. White shirt sleeve under navy jacket. Up a long arm of navy to a wide shoulder. Clean shaven, angled jaw. Lips that are just a little uneven but smiling. Straight nose.

I've just made it to his whiskey brown eyes when he speaks again.

"Mitch Ainsley."

He's holding out his right hand to me and woodenly I reach out for it. My hand slides into his and everything around us fades away. I can't hear the noisy diners surrounding us or smell the heavenly scent of fries and apple pie. I don't see anything beyond the man next to me. His hand, wrapped around mine, feels like falling into bed after a long day. Like a warm hug on a rainy afternoon. Like coming home after being away.

It just feels right and if I'm not mistaking the sparks pinging between us, I think he feels the same way.

"Dana Tolliver." My name comes out in a hushed whisper, reverent to the significance of the moment.

Mitch graces me with a devilish smile, one that has me mentally placing his image on those magazine covers instead of Reed, with the words 'Sexiest Man Alive!' and everything inside me melts. He leans closer and matches my tone.

"It's a pleasure to meet you, Dana."

"Oh, sorry! I didn't introduce you two." Liv gushes across from us.

Reed pulls her back into him and smothers a laugh. "I think they managed it on their own, Sweetheart." He says before kissing her temple.

"Well, good. I was just telling Dana about Sunday dinner."

"I'm surprised you weren't there last week." Reed kids with me.

"I was still unpacking boxes, trying to get as much done as I could before Monday. I wasn't sure how much free time I would have once I started the new job."

"What do you do?" Mitch asks.

I take my time turning to meet his eyes again before I answer. "I'm a paralegal at Wallace, Dunn and Fields."

He adjusts in his chair to face me better and leans his elbow on the table. "Really? I'm in the legal field too."

The space between us seems to grow smaller and my skin vibrates from the electricity buzzing around us. I'm energized and frozen at the same time, drinking in the way being near this man makes me feel.

The spell is broken when the chairs behind us are pulled out and more diners sit, but Mitch never turns away from me. When the noise level drops, I try to pick up where we left off.

"You're an attorney?"

Mitch is focused solely on me. "Something like that." He answers vaguely.

"Something like that," Reed states with a laugh. "He's a US Assistant Attorney General."

Mitch looks at me and shrugs like it's no big deal but I see the stain of pink beneath his tanned skin. He's not flaunting his fancy job, something attorneys are usually known for, in fact, he seems a little embarrassed to have it brought up. Interesting.

A soft kick to my shin alerts me Liv wants my attention. I kick her back, making a subtle 'what the hell' face. Her eyes dart back and forth from Mitch to me, and I know she's asking if I'm interested in him or not. I guess she thinks he can't see her or maybe she just doesn't care. Falling in love has made her bolder and honestly, it looks good on her.

Rolling my eyes, something I really need to stop doing, I hitch the side of my mouth and she practically squeals in her seat with excitement.

"So, Dana, you'll come to dinner Sunday night? Mitch will be there." Liv says, not even bothering to hide her motive.

I give her another kick under the table, this one a little harder.

"It's our Sunday night ritual. You have to come." Reed smirks, playing along with his wife's matchmaking plan.

I feel Mitch lean into me, and I know he's about to close the case. "Yeah, I'll be there, Dana. You should come."

Looking back at his magazine worthy face, I let myself swoon for a second then give them the answer they're waiting for.

"I'll be there."

CHAPTER TWO

MITCH

"How could I say no?" Dana says, smiling coyly at me and it feels like the clouds have parted and the sun is shining directly on me. Interesting.

The waitress stops at our table, looking down as she pulls a notepad and pen from her apron.

"Hi, I'm Melissa. What can I..." Her words trail off as her eyes lift, meeting mine and I hit her with a smile. Three seconds that feel like hours later, she visibly shakes her head to clear it and get back on task.

3
2
1

"What can I..."

She trails off again when she sees Reed. I lift my hand, covering my mouth to keep in the chuckle straining to come out. It's pretty comical, but Reed takes it in stride and lucky for him, Liv does too.

"We both want water," Liv tells her politely while waiting to be noticed.

The flustered waitress nods a few times, looks down at the notepad and pen like she doesn't know what to do with them, then looks to Dana for help.

"I'll have water too," Dana says.

"Make that four," I add on and get Melissa's eyes back on me.

"Four?"

"Four waters," I confirm, then look around the table. "Are we ready to order?"

When everyone says yes, Melissa's eyes widen and suddenly she gets down to business. With our orders written down, she walks away and the table is silent.

"That probably happens a lot," Dana says, looking at Reed with a smirk before glancing at me and giving me a slow once over.

Liv snickers. "You should see what it's like when they're with Dave and Nick. I had lunch with them last month and it wasn't just the waitress. I think every woman there dropped or spilled something, they couldn't focus on anything but our table."

"It wasn't that bad," Reed replies, smiling at Liv who just rolls her eyes.

Dana watches them with an affectionate smile then turns to me. "Assistant Attorney General. That's impressive."

"Youngest in history," Reed adds on like a proud mama. I shake my head at him because it's weird for me to have a friend who isn't competing against me. One who wants me to succeed. Those haven't been common for me.

"That takes a lot of work. Did you always want to be an attorney?" Dana asks. It feels like she really wants to hear the answer and isn't just asking because she knows men like to talk about themselves.

"It was either a lawyer or a history professor slash archaeologist but my dad convinced me that wouldn't be as cool as the movies made it out to be," I tell her with a smile. She doesn't need to hear his method of convincing was berating my other interests and making me feel like a disappointment.

My Dad had very strong expectations of what his sons would be and he pushed us hard to succeed. I was expected to follow in his footsteps, becoming a lawyer and both of my brothers are surgeons. Everything we did from the time we started school was specifically selected to move us forward on our career paths. We didn't play sports, we were on the debate team and in chess club. We didn't have friends, we had peers we competed with and against much like my dad and his colleagues. I followed his rules without question, not wanting to feel his crushing disappointment. The only exception to his rules I ever got was when I joined the Cross Country team in high school.

I argued it would teach me discipline and endurance, both things I would need to be an attorney and he finally gave in although he said it was because I formulated a compelling argument, not because he necessarily agreed, but it didn't matter to me. I finally was doing something because I wanted to do it, not because I was expected to. It was liberating and terrifying at the same time.

The first few weeks, I thought I was going to die every single day but I wouldn't quit. I couldn't quit. If I did, my dad would never let me forget it and that would be the end of me ever stepping foot off of his explicit plan. Eventually, running miles at a time got easier and that one hour after school became the only thing I looked forward to, the only time I really let myself enjoy life.

"Maybe it is overrated but you would've had a cool whip." Dana teases and I'm genuinely shocked. It's the first time a woman has gotten my movie reference. The first time I've ever felt like a woman really got me.

Leaning a little closer, Dana lowers her voice for my ears only. "Not to mention, the sexy hat." She says it with a smile, hinting at the things we could do wearing nothing but that hat.

Damn, I wonder where I can get one.

My phone rings and for once, I'm not eager to answer it. "Sorry, it's probably the office," I say to no one in particular as I slide my cell out of the breast pocket of my jacket.

Jessica.

There's only one reason she's calling and although it's always a mutually beneficial time, I thought I had ended it. When your fuck buddy says she wants to be more you have one of two options. Start dating or call it quits and I voted for the latter.

Jessica said it was fine with her but apparently, she's changed her mind.

Ignoring the call, I slip the phone back in my pocket, always keeping the screen discreetly hidden from my lunch mates. Liv obviously brought us here as a setup and since I'm intrigued by her friend, I don't need any of them seeing another woman's name blazing across my screen.

"My mom and William are officially moving in together," Liv tells Dana.

Dana frowns slightly before responding. "I thought they were already living together."

Liv gives her a look that says 'exactly my point'. "That's why I said officially. She just told me she's moving into his house but I know she's been staying there most nights for over a year."

"Well, good for her. I'm happy for them," Dana says as the waitress returns with our drinks, setting them down and quickly walking away without a word.

Dana raises her eyebrows at Liv and they both smother a laugh then look at Reed and me. We smile back like it's no big deal because really it isn't. The attention is nice but it doesn't mean anything and if a man were waiting on us, he'd be doing the same thing to Dana and Liv.

"What are you doing Saturday night?" Liv asks Dana and I'm suddenly very curious to hear the answer.

With a shake of her head, Dana replies. "Nothing. Why?"

Liv ignores the question and looks at me. "What about you?"

I guess I'm not moving fast enough for the little blond and she's decided to take matters into her own hands. Again.

Raising my own eyebrows at her, I respond letting her know I'm onto her game. "Nothing."

Pretending like she didn't hear the silent 'stop and let me handle this myself' I was sending her, Liv's eyes ping pong back to Dana. "Great! You two can have dinner!"

"Liv," Dana says in a way that would stop most people in their tracks.

With an exasperated sigh, Liv looks to the ceiling then back to Dana and me. "Fine. You can have lunch."

I'm completely amused by the silent conversation Dana is trying to have with Liv who continues to just smile at her innocently. Dana turns to me for help but seeing my entertained expression, she throws the gauntlet down.

"I'm not having lunch with a man incapable of asking himself." She doesn't say it in a bitchy way, more like a challenge and I gladly accept.

Sliding my arm across the back of her chair, I tilt my head down slightly, looking directly into her eyes. "Dana, will you have lunch with me Saturday?"

Holding my stare, she makes me wait until sweat starts to form on my brow. I don't remember the last time I was nervous around a woman since my teenage years. That had more to do with sneaking out to go on a date and lying to my parents about it than nerves over what the girl was thinking. Twenty minutes with this woman and I'm feeling things I've never felt before. The crazy part is, I like it.

Finally, Dana responds. "On one condition."

"What's that?"

Lowering her voice to match mine, she answers. "You wear the hat."

Chapter Three

MITCH

"So, Liv wants to know what you think about Dana. You two seemed to hit it off."

It's the question I've been waiting for since I pulled up to the gym for our monthly game. It's also the woman I haven't been able to get out of my head since yesterday's lunch.

After heading back to the office, Dana was on my mind for the rest of the day. I don't remember dreaming about her last night but when I woke up, I insistently yelled out her name, like I was calling to her and had an image of chasing her through the park. Other parts of my body were thinking about her too. I had hoped a cold shower would take her off my mind but nope, that's where she stayed, front and center through ten hours in the office when I should have had my mind on work.

"She seemed nice," I respond vaguely, not meeting Reed's eyes.

"Who seemed nice?" Dave asks dropping his gym bag on the floor and taking a seat on the bench next to me.

"Dana," Reed answers for me.

Dave doesn't look up, just unzips his bag and starts digging around in it. "Yeah, she's nice."

"But not your type." I quip back at him.

He tips his head up to us and gives a lazy smirk. "Definitely not my type."

"And why is that?" Reed jokes but I hear the undercurrent of seriousness in his tone. Dave must hear it too because he drops his smirk, his eyes going back to his bag.

"You know why."

Confused, I look back and forth between them, waiting for someone to fill me in.

I've been hanging out with Reed and Dave, along with a few other guys they know, for almost a year. There's a standing dinner invitation to Reed and Liv's house every Sunday and we're all there if we're available. I have lunch with Reed, Dave and Nick, an IT guy in our office, at least once a week. On top of that, all the guys get together one Thursday a month for some basketball. In all that time, I've gotten to know these guys pretty well and I've seen the kind of women Dave usually dates. They're beautiful and nice but he doesn't stay with any of them very long. The thing I don't know is why and I think I'm about to find out.

Dave doesn't respond and Reed must be tired of dodging the subject. He drops his keys in his bag, turning to give Dave his full attention. "Because she's more than just a pretty face looking for hot sex. She's someone you could actually like."

Something prickles inside me at the thought of Dave being interested in Dana, but I shove it away.

"You don't date any woman you could potentially have a future with. You go for easy and shallow." Reed finishes still staring Dave down.

Pulling a water bottle out of his bag, Dave takes a drink and shrugs. "So, what's wrong with that?"

I'm a statue, embarrassingly fascinated by the dude drama playing out in front of me and curious as hell what Reed's getting at.

Reed's stare goes unmet as Dave fiddles with his bag and Reed lets out a sigh. "Look, man, I know she hurt you but not all women are going to do that. You can't keep avoiding a real relationship. Someone like Dana."

Dave hammers his water bottle down hard and strides toward the middle of the court. "Let's play."

We watch him bounce the ball a few times and make some practice shots. "Who was she?" The question tumbles out of my mouth.

"His ex-wife."

His ex-wife? "I didn't know he was married."

Reed sighs again and I can tell this is something that's bugged him for a while. "It was a long time ago. He doesn't talk about her."

The question I really want answered is screaming inside my head and I have the thought 'curiosity killed the cat' before I let myself ask it. "You think Dave and Dana would be good together?"

I'm dreading his answer, holding my breath and my body still, eyes on Dave who's greeting the latecomers of our group.

"No."

A glimmer of hope pokes out but I need more information.

"Because she's..." The question trails off while I search for a reason why dating Dana could be a bad idea.

Reed turns and gives me the same look he was just giving Dave a few minutes before. "Because she's perfect for you. Or so Liv thinks."

Unconsciously, I bob my head, taking that in. "Cool." I let out the single word, trying to keep the weird, happy feeling under wraps. Not ready to dive deeper into that feeling right now, I jump up and head onto the court. "Let's play."

The game helps clear my head and I'm wiped out by the time I make it home. Dave's pissy mood eventually faded, and we spent most of the night giving him a hard time about his former girlfriends. He hasn't loved any of them, I'm not even sure he likes them, they're more of a hobby, so he didn't take any of it personally. But without the game to distract me, the thought of him and Dana together keeps popping into my head and I'm getting angrier each time it does.

The water shoots on and I look at myself in the mirror waiting for it to warm up.

"What's wrong with you?" I say to my reflection. "You're just like Dave. Women don't get to you. You don't do relationships and you don't give a shit if the woman you're banging is with someone else when she's not with you. Why do you care if Dave thinks Dana's nice?"

The man in the mirror responds. *Because you like her.*

"What am I, twelve? I don't like women. I mean, I like women, I just don't ever feel anything for them beyond a physical interest."

Did you always think it would be like that? The asshole in the mirror asks like I'm an idiot.

"I don't know, I've never really thought about it. I figured eventually I would settle down, start a family, but I haven't thought much about the feelings that would go into that."

You're an idiot. He tells me and I kind of have to agree.

Dana stirred up something in me, something I didn't even know I was capable of.

My grandma would say I fancy her but I'm just going to call it an old-fashioned like.

I like Dana.

Do I want to get her naked and make her scream my name?

Of course, but I also want more. I have a genuine fondness for her, a desire to get to know who she is. To find out what makes her tick and see if I can earn another smile from her glossy lips.

Lips I'm sure can deliver more than just a smile.

Dropping my head, my body is painfully hard, wanting to claim a woman for the first time. Wanting to make her mine.

Steam fogs over the mirror, but I still manage to catch the look my reflection gives me.

Challenge accepted.

Chapter Four

DANA

I 've barely turned off the car when Liv appears next to my door, and I shriek. She starts laughing her ass off as I place my hand over my racing heart and wish unpleasant things on her.

Slowly, opening the door, I cut my eyes her way. "Liv, you scared the crap out of me."

"Sorry. So, what do you think?" Liv asks, like she didn't just scare ten years off my life.

"That you can't get enough of me," I state dryly.

"Obviously, but that's not what I was talking about, and you know it."

Acting aloof, I pretend not to have any clue what she's talking about.

Stopping in front of the restaurant doors, Liv grabs my upper arms like she's going to shake me. "Dana Marie! Don't keep me in suspense! What did you think of Mitch?!"

I laugh out loud at her exasperated expression. Liv can be a bit dramatic, but I love her. She's been my best friend since elementary school, and truthfully, I've really missed not living close to her since she moved to DC. It didn't take long for her to suggest I move too and well, here we are.

"First. You know my middle name is Nicole, not Marie." I say, opening the door for her and ushering her in.

"Apologies," She deadpans.

"Accepted. Second, I'm pretty sure you already know the answer so I'm not keeping you in suspense."

"For the love of cheesecake, answer the damn question!" She cries and I stifle a laugh.

"Table for two?" The hostess asks us with a puzzled look on her face.

"Yes." Liv and I reply in unison and follow her to a table. She leaves us with menus, and I pretend to scan the appetizers.

"For the love of cheesecake? That's pretty serious."

"It doesn't get more serious than cheesecake," Liv says soberly, laying her menu on the table and staring me down. She and Reed have a thing for cheesecake, she's not exaggerating her seriousness.

"Ok, fine. I'm interested," I state plainly. "That would be why I said yes to lunch on Saturday."

I'm more than interested but I want to make Liv sweat a little. She knew Mitch and I would be into each other and she was so right she didn't even try to hide her self-satisfied smile while we finished lunch. I was tempted to throw my grilled chicken salad at her, but really, I'm thankful she knows me so well.

Since lunch yesterday, I've barely been able to concentrate on anything other than Mitch. It's only been a day since we met, and I can't stop thinking about him. He's funny and intelligent and I felt like we really hit it off, not to mention the way my body reacted to him. I've met handsome men before, men I was attracted to, but I've never had one take over my brain the way he has. It's like flipping through channels and he's the top news story everyone's talking about, referencing his perfect face.

Those eyes.

And his hands.

Not to mention the warm and fuzzies I felt all the way to my core when my hand nestled in his for the far too brief shake. Just thinking about it causes those fuzzies to erupt again and I clench my thighs instinctively. It's been so long since I got off, the little bit of pressure sends a ripple of pleasure through me, and I grip my table hard. A moan almost escapes, and I mentally scold myself.

I need to get laid.

And my mind goes right back to Mitch.

"Dana. I said of course, you're interested." Liv's words draw me back to our conversation. "You would have to be dead not to be interested. What did you think?"

"One of the Senior Partners asked me out, today," I tell her, skimming the menu again.

"What?"

I can't tell if she's incredulous or just thrown off by the change of subject.

"I needed a break," more like a distraction from lusty Mitch thoughts, "and when you work in an office that's either a trip to the restroom or the break room and I didn't need to pee."

"What does that have to do with anything?"

"I was getting a fresh mug from the cabinet when I heard the door open." I continue, setting the menu down.

"A male voice asked if I was Dana and when I turned around..." My eyebrows raise and jokingly I fan myself.

"...an extremely handsome man stood in front of me. I'd already met so many people at work, I had lost track, but he wasn't one of them. I would have remembered meeting him. He's probably a decade older than us with dark hair starting to gray on the sides in that totally sexy way only men can pull off. And he has those crinkle lines around his eyes which makes me think he spends a lot of time in the sun. And that smile, damn, that smile is luring. I'm sure many women have fallen victim to it."

From the subtle eye fuck he was giving me, I could easily be one of them.

Liv is still staring at me like I'm from outer space, so I go on. "He introduced himself, Peter Moore, Senior Partner and held out his hand to shake."

I leave out the fact there were no warm and fuzzies when our hands touched but I did note Peter had nice hands. Hands that probably know exactly where to touch a woman.

I haven't been touched in so long but it's not Peter's hands I'll be dreaming about tonight.

"Peter gave my hand a little squeeze," and inwardly I cringed. I hate when men don't really shake my hand. I guess they think because I'm a woman, I won't know this dainty squeeze implies I can't handle the real thing. Mitch gave me a real handshake, the way my mom always told me to shake someone's hand. Not overly firm or limp or just a light squeeze of my hand. Mitch's handshake was nice, a good solid shake.

And... I'm thinking about Mitch again. See how it happens?

"And I felt something graze over the back of my hand. I looked down and saw Peter still held it and was running his thumb back and forth in a very unprofessional manner."

"Really?" Liv's totally into the story now.

"I didn't realize he was doing it at first, my mind had wandered. And then I told him that and he got a smug look on his face. He thought I was fantasizing about him."

"Were you?"

I keep her in suspense until her eyes look like they're about to pop out of her head. "No."

Yes, Peter is attractive, but I wasn't feeling anything. No goosebumps up my arms, no flutters in my core, no tingles in my hand when we touched.

"He said we should go out sometime." I finish with a little shrug.

Our waiter approaches, introduces himself as Scott, and takes our order. Liv and I both notice his eyes lingering on me and I smile politely but don't encourage him.

"So, you're not going to go out with Peter?" Liv asks when it's just us again.

Ok, enough prolonging, time to tell her the truth. "Probably not. I didn't feel anything for him except appreciation for his good looks. Even his panty melting smile didn't do a damn thing for me." I found him attractive like a beautiful piece of art I had no intention of buying. Which is weird. "Usually, I would totally go for someone like him."

"Or someone like Mitch," Liv says but I just keep on talking.

"Maybe it's because we work together. I try not to get involved with co-workers." I say, rationalizing the lack of lust for Peter. Dating someone from work can get messy, something I learned in the past.

"I mean, what else could it be? He has all the physical qualities I like in a man, and he's definitely interested in me. If I gave him the signal, I could break my dry spell tonight." Which doesn't sound appealing at all.

"Maybe you're already falling for someone else." Liv practically sings.

I roll my eyes. "Someone I haven't even had a date with?" I ask but can't stop myself from grinning. "Ok, fine, I'll admit it. I would rather Mitch be the one breaking my dry spell."

I really, really want Mitch to break my dry spell. If I get full body tingles just sitting next to him, and warm and fuzzies when he shakes my hand, my body will explode into blissful oblivion when he puts his lips on me.

Or his tongue.

Or...

"Maybe you're hoping it could be more than that. Like what Reed and I have."

I blink, trying to focus back on my friend. When did it get so hot in here?

"Not many people find love like what you have with Reed," I say, taking a healthy sip of water.

"That doesn't mean you won't."

Scott comes back with our drinks, placing a few cocktail napkins next to mine. He smiles intimately at me and walks away.

"That was weird," I say and Liv waves it off.

"Back to you and Mitch..." Her comment is cut off when she picks up one of the napkins in front of me. "Looks like Mitch has more competition." She jokes and turns the napkin around so I can see it.

In black ink, there's a phone number and Scott's name. Before I can say anything, Liv shoves it in her purse. Seconds later, Scott's back with our food. I thank him without making eye contact, not trying to be rude more like politely distant.

"If things don't work out with Mitch, you can give Scott a call," Liv says before shoving food in her mouth. She makes a sound that has the men at the next table looking our way in interest. Liv loves food and isn't shy about it.

"You know that's not going to happen," I say and take a bite too.

Liv doesn't hold back, going right to the heart of it. "Because of Scott's job or Mitch?"

"Both," I tell her honestly. She knows all my faults and still loves me. I can tell her anything.

"I don't want to have to support a man financially. What kind of future would we have? A waiter can't support a family, provide insurance, or pay for college. I shouldn't have to do that because he chose a career that doesn't pay well."

It's an old argument, one we've had many times, but I'm not changing my mind on this. I know what happens when a woman has to not only take care of herself but of a man too.

"A. You have no idea if being a waiter is Scott's career. He could own the restaurant or maybe his family does and he's just helping out."

I don't respond, just take a sip of my wine.

"B. Tell me what you think about Mitch. Not just that you find him attractive or want to have sex with him, but what you really think about him."

"I am attracted to him, what more do you need to know?" I reply with some snark, setting my glass down.

Liv makes a sound of exasperation. "Like, what do you think of him as a person, and did you feel anything besides lust?"

The last time I admitted feeling anything beyond lust for a man and blabbed all about it to Liv, I felt like a damned fool when it was over a few months later. Talking about attraction and sex is easy. It's opening up and confessing to deeper emotions that I have a harder time with.

Liv's the only person I can even kind of talk about my feelings with and it's still uncomfortable for me but I'll try anyway because I love her.

"I like that he has a great job."

"Somehow, I knew you'd say that." She replies with a bit of sass herself and I get a little offensive.

"No. I meant his job is impressive because he must have worked really hard to get there. That shows a lot of dedication and drive."

Liv nods her agreement. "Ok, go on."

"I liked his sense of humor and talking to him felt comfortable, natural. There wasn't the awkwardness you get sometimes with new people. He and Reed seem to have a great friendship and even though we were all there, talking to each other, when Mitch talked to me, it was like he was hyper focused on me. Like he was really interested in what I had to say and wasn't just pretending to get in my pants." Although, with the way my body came alive when we touched and how his voice rolled through me, waking up parts I thought were dead, he'll be getting in my pants very soon.

Maybe Saturday.

"You like him." Liv teases and I feel my cheeks warm. There's no use denying it.

"Yes, I like him. A lot." I admit. "It's crazy, Liv. We just met."

"It's not crazy." She says back, knowingly.

"It feels different than when I've liked someone in the past." Different how, I don't know.

Liv reaches over and grabs my hand, squeezing it lightly. "Maybe that's because it is different."

The last real relationship I had was a few years ago. I would say it ended badly but he didn't care enough for it to be bad, it was just over. I don't think he even cared at all when it was over, not like me. I was the emotionally invested one. Since then, I've dated other men, men I found attractive but didn't trigger anything deep inside me and it's been fun but shallow. I didn't realize I wanted more until I moved here.

Until you met Mitch.

"Maybe even love?" Liv draws out the word love and I think she's about to start chanting the letters to spell kissing.

"I wouldn't use the word love. I just met the guy." I retort.

It's Liv's turn to roll her eyes. "Fine. But it's something. Something different and maybe a little scary but something you want. I saw it as soon as you looked at him."

I can't hide my feelings from her just like she can't hide her's from me. We've been best friends too long, gone through too much together, not to know each other inside and out. She proved it again by setting me up with my perfect man.

"I do want it. I want Mitch more than I want another glass of wine." I confess, confidentially.

"More than a glass of wine? That's cheesecake level serious." She mocks.

She has no idea. My hormones are acting like rowdy teenage cheerleaders, screaming Mitch's name, and yelling for me to score while my heart is starting to make plans about our future.

Liv gives me a smirk before taking a drink and I realize she probably does know how I feel. This is probably how she felt about Reed and look at them now, happily married and more in love every day.

My heart finds that very optimistic.

Chapter Five

MITCH

T he past few days have been a blur. I know I've worked on things, I had to. You can't just flake off in my line of work. The problem is, I don't remember much of it. The only thing I can remember doing is thinking about Dana.

And jacking off to thoughts of Dana.

I feel like a total perv, but I couldn't walk around all day stiff as a board. People would talk.

When I woke up this morning, Dana was already on my mind. I was hard as a rock and aching with the need to release. A clear picture of her seated next to me at the diner projected in front of my eyes.

The sun was shining in the window behind her, giving her a glowing effect, adding to the almost holy feelings running through me when we touched. I was mesmerized by her chocolate brown eyes. Captivated by her smile. Her lips. Her lips covered in cherry red lipstick.

Her lips covered in cherry red lipstick wrapping around my favorite body part.

I thrust into my hand, but it's Dana's mouth I felt on me.

Her red lips sliding up and down.

Her lips leaving a perfect red ring around me.

Her red lips...

FUCK. Pleasure crashed through me so hard my vision went hazy.

Taking a ragged breath, I closed my eyes and there she was again. That release was phenomenal but wasn't enough to get her out of my head.

I think I'm infatuated with her. I've never been like this with a woman before and hell if I know why it's happening now, but it is. She's consumed me and it's driving me nuts.

I had hoped my usually six-mile jog around the park this morning would help clear her from my head but it's not working. I'm halfway through and this morning's fireworks show for one is playing on constant repeat in my head. Dana's face, those fucking red lips, kept swimming in front of me.

Distracted, I step on a rock and almost bust my ass. Recovering quickly, I automatically look around to see if anyone saw me. There's no one behind me on the trail and the couple ahead of me don't turn around. I'm good.

Picking up my pace, I focus on the ground in front of my feet. That wasn't the first time I almost face planted this morning, but it will be the last. I'm running. Putting one foot in front of the other. Deep even breaths. I'm halfway through.

With that last thought, I'm feeling better and gaze ahead of me. The couple is still there but they've put more distance between us. I will easily make it up with the speed I'm at now.

Gaining on them, I see a woman run across the main trail and take the hiking trail into the woods. Her brunette ponytail swinging behind her.

My steps falter and I blink. Is it really her or do I just want it to be?

"Dana!" I yell and start running after her.

"Dana!" I call out again.

The brunette doesn't turn around, continuing to jog away from me and I stop.

"I really thought it was her," I say to no one but myself.

Fuck, I am infatuated if I'm hallucinating her.

Giving myself a mental slap, I get back on the main trail and set off to finish my run.

"Focus, Mitch," I tell myself but it's no use. Dana Tolliver is front and center of my mind and stays there until I'm driving home to shower and change for our date. In the rearview mirror, there's a weird look on my face.

Excitement.

When was the last time I was excited to go on a date?

Usually, I already know the outcome, choosing to date women married to their careers like I am and only looking for an appropriate date to a function or straight up sex. There's never the question of what does she think of me or will she want to see me again because it doesn't matter. None of those women are looking for long-term any more than I am.

But with Dana, the idea doesn't make me want to block her number from my phone.

Ok, that's a little harsh, and I've only had to do it once, but seriously. Not only am I not looking for exits, trying to extract myself from a date with a woman I could potentially see myself in a relationship with, I'm excited about it.

"Calm down, Mitch. She's just a woman."

A beautiful woman you had an instant spark with.

"A spark that went farther than physical attraction." I agree with myself.

She got the movie reference and even used it when she flirted back.

"That's never happened before."

Although, I learned to keep the history and related movie references to a minimum in college. Women do not find history facts a turn on.

Maybe Dana won't mind. I muse, thinking it would be nice if I didn't have to hide my inner history nerd from a woman.

And if she does mind, I have to get to the office anyway so lunch will be quick.

Walking into my house, I'm jogging up the stairs when my phone rings. One look and my good mood is gone, replaced by dread and a touch of anxiety.

Might as well get it over with. "Hi, Dad."

"Mitchell. How is work?" He's started every conversation with me this way since I began first grade, only then it was 'Mitchell, how is school.'

"Good, busy as usual," I tell him. He knows I can't give him details about anything I work on, but he always asks anyway. Work is the only thing he's capable of talking about. Mom only talks about their social standing and the people and events needed to maintain or elevate it. I used to wonder if they ever had conversations about anything else. One time I tried to change the dinner topic to travel or hobbies but they managed to turn both subjects back to networking with colleagues and impressing their frenemies. I never tried again.

"Good, good. Did you have meetings with the President this week?" He asks as I walk through my bedroom. It's the only part of my job my dad is somewhat impressed by.

Opening the door to my bathroom, I start to answer him. "No. Not this week but I'll..." My voice trails off as my brain tries to understand why I'm splashing in water. "What the fuck?"

"Mitchell. That language is not tolerated." Dad chastises me just as I see the waterfall coming out of the cabinet below the sink.

"Shit!" I yank open the cabinet door. My eyes go from the gush of water I release onto the floor to the heavy flow coming out of the pipe sink.

"Mitchell!"

"Dad, I have to go. I have a busted pipe." I say quickly looking for the shut off valve located above the pipe. With a quick twist, I turn it and lean back, expecting the water to stop.

"Call maintenance." He instructs like I'm an idiot. The gushing from the pipe seems to get worse and I reach back and turn the valve the other way. "They should be taking better care of government offices."

With the water still pouring out of the pipe, I stand up and slosh over to the cabinet next to the shower. "I'm not at the office, I'm at home," I tell him absently grabbing a towel to tie around the pipe until I can shut off the main water supply to the house.

"On a Saturday? Mitchell, if you ever plan to get the Attorney General position, you need to put in more effort. I work six days a week, minimum twelve hours a day. Sunday is the only acceptable--"

Needing to take care of the lake forming in my bathroom, I cut him off. "I know Dad. I have to go." It comes out brusquely and I hear him say my name with a sharp edge before I hang up.

"It's not like I haven't heard it all before," I mutter to myself, setting my phone on the counter to wrap the towel around the pipe.

It doesn't matter I was the youngest Assistant Attorney General in history or that I'm on track to get the promotion to Attorney General with the time comes. My dad will always expect more, demand more, despite what I've already achieved. Just once, I'd like to hear him say he's proud of me instead of telling me to work harder.

Immediately, my phone rings again. I'm already kneeling in water, reaching for the pipe. I don't have time for a lecture. With one hand, I blindly reach up and answer the call loud and irritated. "Dad. I can't talk right now. I'll call you back."

"Mitchell?" The female voice halts my hands, one holding a wet towel to a busted pipe, the other holding the phone above my head. Slowly, my head rears back and I look at the screen just as Jessica calls my name again.

"Jessica. I can't talk right now." I tell her, hanging up before say can respond.

"I really don't have time for her either,." I mutter to myself setting my phone back down.

The water is getting deeper every second and the towel is only mitigating the flow by a fraction. I need to shut off the water to the house now before things get worse. Running through the house and out the front door, I scan the yard. Seeing the metal cover by the road, I sprint to it, yanking it off and turning the knob hard. Hoping it worked, I run over to the outdoor faucet and test if anything comes out.

A stream falls to the ground but slows to a trickle and I breathe in relieved. Now I need to see how bad the damage is. Water damage can be bad and if I don't get it all dried out properly, I could end up with mold and that's a much bigger problem to clean up.

Trudging back upstairs, I step into the bedroom when I see the puddle expanding across the hardwood floor. A curse escapes me as I survey it, carefully walking through the growing mess to the source of the problem.

The bathroom has standing water wall to wall and my first thought is I don't have enough towels. Second is, I need to call a plumber, followed quickly by another call I need to make. I spread towels on the bedroom floor before calling the number I haven't used before.

Dana answers on the second ring, a smile in her voice. "Hi, Mitch."

"Hi, Dana." Damn. I don't want to do this. "I have to cancel lunch."

"Oh... Ok." The hesitation does little to hide the question she doesn't ask. Why?

"A pipe burst in my house. I have water everywhere and need to get a plumber over here. I don't know how long it's going to take."

When she responds it's with understanding and empathy. "Oh, no! That sounds like a mess. Do you need help?"

Having Dana in my house, all to myself, is exactly what I want but making her clean up this mess before I've even taken her on a date is not what I had in mind. Irritated with the situation, I close my eyes and quietly exhale. "I'll manage."

There's no response for a beat, then another. I'm wondering if I should tell her I do need her help when she speaks. "Ok." I can't detect what emotion I'm hearing but I hope to hell it's disappointment and not something else.

"I'll see you tomorrow night at Reed's," I tell her, trying to end on a positive note and a reminder this is just a minor setback.

"See you tomorrow." Her voice is lighter and for a moment I forget about the water I'm standing in and the damage it's doing to everything it touches.

Tomorrow can't get here fast enough.

CHAPTER SIX

DANA

I'm nervous as I knock on Liv and Reed's front door and I tell myself it's because I'm about to meet all their friends, not because I get to see Mitch again. My hand is still suspended when the door swings open, like Liv was waiting on the other side.

"Were you watching me walk up through the peephole?" I tease her, handing over the bottle of Merlot I know she won't drink. She's not much of a wine drinker, that bottle is more for me, but my mom drilled it into my head you never show up at a dinner party without a gift.

"No." Liv tilts up her chin and spins away. "But maybe I was checking out the window."

I follow her down the hall, past the living area and Reed's home office, to the back of the house where the party seems to be. The back doors off the kitchen and dining room are open and people are hanging out on the back deck, their voices and laughter floating inside. Just before we step out, Liv stops and whispers to me. "Mitch isn't here yet."

A light mixture of confusion and disappointment passes through me. "Ok?"

"I didn't want you to be disappointed when you didn't see him." Damn, she knows me too well.

With a little shake of my head, I try to convey how wrong she is. "Why do you think I'd be disappointed if he wasn't here yet?"

She snorts, not buying my supposed disinterest. Leaning in and looking me dead in the eye, she confirms that. "You like him." She leans back, looking smug. "And he likes you."

He likes me? The giddy teenage girl in me asks.

"He may have canceled your lunch yesterday, but he'll be here."

Grabbing my hand, Liv pulls me through the door. "Now, let me introduce you to everyone." She says this loud enough it gets everyone's attention, and they all stop their conversations and look at us expectantly.

"This is Brent and Emily Russell," Liv says, gesturing to the couple standing next to Reed. "They live across the street. He's a stoke broker and she's a vet."

They both say hi as a few chuckles emerge from the group. "What? I'm just giving her some basic information so she's not completely at a loss." Liv defends herself.

Flinging her hand out, she continues. "You know Dave."

He says "Hey" as Liv points to the blond woman next to him, "and that's..."

"Kaitlyn." Dave supplies.

"Yes, Kaitlyn! Sorry." Liv says and hurries on. "That's Nick Fisher and Hannah Bell, they're not married but." She gives them an overly encouraging smile. "Maybe soon!" More chuckles come from the group, including Nick and Hannah so I guess Liv's not too far off. "They both work for the DOJ. He's in IT and she's in HR."

"Hi."

"Nice to meet you."

I smile back and Liv waves her hand towards the last couple. "And this is Jake and Suzette Powell, they live next door. He's an Orthopedic Surgeon and she's a reporter for Channel 6 News."

"Oh, yeah, I've seen you!" I tell her and get her camera perfect smile.

The chatter picks back up and Liv heads inside to get me a wine glass. The other women make their way over to me like a pack and form a huddle around me to match the one all the guys just made.

"Dana, it's so great to finally meet you. Liv has talked about you so much. I feel like I already know you." Emily says.

"I know. We were so glad you decided to move here, almost as much as Liv." Hannah agrees and all the ladies laugh.

"What are we laughing at?" Liv asks, handing me a full glass of Merlot.

"Just that it's good to finally have Dana here," Suzette says, giving me a wink.

Holding up her own glass, Liv makes a toast. "To finally having Dana here."

We all raise our glasses and right before they clink Liv adds more. "And to getting Dana and Mitch together."

Eyebrows raise and five sets of female eyes look at me, each with an eager look on their face. Well maybe not from Kaitlyn, she seems to just be going along with the rest of the group, but the other four women are certainly interested in Liv's little proclamation.

"Really?" Suzette asks.

"You should have seen the sparks popping between them at lunch on Friday." Liv helpfully declares.

"I can totally see you two together." Hannah agrees before taking a sip of her own wine.

"He needs a good woman, someone who will make him take the time to enjoy life. He works too much." Emily tells us.

"They all did before they met us," Suzette adds, flicking a glance over at her husband.

"Dave works all the time too, but we still spend a lot of time together," Kaitlyn says. I've just met this woman, and I can already tell there's only one thing she and Dave spend time doing together but she seems nice. The other ladies must think so too because no one says anything, they just nod their heads and take another drink.

Emily picks the conversation back up. "So, back to you and Mitch. You would be perfect for him."

"Yeah, I mean, I don't know what his type is, he's never introduced us to anyone he's dating, but I think you would be it," Hannah says.

"I don't know if Mitch has dated anyone since we've known him. He's always working." Suzette states.

That's the second time one of them said he's always working, and the word workaholic flashes in my brain.

"Or he's hanging out with the guys." Liv defends him.

Ok, so that's something. Maybe he's not a complete workaholic.

"When he can get away from work," Emily adds.

Ugh! I'm getting whiplash from this conversation.

"Didn't Brent work a lot before he met you?" Suzette asks her pointedly but politely.

Emily finishes her sip and nods. "Yes, he did. He still does but he's gotten better about making time just for us. Especially since we found out about the baby."

The other women start gushing over the first baby in the group and I smile but refrain from saying anything. I always thought I would have a family but it's seeming less likely the older I get.

Mitch's whiskey-colored eyes and perfect jawline appear in front of me and for a second, I'm lost in the fantasy.

That is, until I realize he's really here, standing behind Liv.

And there's a gorgeous redhead with him.

CHAPTER SEVEN

MITCH

It's a good thing I don't spend much time at home. The sound of the blowers drying the floor and walls upstairs is loud and nerve wracking.

Grabbing my keys off the counter, I flick the lights off as I head out. I left my car in the driveway since I was just running in to change and with one foot out my front door, I hear a car door shut. Looking up, I see a woman coming toward me. Not just any woman. Jessica. The one I was occasionally having dinner and other things with when we were both free and in the mood.

"Hi, Mitchell." She calls to me, stopping next to my car, waiting for me to come to her. She likes being in charge and the littlest things, like making me come to her, are power moves she gets off on.

"It's been too long." She adds, in a softer voice, looking me up and down.

I have no idea what she's doing here. She's right, we haven't seen each other in weeks and the last time we were together, we didn't leave things off so well. I was getting dressed to go home after a few hours of fun and she said she wanted me to stay. I had never stayed. We weren't like that, but she decided it was time things changed. I told her no then walked out and hadn't heard from her since. I was under the impression we were done so what the hell is she doing here now?

Stopping a few feet away, I tip my head and simply say her name in greeting. "Jessica."

She doesn't say anything, just looks at me, another one of her power moves, one I use myself. We could stand here for hours, facing off, but I have places to be.

Walking to the driver's side of my car, I tell her. "I was just heading out."

"Where are you going?" She asks with almost no emotion or curiosity in her voice, like the answer doesn't really matter.

Hitting the unlock button, I reach for my door. "To have dinner with friends."

Before I'm seated behind the wheel, she slides into the passenger seat and buckles up. "Great, sounds like fun."

I'm momentarily dumbfounded, my hand and seatbelt frozen in front of me.

"Let's go, I'm starving." She says, flipping the visor down and checking her makeup.

I don't know what possesses me to start the car and back out with her next to me except maybe the fact I'm feeling completely blindsided and not thinking straight. We're almost to Reed's house when my brain finally gets its shit together, and I realize I'm taking Jessica to dinner with my friends. This is a bad idea. A very bad idea. The wives are going to be all over this, thinking it's so much more than it is. They're always telling me I need to date more.

Shit! Dana. She's going to be there. What the fuck am I going to tell her?

I glance over at Jessica and think how much of an asshole it would make me to pull over and tell her to get out. It's not like we're in a bad neighborhood or anything. She would be perfectly safe waiting for a car service to pick her up.

I'm tempted to do it, tugging the wheel to the side when I shake my head at myself and keep driving. I may be an asshole but I'm not so much of an asshole that I would just leave her on the side of the road.

"Jessica."

She cuts me off. "You know the case I've been working on, the one with the contaminated food supply chain?" Not waiting for a reply, she hurries on. "They're finally ready to settle and Robert wants to pull me off the case. Me! I've been leading the case from the beginning, and he comes into my office on Friday and says that John is better equipped to reel it in. John Daly, not Sturgis. If it was him, I would understand, but Daly. Really?"

"That sucks." It's all I can say and really, it does suck. Jessica is a great attorney, but she can be like a dog with a bone. I've heard of a few cases where she wouldn't agree to settlement terms and her clients ended up getting a shit deal.

"It more than sucks, Mitchell." She says bitingly.

Dropping her off on the side of the road doesn't sound so bad anymore and I flick my eyes that way but we're already on Reed's street. I wouldn't put it past her to watch which house I go to and follow me there.

I'll just make sure Dana knows Jessica and I aren't together. Not that we were together in the first place. Hell, I didn't think we were anything at all anymore but here she is in my car. Dana and I just met so no commitments have been made, it'll be fine. I'll introduce Jessica as my friend and hope everyone leaves it at that.

Parking in front of Reed's house, I want to make this perfectly clear. "Jessica."

Before I finish saying her name, she's already getting out of the car.

"Jessica!" I say more aggressively and get a door closed in my face. "Shit."

Hurrying out of the car, I'm steps behind her when she knocks on the front door. I expect it to swing open so I keep my mouth shut, neither of us saying anything. Jessica becomes more rigid with each passing second and I hope she's thinking this was a bad idea too and we should just leave.

When no one answers the door, I'm ready to push Jessica back in the car and get her the hell out of here but she has other ideas. Reaching out, she turns the know and opens the door. Again, I'm dumbstruck as she walks in but I go after her anyway. She quickly follows the noise through the house, to the open back doors and stops in the doorway. Taking a step around her, my eyes find Dana like a homing beacon, and she her standing in the middle of the other women.

God, she's beautiful.

I'm transfixed by her, watching different emotions play across her face, and I wonder what she's thinking about.

She looks past Liv and like an arrow to my chest, I feel her eyes lock onto mine.

Then slide to my left.

"Hi everyone. I'm Jessica."

My blood freezes.

"Mitchell's girlfriend."

CHAPTER EIGHT

DANA

G irlfriend.

The word drops like a bomb.

For a few seconds, no one moves, no one makes a sound. Like me, they're probably staring at this mythical creature who isn't supposed to exist.

I can't make myself look at Mitch. I can feel his eyes boring into me but I'm not sure why. He has a girlfriend, why would he be looking at me?

Suddenly a bigger question roars through my head.

If he has a girlfriend, why did he ask me out?!

Busted pipe, my ass!

Anger washes over me followed quickly by the disappointment Liv was trying to keep me from and I squash it down. It's completely absurd to have these feelings for a man I barely know. We've had lunch together once, with friends, and didn't even make it to a date yet, I shouldn't give a shit if he has a girlfriend.

Except I thought there was something between us. Or the possibility of something.

Maybe that's his thing. Maybe he likes knowing he can get a woman to say yes but has zero intention of following through. His looks alone could get him any woman he wants but add in the instant connection superpower he's honed to a fine point and he's basically a rock god in a stadium full of adoring female fans. Panties are flying at him from every direction. He must be drowning in women eager to say yes and he loves hearing it every damn time.

All the while, he's in a committed relationship with a tall, gorgeous, redhead who has fake tits that are big but still tasteful. She looks impeccable, her clothes chosen to emphasize her body type perfectly without giving off a total bitch vibe. She's someone I would maybe be friends with if I didn't have the irrational urge to put my fist in her face.

Reed's voice breaks the trance. "It's nice to meet you. I'm Reed and that's my wife Olivia." He shakes her hand and then points to Liv.

She's still standing next to me and I hear her squeak when he says her name. Liv recovers quickly and offers a small wave. "Hi... ummm, welcome." I cringe for her, knowing she's feeling awkward, but she recovers quickly. "Do you want a drink?"

Jessica relaxes a fraction and I realize she was probably nervous to be meeting Mitch's friends just like I was and here we are all staring at her. "Yes, that would be great."

Liv instructs her to follow as she heads back into the house and as soon as she's gone, a flurry of hushed voices fills the space. I can't hear what the guys are saying to Mitch but the women around me have enough to say on their own.

Suzette is the first to attack. "Who is that?"

"He has a girlfriend? Since when?" Emily questions, looking at each of us like we have the answer.

Hannah shakes her head and sends a puzzled look toward the guys. "She's not right for him. Not at all."

I look at Hannah, wanting to hear more. "Why do you say that?"

"Because she's all prim and proper, looks like she has some high paying executive job. And yeah, Mitch looks that way too, but underneath he's just a normal guy who likes to hang out with his friends, play basketball, and eat burgers off the grill. Does she look like someone who eats burgers off the grill?"

"No," Suzette states emphatically.

"Exactly." Hannah agrees punching the air and Emily shushes her.

"Exactly," Hannah says again a little quieter. "She's only into Assistant Attorney General Mitchell Ainsley, not the Mitch underneath. He needs someone who wants all of him and will bring out the real Mitch, the one he isn't comfortable showing just everyone."

Three sets of eyes look at me, waiting for me to say something. Luckily, or not so luckily, I'm saved by Liv's voice.

"So, this is Emily, that's Hannah, Kaitlyn, Suzette and this is Dana." She points us out to Jessica. None of the others say hello, just give her a tight smile or dip their head in greeting. There's a tense pause as we all look at her and she looks at each of us. When her eyes land on me, I automatically murmur hello. Damn manners.

Jessica smiles huge and speaks directly to me. "Hi. It's nice to finally meet Mitchell's friends."

Ummm...what am I supposed to say to that? I just met the guy so I don't think you could call us friends and I'm certainly not happy to be meeting his girlfriend when I was planning to get down and dirty with him myself.

Suzette, ever the brazen one, saves me from responding. "How long have you and Mitch been together?"

Jessica directs her perfectly made-up face to Suzette. "A few months."

A few months! I feel the statement strike my new group of friends, all of them jolting with the impact.

"A few months?!" Hannah exclaims before getting a not so discreet elbow to the ribs from Emily.

Recovering quickly, Hannah asks. "How did you two meet?"

"A colleague introduced us. She thought we would have a lot in common since we're both in law. I'm a Junior Partner at Matthews and Sterns, Law Group"

"Oh, Dana's in law too." My best friend jumps in, pointing at me.

Jessica looks back at me expectantly and I answer the silent question. "I'm a paralegal at Wallace, Dunn and Fields."

I know her next question before it comes out of her mouth. "A paralegal? Are you in law school so you can actually practice law?"

Her tone isn't snide, unlike most of the people who ask me that question, but it's loud enough to get the attention of the men standing next to the grill. All six of them have turned their attention to us, faces in varying degrees of bafflement.

I let the question roll off my back, not feeling the slightest sting. There's a reason I'm a paralegal, not an attorney, and I have never questioned that reason, not even now.

Giving Jessica the same smile I use on all attorneys who can't begin to understand why anyone would disagree with them, I tell her. "I enjoy being a paralegal. Doing the research and digging up information to support a case. Finding ways to make it stronger. It's like a game for me, a treasure hunt for information. If I was an attorney, someone else would be doing that and I would have to do the boring stuff."

"That is the boring stuff." She says like I'm too ignorant to understand.

I brighten my smile a bit more. "Not to me."

Reed suddenly announces the food is ready, and I catch his eye as everyone starts heading to the table. He gives me the slightest of head nods before moving all the meat to a large platter.

As everyone sits down, Liv makes a point to put us at the opposite end of the table from Mitch and Jessica. She and Reed are trying to protect me and for once, I don't mind.

Maybe they feel bad for setting me up with a guy who was already seeing someone.

It's weird they didn't know.

The conversation around the table bounces from sports to movies to lawn care and I try to enjoy myself, focusing on the people sitting closest to me. My plan is to ignore the other end of the table but that only lasts so long. When Jake and Suzette start telling a story about her latest cooking disaster, I look their direction. And find Mitch looking right at me.

For a second, I freeze, locked in on him, and my chest tightens. He has no expression. His face is an indecipherable mask, but I see a glint of something lurking in his eyes before I blink slowly and turn away to take another bite.

Chewing deliberately, I set my shoulders back. *You do not care about some man you just met who had the audacity to flirt shamelessly with you when he already had a girlfriend.* I order myself.

You are an intelligent, interesting, confident woman. It's his loss, not yours.

The pep talk helps set me straight and I manage to block out the person sitting at the other end of the table while talking with everyone else and enjoying dinner.

As soon as the last fork is set down, Mitch stands up, telling everyone he has an early day and needs to head out. He pauses long enough for Jessica to say goodbye and the other usual crap people say when they've just met a group of strangers and everyone else gives their responses.

When the click of the front door reaches us, an audible exhale is released from everyone around the table. I don't dare move. It was bad enough having Emily, Hannah and Suzette give me those pitying looks earlier, I can't take the whole group looking at me like that. A quick scan of the faces surrounding me tells me it's already too late.

Liv takes a breath indicating she's about to make an announcement, so I go ahead and cut her off.

"It's fine."

"It's not fine." Liv counters back.

"We just met." I see she wants to butt in again, so I keep going. "Jessica seems nice, maybe we can all be friends."

Liv is staring at me, her eyes hard then softening with concern or worse, pity, and I hate it. Once again, I told her how I felt about a man, that it wasn't just lust but something more, and now I look like a fool.

"You want to be friends with her?" Brent asks, dumbfounded. I didn't realize the guys would have an opinion on this but looking around, it appears they all feel the same way.

"Sure," I say boldly and see the glances shot around the table.

Suzette leans over and squeezes my hand. "Don't worry, she won't last long."

"It will be over before you know it." Liv decrees and everyone agrees in return.

I manage to get out of there after a few more attempts at convincing them Mitch showing up with a woman is not big deal and we could maybe be friends. At home, I change into comfy pajamas and settle in to watch the History Channel. I love all these shows and usually get lost in them for hours but tonight they're not holding the same appeal. My mind keeps creeping back to Mitch, to what might have been, and for the hundredth time tonight, I tell myself it doesn't matter. Whatever I thought was there wasn't.

He has a girlfriend and I have the History Channel. The History Channel never leads me on then makes me feel like an idiot for being interested in it.

It sometimes makes me feel like a nerd but never an idiot.

CHAPTER NINE

MITCH

W hat the hell? It's the question I've been asking since night.

When Jessica and I left Reed's house last night, the question was directed at her. At how she could think it would be ok to introduce herself as my girlfriend and act like everything was perfect between us when we've never been more than occasional dinner dates and sexual partners.

By the time we pulled up to my house, I was ready to get out of my car and never see her again. I had parked in my darkened garage and waited for her to exit the car, ready for her to leave but she had other ideas.

"Can I come inside?" She asked in a voice that usually seduced me.

Slipping my keys in my pocket, I tried to be firm but gentle. "No, I don't think..."

And then her tongue was licking a path down my neck and her hand was in my pants.

I gritted my teeth against the sensations and gently tried to push her away. "Jessica."

But she pumped her hand up and down and my traitorous body short-circuited, my sharp inhale cutting off the rest of my words.

I'm not proud of what I did next but really, I didn't think it mattered. Not after seeing the look in Dana's eyes. The one that told me I had missed my shot with her and wouldn't be getting another one. The look that said I'm an asshole and she's better off without me.

So, I did what any asshole in my place would do and fucked Jessica against my car.

When it was over, I told her I had an early morning, the same thing I always told her afterward, so there would be no expectation of a sleepover. For a second, disbelief flitted across her features, but she composed herself quickly and said she'd see me soon before walking to her car with a pronounced sway of her hips.

Yeah, I looked. I'm an asshole.

I barely slept, my mind and my gut churning all night with something I don't ever feel.

Guilt.

Since I started dating, I've made sure I didn't have any reason to feel guilty, letting women know what they could expect from me and not promising more than I was prepared to deliver. But somehow, I still spent last night wide away and feeling like a cheater.

Not that I'm a cheater, I justify. I barely know Dana. We've spent less than three hours together, none of them alone, and hadn't made it to a date yet. But none of that matters to my conscience. It's calling me out for fucking Jessica, who, of the two women, is the one I've actually gone on a date with.

If it was just physical attraction to Dana, none of this would be happening. Attraction doesn't mean much, it's the other feelings that make things complicated.

I've been attracted to women before and none of them have infiltrated my brain the way Dana has. Hell, I was attracted to Jessica, but that is nothing compared to the way I felt when Dana placed her hand in mine and looked up at me. It was so much more than just attraction.

Dana isn't just a beautiful woman I want physically. It's deeper than that and I knew it the second our hands touched. Then we started talking, the connection between us growing, and by the time lunch was over I knew what I felt for Dana was different than anything I've felt before.

And that's what plagued me through the night. Guilt over feeling this way about one woman and fucking another.

This morning, I knew what I had to do. I left the house early, grabbed a cup of takeout coffee and went to Jessica's house to catch her before she left for work. When she answered the door, her smile gave away her pleasure to see me, thinking I was there for a different reason.

I was there to end things with her for good and make sure she understood that. I had to spell it out for her, something I should have done last time instead of just saying no and assuming she understood. It only took two minutes before I was on the receiving end of a slammed door and feeling pretty damn happy about it.

Like I said, I'm an asshole but at least now I'm an asshole who's completely unattached and, if granted another chance, can go after the woman I want.

"Mitch! What. The. Hell?"

Liv's voice brings me back to the present and I set my club sandwich down on the plate. I knew, when Reed called earlier and invited me to lunch with him and Dave, it was a ploy to talk about last night. I just didn't think he would hold off on the subject so his wife could show up and attack me.

"Liv," I say, wiping my hands on a napkin.

"I mean really, Mitch. You have a girlfriend! That you never mentioned! And you asked Dana out!"

"No. Jessica and I were seeing each other occasionally. Whenever we would have a mutual free night, we would get together for dinner." I avert my eyes and lower my voice a tad. "Or whatever." Dave, the smug bastard, smirks. "It was never serious and she was never my girlfriend."

"She seemed to think so." Liv's biting tone slashes at me.

"I never thought so. We've never used that term before. We were just two adults who enjoyed each other's company if nothing else was going on."

"That's not what she thinks."

"It is now. I can't help what she was thinking last night, but we talked," no need to mention it was this morning, that may raise other questions, "and I ended it with her."

"So you're single?" Liv asks skeptically.

"I've always been single." I remind her.

Liv's accessing eyes take my measure and I see I'm not completely back in her good graces. "Why did you bring her then?"

I longingly look at my sandwich knowing I'll probably have to get a to-go box for it. "She showed up when I was getting in my car. I told her I was on my way out to meet friends for dinner, and she was buckled in the passenger seat before I could stop her. I admit I should have made her get out, but I didn't really know what to do. I thought I could just say she was a friend and she'd go along with that." Jessica's always been a reasonable, mature adult. I didn't think she was going to tell everyone she was my girlfriend.

I still can't believe she did that.

"You really think you could show up to dinner with a woman, claiming she's just your friend and we wouldn't question it? You've never brought a woman to dinner before."

A sigh rolls out of me as I deflate in my chair. "I know. Again, I didn't really know what to do so I just went along with it."

Looking up from my plate of uneaten food, I watch Liv's face for clues. "Look, I know this didn't help me with Dana."

"You think you still have a shot with Dana!" She scoffs.

I'm not really a lay it all out there kind of guy but sometimes that's the only card left to play. If I'm ever going to get another shot with Dana, I'm going to need Liv's help. "I would like to." I honestly admit.

She gives me another hard look then relents. "Ok. I'll talk to Dana, explain everything."

I blink, then blink again. That was surprisingly easier than I thought it would be. "Thank you."

She cuts me off with the slice of her hand. "But I can't guarantee anything."

"I understand," I tell her and the truth is I really do. Dana has no reason to give me a second chance except for one tiny thing. I know she's just as interested in me as I am in her. We had... something, a moment, I guess, and you can't just pretend that didn't happen.

Now I just have to prove I'm worth a second chance.

Chapter Ten

DANA

I've only been at my new job for two weeks now, but I've officially been thrown to the wolves. We're working on a huge case and since I didn't need a lot of handholding given my previous experience, Monday morning my boss briefed me on the case then assigned me a month's worth of work. Knowing how this business is, every week that list will grow longer, and the expected completion date gets closer, so I've worked crazy hours all week to get a head start.

And avoid Liv. The irony of that isn't lost on me since I just moved halfway across the country to be closer to her.

Maybe avoid isn't the right word. More like, sidestep unwanted conversations.

Whatever the proper term is, my stress level was getting high, and I needed this morning's run more than I've needed one in a while.

I've been a runner since high school, since my dad died, and I was so fucking angry my mom told me I either had to go to therapy or find a way to deal with my anger on my own. I was pissed at her for saying it and took off out the front door and just ran. I ran for miles, until I couldn't feel anything except the burning pain in my legs and the desperate need for a deep breath. The next day, when the anger started to take over, I ran again and again the day after that.

Running helped me get through the worst time of my life and now the feel of my shoes hitting the ground is the best way I know to relax after a stressful week. No matter what else is going on in my life, I get up and run every Saturday. It's my happy place no matter where I'm at.

I found this park when I was looking for a house. Just driving by I knew this is where I'd spend my Saturday mornings, recharging. Last weekend, I veered off the main path, to jog the hiking trail through the wooded area but today I need more.

The main path follows the tree line and goes around the far side of the manmade pond and back around making a six mile loop. Several people are fishing with little kids, teaching them the basics of casting and ducks of all sizes are gliding across the water, ducklings trailing behind their moms.

It's a beautiful morning, the kind that makes you happy to be a part of it and the fresh air and sunshine fuel my energy. My legs are pumping, the music streaming from my earbuds pushing me faster, driving me to a speed I won't be able to maintain much longer.

Halfway around the pond, my lungs are burning, my muscles reaching their peak. I have to slow down and give myself a minute to catch my breath. Moving off the path, I lean against a tree to stretch. The new song in my ears is blaring as I press my foot back and start to feel the tense muscles ease.

A hand lands on my shoulder, ripping a strangled yelp from me and I spin, arms up and ready for an attack. I've taken self-defense lessons but when you're in that moment, everything you've been taught vanishes. I don't know what I'm preparing to do, but my arms must think they're going to hit someone.

"Mitch!"

The man I've spent the last week trying not to think about is backing away from me with his hands held out in surrender.

"Woah, sorry, didn't mean to scare you." I barely hear the words over my running playlist and yank the earbuds from my ears.

"What are you doing here?" I ask, accusing him of wrong-doing with my tone.

Dropping his hands, he takes a step closer. "I run here every morning before work. Saturday's too, but not so early."

"Oh. Ok." I say, turning to go.

He steps to the side and cuts me off. "You shouldn't run with both earphones in. You can't hear if someone sneaks up on you."

That old friend anger flares up inside me and I glare at him, wondering who he thinks he is to scold me. Genuine concern is looking back at me and maybe it's my pride, but I don't want to concede the point.

But a point, he does have. I didn't hear him at all.

Huffing out a breath, my eyes laser into his. "Noted," I say stepping around him.

"Let's run together." He suggests and my feet stop moving on their own.

It's a bad idea even if parts of my body disagree. I say the first thing I can think of to dissuade him. "I don't run that fast. I'll just hold you back."

Mitch smiles and I know I'm not getting the answer I was looking for. "No problem. I don't mind going slower."

Even if it's a bad idea, part of me still wants to be around this man. Giving him a single shoulder shrug, I put one of my earbuds back in and start running. He's beside me within seconds and we settle into a comfortable speed. For me at least.

I don't notice the ducks floating by or the people fishing in the pond anymore. At some point, we pass the playground, but I don't see it or the other joggers passing us, running in the opposite direction. My brain can only concentrate on the man silently running beside me. The knowledge he's there distracts me from everything else and I pray I don't trip and embarrass myself.

I already looked like a gullible fool believing this man was actually flirting with me, I will not look like a fool in front of him again.

An eternity later, we finally make it to the parking area, and I wonder if I should say something to him or just get in my car and drive away. What would I even say? Nice run. Thanks for going slow. Or I heard you broke up with her, but it doesn't matter. You're not getting another chance with me.

That last one feels more like it but I think actions speak louder than words, so I say nothing and head straight to my car.

Mitch's voice stops me as I'm opening my door. "Are you going to be here next Saturday?"

Giddiness spikes inside me before I stomp it down and tell teenage Dana to grow up. As much as I'm attracted to Mitch, I'm not falling for that charming smile again. And even if I was going to give him another chance, he was just with someone else. Her perfume is probably still on his sheets, her lipstick still on his... shirt.

"You should probably run with Jessica." I turn around and call out instead of answering his question. I know I'm being catty and a bit unfair, but it stung when he walked in with her, and I want him to know it. Not averting my eyes from his, I wait to see if he'll pick up the challenge.

He does. "We're not together anymore."

That's it. A simple statement, no inflection or apology, just a declaration but what did I expect? We had lunch with friends once, he doesn't owe me anything. He did ask me out but then canceled so it's not like we were even dating.

But it's hard to ignore my intense attraction to Mitch when he's right in front of me. I need to get away from this man before I agree to another date he doesn't deserve. At the moment, I don't have the ability to politely extract myself from this situation, so I roll my lips between my teeth to stop myself from saying something else bitchy.

Mitch is watching me so intently I feel like I have to respond in some way but the only thing I can do is nod and then get in my car and leave. A quick look in my rear-view mirror shows he's still standing there, watching my car drive away. Probably wondering what the hell I meant with that nod.

Hell, if I know.

I'm still trying to figure it out when I get home and see Liv's car parked in front of my house.

"Mitch broke up with her." Her voice comes from behind me as I head to the front door. "He said they weren't serious. She wasn't his girlfriend, just someone he went out with occasionally."

I'm dying to ask questions, just like I was Monday when she text me saying he ended it with her. I didn't respond then and I'm not going to now, but I still want to know if they weren't serious, then why did he bring her to dinner? And why didn't he seem too upset when she told everyone she was his girlfriend?

I know if I let myself ask, it will be harder to not think about it later. And I didn't want to think about it.

Yes, I am attracted to Mitch, like I've never been attracted to a man before, but I don't make the same mistake twice. Saying yes to a date with Mitch proved to be a mistake, one I'm now worried could affect my friendship with Liv. Mitch is part of Reed and Liv's group and now I am too. If Mitch and I dated and things went badly between us, they would have to take sides and I don't want that. I need to keep Mitch in the friend category and draw that line in the sand now, so things don't get complicated.

Hell, they probably already are complicated for Liv and Reed, being in the middle, and I don't want to make that worse. I need to see Mitch as nothing more than a friend, maybe a running buddy, but nothing more. And make sure Liv doesn't keep trying to push it further.

"Liv. It doesn't matter. I'm not going to date Mitch. If things didn't go well, what would happen to your and Reed's friendship with him? To me and you? I just don't think it's a good idea."

"But."

"No, no but. End of story. Let's talk about something else."

CHAPTER ELEVEN

MITCH

I've spent two days trying to figure out what Dana's nod meant.

Did it mean she'll be at the park next Saturday? She heard me when I said Jessica and I aren't together? Or she's willing to give me a chance?

The questions just keep circling, making me obsessed. Damn, that woman knows how to get in a guy's head.

I'm hoping she'll be at dinner tonight and we get the chance to talk. Or at the least, I figure out if she's harboring any unfriendly feelings towards me.

The whole time we were running, I keep waiting for her to say something, have an outburst about the whole mess or make a snide remark, but she didn't. Once I realized that's not how she operates, I was sure she was going to push me in the pond.

I really couldn't blame her if she wanted a little revenge. Nothing harmful, just a little push to show me she wasn't happy about the way things went down.

But she didn't do that either. She didn't rant and rave and make a scene or accuse me of leading her on while having a girlfriend. She didn't tell me to fuck off or stay away from her or even give me evil looks. She just ran.

And I wanted her even more. I let a speck of hope take up space inside me.

Until she threw out the barb about me running with Jessica. It was well placed, hitting its mark, and I felt like the asshole that I am.

Or was. Probably still am even though I'm trying to be a better person.

Since last weekend.

Anyway, that speck flickered out, disappearing before my eyes.

Until that nod. The reason for my current madness.

Anticipation fills me the closer I get to Reed and Liv's house. Walking up to their door, I rub my palms together and an image of me doing the same thing when I was sixteen in front of Bethany Levy's house, picking her up for our first date, my first date, flashes in my head.

I don't think I've ever been this nervous since then. Not when I applied to law school or took the bar. Not when I interviewed for my job or even the first time I met and advised the President. Hell, I wasn't this nervous the night I lost my virginity. Again with Bethany Levy, different night.

But seeing Dana again, knowing this could be my one and only shot at getting a second chance scares the fuck out of me.

I don't have time to examine why because the door flies open, and Liv is giving me angry eyes.

"Did you bring another girlfriend no one knows about?" She asks, making a show of looking around me.

"Left her at home tonight." I joke but Liv isn't amused. Putting my hands up, I try again. "No, no other girlfriends or supposed girlfriends. Just me."

Liv's scrutiny lasts so long I think she's not going to let me in but finally, she steps back, opening the door wider. Following her through the house, we stop in the kitchen where she grabs me a beer from the fridge. She must not be too mad if she's stocked the fridge with my favorite craft beer.

Tipping the bottle, I taste the citrus and hops, enjoying the flavor.

"Dana's not coming."

Those words are like a kick in the chest, one I don't let Liv see. I've worked hard to keep my expression neutral in all circumstances. It's helped me in business negotiations and at poker tables, but something tells me I need to be more transparent about my feelings where Dana is concerned.

"Is she ok?" Well, that wasn't really being transparent about my feelings but I'm a guy, what did you expect? Besides, I'm new to this having feelings thing.

"She's not sick if that's what you mean," Liv says. By the way she's looking at me, I know she's not going to offer anything else. The ball's completely in my court. If I want to know any more about Dana or get Liv's help, I'm going to have to ask.

"Why isn't she coming?"

Liv takes a deep breath like she's about to give a speech and I brace for impact.

"She said she needed to get a head start on work."

I wait but Liv doesn't go on, so I prompt her. "But?"

"But. I think we both know she didn't want to see you. And whoever you showed up with."

Generally, I don't sigh but, in this moment, I can't help it. "I told you, I ended it with Jessica. Not that there was anything to end."

"In your opinion." Liv interrupts.

"Yes, in my opinion. Which I made very clear to Jessica, and I thought to you too."

Liv gives a little nod, begrudgingly agreeing with me.

"Did you explain it to Dana?" I ask although, from the sound of it, she didn't.

Liv suddenly becomes very interested in the glass she's holding, twirling it around on the counter. I have a feeling I'm not going to like whatever she says next.

"I tried. But she didn't want to hear it." I can tell there's more she's not saying. Normally, I would wait her out but there's a crowd of people right outside. I probably don't have much longer until someone comes in.

Leaning my elbows on the counter, I lower my voice, asking in a confidential tone. "What else, Liv? What else did she say?"

"That she doesn't think dating you is a good idea." The words are so quiet I almost miss the disappointment behind them. Disappointment I'm feeling too.

Not even trying to hide that emotion, I ask for more. "Why?" My throat feels raw, my voice coming out hoarse.

"She said if it didn't work out, it would be difficult for Reed and me since we're both of your friends."

I understand what she means. My friendship with Reed and Liv has come to mean a lot to me. I don't want to jeopardize that, and I almost did, letting Jessica come with me last week. What Dana said sucks, but I get it.

Dipping my chin in a nod, I look at Liv. "Thanks for trying."

She says something but I'm already out the door and don't hear it. The rest of my friends greet me with slaps on the back or a raised beer bottle, the smell of grilled meat making my stomach growl.

"So, where's your girlfriend?" Brent asks and everyone goes still. Shit, I have to explain it all again. They're going to think I'm an asshole.

I stare at Brent, thinking of a way to phrase it that doesn't make me sound so bad when Hannah bursts out laughing. Everyone else joins in and I know my fear is unfounded. These people love me, even if I am an asshole sometimes.

"Yeah, yeah. You got me." I admit with a chuckle. "We..."

"No need to explain. Liv and Reed filled us in." Brent assures me and hands me a plate.

I'm surrounded by good friends about to eat some great food, I should be happy. And I am, but a part of me is disappointed Dana isn't here. Disappointed I missed my chance with her, knowing I missed out on something great.

Chapter Twelve

DANA

I'm glad I got a head start on this week's workload, but Liv and I both know that's not why I skipped dinner at her house tonight. I expect a call from her any minute.

My phone rings as soon as I have that thought and I glance at the screen.

"Speak of the devil," I say out loud, answering the call. "Hello."

"Hey. I just wanted to check in, and see how the work's going."

Yeah, right. "It's going. So much to do, so little time." There's no point in really talking about work, we both know that's not why she called.

She doesn't keep the pretense up for long. "Mitch was here."

Teenage Dana squeals inside me but I shut her down. "That's nice."

"He was alone." She prompts.

Too late. Bitchy Dana says silently.

"I thought you said he always came alone. Until last week." That last part is a bit bitchy, but I think it's fair since she was trying to set me up with this guy and he showed up with another woman.

Liv's sigh comes over the phone and I know she feels bad about it. "I'm sorry about that. And he really hasn't ever brought a woman to dinner before."

I'm not sure what to say after that, so I stay quiet, but I can't sit still. Standing, I start cleaning off my cluttered kitchen table. My wallet is out from an impulse purchase earlier and I pick it up, opening my purse to toss it back in. A crumpled napkin is on top, and I grab it to throw away when Liv responds.

"He seemed disappointed you weren't there."

"Oh really?" That comes out with an extra side of sass.

"He asked if I explained he and Jessica weren't really dating and he ended things with her."

"And that makes you think he was disappointed I wasn't there?" I ask a little too defensively because it does kind of sound like he was disappointed, and I don't know what to make of that.

"Yes! And he asked me what you said back, and he was, well, disappointed you didn't want to go out with him."

I try to remember that conversation with Liv. I don't think I ever said I didn't want to go out with Mitch, just that it wasn't a good idea.

"But he understood your reasoning."

I can't remember what reason I gave her, but I know I didn't tell her that for a brief moment I stupidly thought Mitch might be the man I've always been looking for. Until he proved to be just a flirt who already had a girlfriend. He may say she wasn't his girlfriend, but she was something to him or he wouldn't have looked so guilty when she announced it.

"Maybe you should give him another chance," Liv says, her voice timidly hopeful.

"Liv, he just got out of a relationship, like yesterday. One he was in when he asked me out." I argue. Plopping back down in the chair, I throw the wadded-up napkin on top of my notes and watch it slowly loosen up until I see writing on it.

When did Liv put that waiter's phone number in my purse?

"It wasn't like that." Liv defends him. "I told you he wasn't really with her. She was never his girlfriend. It was so nothing it didn't even occur to him he needed to end it with her." She defends him, and it ticks me off a little.

"Until he brought her to dinner and introduced her as his girlfriend!"

"He didn't introduce her that way, she did. I explained all this. He really feels bad about that which you would know if you came to dinner tonight." She says with another sigh.

All the righteous indignation goes out of me with that sigh. Not because I think I'm wrong but because I know my friend just wants me to be happy and she thought it could happen with Mitch. I don't think he's a bad guy, more a womanizer who dinged my pride and no self-respecting woman should sacrifice her pride to be with a man.

But if I don't give Liv something, she won't let this go. "I did see him yesterday," I tell her blandly.

The surprise shows in her voice. "Really? Where?"

"At the park, when I was running."

"What? Why didn't you tell me yesterday?"

I hesitate for a beat but decide to just give her the highlights. "He was running too and turned around so he could run with me."

"That's great! So, you too talked?" She's so excited I feel a little bad I'm about to squash that.

"No. Not until we were back in the parking lot."

"Did he ask you out?"

"No." But maybe I wanted him to.

Until I thought about seeing Mitch with Jessica and how much it stung. Yes, I know he broke up with her and maybe he broke up with her because of me, but no matter what I tell myself, I keep picturing them together.

Naked.

Naked on Saturday when he was supposed to be having lunch with me. A lunch I was looking forward to, and that makes me feel foolish. And feeling foolish makes me angry. Like I could hit something. Hard. Repeatedly.

Maybe I should go to kickboxing...

Or maybe I should go on a date with someone else. Someone like Peter. Yes, we work together but a few dates won't hurt anything.

Even if it's Mitch you want to get naughty with?

Stop it, Dana! I scold myself, hardening my resolve to date someone else. Nothing serious, I'm not looking for a marriage proposal, just dinner, drinks and some good conversation.

"Oh, ok." Liv sounds defeated but she rebounds quickly. "What about that Peter guy at work?" She suggests, reading my mind. "You said he was interested."

The idea of going on a date with Peter doesn't hold much appeal but it's exactly what I need right now. "I was thinking the same thing. I'll ask him out tomorrow." I tell her and Liv, being the great friend she is, wishes me luck.

***

The next day is busy and I barely have time for a restroom break much less time to find Peter.

"Hey, Dana." Leslie leans around the cubical wall separating us. "You want to go have drinks with us after work?"

I don't even bother asking who us is. "Yes."

"Great!" She smiles and turns back to her workspace.

At four fifty-nine, I'm watching the clock, waiting for the last minute to tick by. It's unusual for us to leave right at five pm but these ladies are serious about their happy hour.

"It's five o'clock bitches!" Gina shouts and a whoop goes up from her fellow cohorts. I click the clock out button on my timesheet app and power down my computer.

"Dana, it's about time you went out with us," Allison says as we're making our way out of the cubicle maze.

"I've only been here a few weeks but yeah, it's time I get out and make my presence known." I toss back with a smirk.

We're heading down the back hall and as we pass the break room, I notice its lone occupant. It only takes a second for my thoughts from last night to run through my mind and then I'm stopping in the middle of the hall. "Hey, I'll meet you in the parking lot, I just need a minute." I call out to the group and get an "ok" and a thumbs up in return.

"Here goes nothing," I tell myself and take a steadying breath before opening the door.

Peter turns and I see the second his brain processes who's just walked in and his friendly smile settles in place. He's keeping it professional since I turned him down but that's fine. This isn't the first time I've asked a man out.

"Hi, Peter."

"Hi, Dana. Heading out?" He asks then takes a sip of his coffee. Who drinks coffee at five pm?

Shaking that thought off, I take a step closer and see him survey me, probably wondering what I'm doing here. Deciding not to keep him guessing, I just get it out. "If you're still interested, I think we should go out sometime."

For a few seconds, Peter is frozen, and I wonder if he changed his mind but then his panty melting smile slides into place. Too bad it still doesn't do anything for me, but we can have a few drinks and get to know each other. You can't always expect fireworks and tingles when you meet a man.

"How about Saturday night?" He asks, letting his eyes roam over me again, and this time there's no question behind his gaze. He's taking in all that is Dana Tolliver and I have to admit, it feels good to get checked out by a handsome man. I work hard to look this good.

"Saturday night works for me," I reply with a flirty smile and give him my address.

Making my way to the staff elevator, I head to the parking garage thinking about my new plans for the weekend. Now that the adrenaline from asking Peter out is wearing away, I'm not feeling very good about it.

"You're having dinner with a sexy lawyer." I scold myself.

Yeah, but it's not the sexy lawyer you really want.

CHAPTER THIRTEEN

MITCH

I 've known I would be a lawyer since I was six and my dad showed me his office for the first time. 'Mitchell, someday, you'll follow in my footsteps and be a lawyer too. Anything else is unacceptable.' He said, letting me sit behind his big, wooden desk. I never questioned it. I wanted to make my dad proud, and I sacrificed everything to do it.

There were a few weeks when I was ten, that I ran around the house with a hat, dodging imaged boulders, stealing price-less artifacts and cracking a fake whip but like I said, my dad didn't tolerate that silliness, as he put it, and convinced me to leave that kind of work to the movie stars.

I may have given up the dream of being the next history professor slash archeologist, but my love of history was born when I watched that movie and has grown over the years.

But after Dad's talk, I was determined to get into Harvard Law, like he did, and I worked my ass off to get there. Everything I did from the electives I chose to the volunteer work I did as a teenager was all to earn my acceptance.

And it worked. I rarely dated, girls were a distraction, one I couldn't afford and the few times I did date, my parents wanted to make sure the girl was a "suitable" match. Most of the girls I was interested in fell into their "unsuitable" list except Bethany Levy since her father was a big client of my dad's.

My parents still remind me every relationship from acquaintance to spouse should support my career goals. They're a match made in country club heaven.

After I passed the bar, my focus was on working my way up the ladder. I started dating more, something I don't mention to my parents, but I've never had a girlfriend. Never been on more than a few dates with a woman knowing a relationship requires something I can't give. Time. And my time belongs to my job.

For me, work has always come first and that's how I've lived my life, solely focused on my career and my ultimate goals. Everything else was secondary and all that secondary shit never crossed my mind when I was in the office.

But today, the secondary shit is taking over. I've been staring at the same document for almost an hour, rereading it at least ten times and still have no idea what it says. My mind is on a woman I can't have and how, for the first time in my life, I want more than a few random dates and a casual fuck. I keep hearing Liv telling me Dana doesn't want to go out with me. I don't like it but there's nothing I can do.

Looking back at the paper in my hand, I skim it again, trying to find my place but it's no use. My head's not in it today.

Frustrated, I shove back from my desk and pace in front of the window. I don't know if I'm angry because I blew my shot with Dana or because I can't separate myself from it and focus on work. A knock on my office door irritates me even more and I growl out a greeting.

Thomas Sherman walks through the door and my shitty attitude immediately disappears.

"Thomas! What are you doing here? I figured you'd be on a golf course somewhere." I joke with my old mentor.

Shaking my hand, Thomas slaps me on the back. "I usually am but I had lunch down the street and thought I'd stop in and see how you're doing."

"I'm good. Work is going well. We've had a few issues that required some extra time, but you know I don't mind that." I tell him, smiling, proud of my commitment to the job. The commitment I learned from him and Dad.

Thomas' lips quirk, not really a smile and I feel like I just gave the wrong answer.

"I'm not surprised, you're a hard worker. You outshined all the other candidates and earned this job by your own merit." I appreciate him saying that, but I feel a "but" coming. "But I wasn't asking about the job. I know that's going well for you, it always is. I was asking about you. How are you doing?"

How am I supposed to answer that if he doesn't want to hear about work?

My lack of a response doesn't go unnoticed, and Thomas tries to help me out.

"How's your personal life?"

Did he just read my mind? In all the time I've known Thomas, he has never asked about my personal life. A friend of my dad's, they share the same philosophy on careers and relationships. Now Thomas shows up at my office, out of the blue, on the one day my personal life has taken over my brain and asks about it.

I know I'm staring at him with a strange look on my face but I'm a bit baffled. Being the great attorney he is, he gives me a more direct question.

"Have you read any good books lately?"

"Ummm... no, I haven't read anything that wasn't work related in a while."

"You should make more time to read. It's a great escape for the mind." He says, tapping the side of his head.

Who is he? The Thomas I know doesn't give a shit about reading or finding a great escape for the mind.

"What about a vacation? Have you taken any time off?" He asks.

The question is so ridiculous, I can't help but repeat it. "Have I taken any time off? No. I don't ever take time off."

"You should. It would do you some good."

"When's the last time you went on a vacation?" I sling the question at him.

"Evelyn and I just got back from Aruba. We were there for two weeks, it was great. You really should go on a vacation. You work too much. Spend all your time in this damn office."

My jaw drops and I make little effort to hide it. Go on a vacation? Thomas never took a single day off that I can remember. Not even a sick day. Of course, he's retired now so he has all the time in the world to visit tropical islands, but I have shit to do.

"Are you at least seeing someone?"

Immediately, I think about Dana for the six thousandth time today but shake my head. "No."

"No? Not even casually?"

He knows how I operate, that I don't have time for relationships. "No. There was someone I would see occasionally, but that's over."

"I would ask why but it sounds like you weren't really interested in her."

"You read my mind," I say with a smirk, trying to keep this from going where I think it's going.

"You haven't met anyone who does interest you?"

The way he's looking at me, I know he could answer that question for himself, which he does.

"You have. But..."

There's no point in denying it so I go for nonchalant. "It just didn't work out, but it's fine. I don't have time for a relationship right now." Not the first time I've said that today.

Thomas studies me for what feels like an hour. We're already in uncharted territory and I don't dare say anything, too afraid of where else this could go.

Finally, he speaks. "Mitch, you are one of the smartest and quickest legal minds I've ever had the pleasure of working with and I couldn't be more proud of you and how far you've come."

"But?" *Shut up, Mitch.*

"But you're an idiot."

"Excuse me?"

"I know I didn't set a very good example. Hell, I set a pretty awful example, working eighty, ninety hours a week, eating breakfast, lunch and dinner at my desk most days. I never took a day off, not even when I was sick. I neglected my marriage, missed seeing my kids grow up and my grandkids too. I just kept pushing myself harder, thinking if I could put in a few more hours, I would finally have some extra time for myself. Be able to spend quality time with my family. Go on a vacation. See something besides the inside of my office. And do you know what happened?"

I have a feeling but, "No."

"I woke up one day and wondered who the old man looking back at me was and where the hell my life went. My kids were grown, and their kids were almost grown too. My Evelyn, God, that woman is a saint. She was old too. But don't you tell her I said that. I mean, she's still the most beautiful woman I've ever seen but she's not young anymore. She spent her whole adult life raising our kids, taking care of me and how did I replay her? I just worked longer hours until most of our life had passed us by. What a bastard I was."

I squirm in my chair, very unlike me, fighting the uncomfortable feeling rising up my chest. I have the distinct need to jump up and run out of here before Thomas can say anymore. This man that I idolized, that I patterned my career after, is telling me it was all a mistake. That the way I'm living my life, the choices I've made, are wrong.

Is Dad feeling the same way? That would explain why he's been calling me more.

Thomas gives me a hard look, then goes in for the kill.

"Don't wait until you're old to start living your life, Mitch. Don't waste all your youth on building a career because let me tell you. One day you're going to wake up and see an old man in the mirror too and you're going to wonder where all the years went. I don't want you to have the same regrets I do. Your career isn't going to sit next to you when you're old and tired and hold your hand. A job is never going to love you. Don't put it before everything else. It's not worth it."

Thomas leans closer to my desk, and I know his next words are going to alter my life.

"If you find someone who makes you happy, don't put them behind the job. Make time for them, for yourself. You understand?"

"I understand, but there's more to it than that," I tell him.

"There always is, son." He says as he stands and reaches for my hand.

We agree to get together soon and as he's walking out the door, he gives one final piece of advice. "If you want to be with her, be with her." Then he turns and walks away.

"But she doesn't want to be with me," I say to my empty office.

Liv's words from Sunday night go through my head again. 'She said it wasn't a good idea. If it didn't work out, it would be difficult for Reed and me since we're both of your friends.'

If it didn't work out...

Wait. That doesn't sound like Dana isn't interested in me, but that she's concerned about the fallout if things don't go well. Maybe I do still have a shot.

I just can't blow it this time.

Chapter Fourteen

MITCH

After Thomas' visit and my revelation that Dana never said she didn't want to go out with me, I was able to get some work done. I guess thinking I didn't have a chance in hell with her was eating me up and stealing all of my focus. Once I knew it wasn't hopeless, things settled down.

I still think about her constantly and that has led to more intimate times with my right hand and a few cold showers but at least I've been somewhat able to block those thoughts when I'm in the office and get some shit done.

Even though it's Saturday, I have to head back to work for a few hours, but I'll go after my run. I run every day, it not only keeps me fit, it keeps my stress levels down and I fucking need to keep my stress levels down. This job is a heart attack waiting to happen. But Saturday runs now have a new purpose.

My contractor wanted to start working on my new floors this morning but I pushed him off until Monday. I have more important things to do today. Like see Dana.

She didn't exactly say she would be here again today but I'm not willing to miss out on seeing her if she does. I've been here for almost an hour, just in case she decided to come earlier than she did last week. I've stretched three times, cranked out a hundred push-ups and updated my running playlist.

Checking my watch again, only four minutes since the last time I looked, I scan the streets for her car. I refuse to believe she's not coming and with no sign of her, I start stretching again.

A dark blue car turns into the parking lot, and I try to keep the smile off of my face. I knew she'd be here.

I'm standing near the entrance to the main trail when she gets out of her car and walks toward me. I want to go to her, pull her close and kiss the hell out of her but I can't. *Maybe one day if I play my cards right.* Forcing myself to stay where I am, I shove my hands in my pockets and wait.

If she ignores me, I'll just keep my mouth shut and run next to her. If she doesn't ignore me, well, things are delicate. I'll take my cues from her.

She's coming closer.

Dana looks at me and is that... yes, it is. That's a smile on her face! Fuck yeah!

There's cheering in my head but I keep my celebration inside. I don't want to scare her off or piss her off which is more likely so I just smile back instead.

"Hey, Mitch." She says, stopping a few feet away.

I'm momentarily speechless, watching her bend at the waist and touch the ground. Damn, that ass is perfect.

Dana turns her head to the side and looks up at me quizzically. Oh shit, I was supposed to say something back.

Giving myself a mental slap, I seem to do that a lot lately, I respond. "Hey. Dana. I was hoping you would be here." Did that sound creepy? Fuck, is she going to think I'm stalking her?

"Really? And why is that?" She asks. It almost sounds like she's flirting with me.

Do I answer honestly and tell her I can't stop thinking about her? Do I apologize again for the "misunderstanding" with Jessica? Do I tell her I would do just about anything to see her again? No, that does sound like a stalker.

She's in another stretch and I drag my eyes away from her body and stretch my quads for the fourth time.

"I thought we could run together again." That was casual, not too stalkery, right?

Dana stands and does one last stretch. "Ok."

That's all she says and then she's taking off, running away from me in very tight pants. Did I mention how perfect her ass is?

I easily catch up to her and match her pace. We make it about halfway around the lake before any blood travels back to my brain and I can come up with something to say that doesn't involve parts of our anatomy and caveman noises.

"There's an event at the Smithsonian tonight. At the National Museum of American History. They're unveiling a new exhibit on Prohibition. I was planning on going, maybe you could go with me." *Unless you already have a date for tonight.* "If you aren't already doing something else." I tack on real fast.

We keep running and Dana doesn't respond which doesn't do my self-esteem any favors. I don't generally question myself, especially not when it comes to women, but I also don't show my nerdy side to many people either. What was I thinking, asking her to go to a history museum with me?

"It's probably not your thing..."

"Actually, it sounds interesting." She says, still running. "I just already have plans for tonight."

"Of course, it is kind of last minute." I want to ask if she's going out with another guy, but keep my mouth shut. Neither one of us says anything for the rest of the run.

When the end of the trail is in sight, we both slow down to a walk. A breeze comes through the trees, blowing Dana's long ponytail my way and I can smell her shampoo. Coconut and something minty. It smells like relaxing on the beach and I picture us laying in the sand, her in a bikini. My hands massaging suntan oil onto her skin.

I choke back a growl and Dana glances at me.

Not the time for those kind of thoughts. But it is the time to ask her out for next weekend, get on her calendar before someone else does. We're almost to the parking lot so if I'm going to do it, I better do it now.

"How about dinner with me next weekend?"

She stops and fully turns, all her attention focused on me. This is good right?

"No." She says and it totally catches me off guard.

"No?"

"No." She repeats but it doesn't have any heat behind it, like she doesn't want to be saying it.

"Bye Mitch." She tells me, a little frown wrinkling her brow, and heads to her car. As I watch her walk away from me, I only have two thoughts.

One, she really does have a perfect ass.

Two, she may have said no, but her confused frown said something else.

And that's all the hope I need.

***

Hours later, I wander around the American History Museum with a drink in my hand. The new exhibit on Prohibition is already a hit, but the back half of the space is a speakeasy so it's not really a surprise.

Reed and Liv are supposed to be here, but I haven't seen them yet. Pretty sure Reed's only coming for the alcohol and the fact he's wrapped around Liv's finger. She's the one who seemed excited when I mentioned coming tonight, although now that I think about it, she did say Dana would love this. Maybe she thought it would be a good way to get the two of us together again. If so, neither of us accounted for Dana having other plans tonight.

Sipping my whiskey, I study the display in front of me. There are actual prescriptions from the 1920's listing whiskey as the medication with a few government stamped one hundred proof whiskey bottles next to them.

"It's amazing what some people will do for a drink," a feminine voice says to my right.

Looking down, I see she's beautiful and now leaning into me.

"I'm Mara." She says, holding out her hand.

Switching my glass to my left, I shake her hand and introduce myself.

"Mitch, tell me you're here alone." Even if I didn't catch her not so subtle cues, there's no mistaking what she just said. She wants to fuck me.

A month ago, I would be escorting her out of here within five minutes but not now. Looking at her I don't feel a thing. Which is weird since that's how I always wanted it before. I've never felt anything for the women I've had sex with except maybe lust. If I met a woman and even thought I might feel more for her, I walked away. Too complicated, not worth the trouble.

But all that's changed. I barely know Dana, I sure as hell can't explain my feelings for her, but now that I've felt something, the thought of having sex with a random woman I don't give a shit about turns my stomach a bit. It started with Jessica in my garage but I went through with it anyway and it's something I'm not proud of. I won't be making that mistake again.

The woman, I can't even remember her name, moves closer, pressing her tits to my arm. I could probably fuck her in the bathroom or a storage closet somewhere if I was still that guy. But I'm not.

Suppressing a sigh, I try to let her down easy. "I'm not available but I am flattered. Have a good night."

I give her what I hope is a friendly but standoffish smile and start to turn away. Her hand latches onto my arm.

"I haven't seen you with anyone else. She must not be here." Her voice has a seductive tone matching her body language and the knowledge she's trying to entice a man to cheat makes me disgusted.

Leaning down to make sure she hears me over the growing party, I make myself clear. "I'm. Not. Interested." I hold her stare long enough to get the point across then walk away.

I know people cheat all the time, but I never wanted to be one of those people. I may have stayed away from relationships but that doesn't mean I don't value commitment. Knowing just a few weeks ago, I would have left with this woman pisses me off even more. I may have been single but my judgment was lacking, something I already figured out by the mess with Jessica.

I'm still berating myself with I spot Reed and Liv walking in. Dodging other guests, we met in the middle of the space and after a hug from Liv and a handshake from Reed, he heads to the speakeasy to get them drinks.

"I asked Dana to come but she had other plans." Liv says, confirming my earlier suspicions. At least it seems like Liv is team Mitch again.

"I know. I saw her this morning and asked her too."

Liv's eyes get huge, and she blinks once. "You did?"

I'm not sure why she's so surprised, it's not like I haven't made my interest known.

"Where did you see her?"

"At the park. We both run there."

Liv rolls her eyes and swats her hand through the air. "Oh, yeah. You're both runners. I'm a yoga girl myself."

"It shows." I tease her and get a swat to the arm.

"Well, good for you asking her out even though I told you not to."

"You didn't tell me not you. You said she didn't think it would be a good idea for us to date because things could be awkward if we broke up."

"Exactly. But you asked her out again anyway!" She says with enthusiasm.

I don't have a clue why she's so damn happy about me getting shot down even after telling me, just last week, Dana said going out with me wasn't a good idea.

Liv shakes her head at me and tries to explain. "Look, I think you are perfect for each other and if you wouldn't have shown up to dinner with Jessica, you could be here with Dana now, but that's beside the point."

"But you still had to bring it up." I deadpan.

"Of course. But... back to the point. Dana said you should put some time between your last relationship and your next one."

"It wasn't a relationship." I try to defend myself, but Liv talks over me.

"And honestly, I think she really likes you but you showing up with another woman stung and she needs time to lick her wounds." I know what she's trying to say, but those words conjure a very different image in my head. "Which means eventually she'll be ready to jump on the Mitch train even if she won't admit it right now. But until then, you have to be patient. Without giving her too much space. You don't want her to think you're not interested anymore."

I stare at my friend's wife, a lady I consider a friend and let her words sink in.

Be patient and give Dana some space while still making it obvious I want her.

I can do that.

"See, it makes sense, right?" Liv says, smiling and nodding her head. I mirror her and that's how Reed finds us, smiling and nodding at each other like two bobble heads.

"What is happening here?" He asks, handing Liv a drink.

She wraps her arm around Reed's and gives him a kiss. "Just imparting some of my relationship wisdom on Mitch."

Reed raises his eyebrow at me and offers his own piece of wisdom. "Good luck."

CHAPTER FIFTEEN

DANA

"Here we are. A glass of Sauvignon Blanc for you." The waitress says, setting the glass in front of me. "And a bourbon neat for you." She leans over the table a little more as she sets Peter's drink down, giving him a clear shot of her cleavage but he just thanks her and looks back at me.

"So, Dana. I know you haven't been with WDF very long, where were you before that?" Peter asks me. The waitress rises stiffly and mumbles something I assume is our food will be right out before walking away. Peter never takes his eyes off of me.

He's solely focused on my face, and I can tell he's doing it not because he finds me so beautiful he can't look away but because he knows women eat that kind of thing up. Having an attractive man ignore the pretty flirtatious waitress and only have eyes for you is an incredible boost to your confidence, something all women crave.

The problem with me is I see right through it. Peter doesn't give a shit about where I worked before WDF or what I like to do in my free time, it's just his move to score with women. Ask them questions about themselves, make them feel special, like they're the only women you notice, and they're putty in your hands. Yep, he's one smooth player.

Reminds me of someone else.

Honestly, it's a good move and I can't really fault him for it. If I thought for a second he really wanted to find out what makes me tick, I would be all in, but I can see this guy for who he really is. Insincere flattery and bullshit.

At least Mitch seemed more genuine or genuine enough I actually fell for it.

Anyway, I figured Peter out pretty quickly on the ride to the restaurant. Every question I asked him he answered quickly and with few words only to turn around and ask me three more questions. At one point he even told me I didn't want to hear what he had to say and that I should tell him more about myself.

He's either trying to gather my personal information to steal my identity or he's figured out most women have self-confidence issues, and he can use that to get them naked. Make them feel pretty and special and their clothes come right off. Hell, it even works on women who aren't self-conscience. We all want to feel special.

Too bad it's not working on me tonight. That dry spell's going to last a little longer.

Taking a sip of my wine, so good, I set my glass down before answering.

"I was at a firm in Dallas, I just moved here last month."

"So, you're new in town." He smiles at me again and I see him gearing up for another question. I beat him to it.

"How long have you been at WDF?"

"Twelve years." He starts to say something else, but I cut him off again.

"How long did it take to make Senior Partner?" Most men love to brag about themselves, but Peter looks a little annoyed by the question.

"Six years."

"You must have worked your ass off."

I know the moment Peter realizes I'm onto him. His slick smile drops, and he sits back in his chair. We have a stare off until he changes his game plan.

"I did. Put in eighty and ninety hour weeks for years. It cost me my marriage."

Hmmmmm, so he's going for direct honesty. That's my preferred method of communication too. Now we're getting somewhere.

"I'm sorry to hear that," I tell him in a softer voice and see the confusion behind his eyes. Peter Moore doesn't know what to do with me. His flattery put me on guard but talking about his divorce softens me. Taking a sip of his bourbon, he decides to continue with the honesty tacit.

"Like I said, I was working at least eighty hours a week, trying to get the promotion we both wanted me to have so I could buy her the big house, the luxury vacations, the fancy jewelry. But she ended up leaving me anyway. Said I never made time for her, that I was a workaholic. But have you ever met a lawyer who wasn't a workaholic?" He asks this matter of factly, and it hits me hard.

No. No, I haven't met a lawyer who wasn't a workaholic, or in the case of my ex, Chris, "dedicated to his career" was how he put it. I put it "selfish, money whoring asshole" when we broke up. Not that it bothered him, his career was the only thing he cared about. I was never a priority in Chris' life. His work always came first so I can understand why Peter's wife left him. Of course, I'm only hearing one side of the story so who knows what really happened.

Peter extends his hand across the table and runs a finger over the back of my hand. He must think his honesty is going to pay off. And it is on a getting to know you level, but my panties are staying in place tonight. And probably forever for this guy.

Before I moved here, I would have been all over someone like Peter but I'm just not feeling it now. And not because I know Peter's game and see him for the workaholic man whore he probably is but because I can't stop thinking about Mitch. Part of me wants him to be the one I'm getting to know and wishes it was him flirting with me. The other part of me is pissed at myself for wanting him.

I spend the rest of dinner making conversation and walking the fine line of letting Peter know nothing is going to happen between us and trying not to offend him. I don't want my lack of interest to affect my job.

This is why you shouldn't date men you work with, Dana.
Thanks Rational Dana, I'll remember that.

***

Sunday night, the door flings open. "You were supposed to call me."

"Hi Liv, it's great to see you too," I say with extra sarcasm, walking into her house.

"I can't believe you didn't call me after your date."

"Was I supposed to? I don't remember that."

She doesn't even try to hide her exasperation with me. "Dana!" She wails flinging her hands and huffing out a huge breath. I try to keep a straight face, but the chuckle escapes me.

Liv, standing there with her hands on her hips, literally tapping her foot, tries to keep the aggravated look on her face too but she can never stay mad at me. We're both laughing when Reed walks by.

He doesn't bother to stop on his way to the back deck, just says over his shoulder, "I'll just be out here, lighting the grill."

Liv wipes tears from her eyes and calls out to him. "Thanks, honey!" Turning back to me, she's all business. "Ok, spill."

I know I have to give her details, or she'll badger me until I do. I used to do the same thing to her so it's payback. Wondering how best to sum up my dinner with Peter, I grab a glass from the counter and hold it out to Liv. She quickly fills it and plunks the bottle down. "Ok, now spill."

Picturing Peter across the table from me, I try to sum it up. "Like I said, he's a Senior Partner at work, good looking, probably in his late forties."

"Ok, good. Go on." She encourages me.

Shrugging, I watch my wine swirl in my glass. "There's not really a lot more to say."

"Not more to say? There's a lot more to say. Where did you have dinner? What did you talk about? Are you going out with him again? Did you kiss him? Did you sleep with him?"

This last question is asked with a bit of dismay.

"No! I didn't sleep with him." I hiss back at her. No one else is here yet but I still feel weird talking about my sex life, or nonsex life, in front of her husband. I may act all ballsy and like I'm an open book but Liv's the only person who gets the intimate details. Everyone else can just assume whatever they want.

Giving a dismissive hand toward the open back door, Liv leans across the bar towards me. "Out with it."

"We went to Le Diplomate, some trendy French restaurant. The food was good, the wine was better." She's nodding her head and murmuring for me to continue.

"We talked about work. No not like that," I say to her sudden frown. "We talked about how long he had been there and where I worked before." This next part she's not going to like. "And his ex-wife and the reason she divorced him was because he's a workaholic."

"That sounds familiar." She mutters.

"Chris and I weren't married." I remind her like she's forgotten.

"I know but workaholics seem to be a trend for you." She sees my frown and reaches over and grabs my hand. "I just want you to be happy. To find someone who cares about you and makes you feel special."

Clasping my other hand on hers, I give her a smile. "I know."

The doorbell rings and Liv pulls away. "Real quick, what happened after dinner?" She asks.

My eyes roll thinking about that awkwardness. "After dinner, he drove me home and tried to kiss me, but I dodged it and told him we should just be co-workers."

"Good," Liv says and starts walking towards the front door. "Now you can go out with Mitch." She practically yells on her way to the front door.

When she opens it, I hear several voices, but can't tell who it is. I haven't been around this group enough yet, so I'm a little surprised when the topic of Liv's last statement walks into the kitchen. As soon as he sees me, a smile covers his face, and he says, "Hey."

Inwardly I'm cringing, I really hope he didn't hear what Liv just said. My hand goes up in a little wave and I manage to get out a "Hey" in return.

Mitch comes closer, charming smile still in place, and my heart starts beating a little faster.

He looks so good. Is he going to sit next to me? Is he going to kiss me?

I'd like to say I don't know why my inner teenager is making another appearance after I told her he is off limits but let's be honest. It happens to every woman when a cute boy, or handsome man, looks at them like Mitch is looking at me right now, especially if the guy is labeled off limits.

Stopping just outside of my personal space, Mitch looks directly in my eyes. "We missed you last night at the history museum."

For a moment, I'm in a trance. His eyes holding me in place until the doorbell rings again.

"I'll get it," Liv calls out to whoever else is here, something I would know if I could stop staring at Mitch.

Flicking my gaze away, I try to swallow my fluttery nerves. As my eyes roam back up to his face, they take the path that travels over his body and holy shit, this man is hot. A slow deep breath steadies me a tiny bit more and draws his eyes to my chest for the briefest of moments.

Good, let him see what he's missing.

"I missed being there," I tell him, honestly and his returning smile lights something up inside me.

Off limits, Dana! I tell myself and turn the conversation in another direction. "I love history. The History Channel is my favorite thing to watch."

Mitch gets a perplexed look and I shut my mouth fast, looking away. Damn, it. Now he's going to know I'm a big nerd. I usually keep my love of the History Channel under wraps for just this reason. Hmmmmm, maybe it will work to my advantage, and he'll lose interest.

Do you really want that?

"Me too," Mitch says and my gaze snaps back to his. "I love the shows about the founding of America, but History's Mysteries is my favorite. I watch the reruns over and over."

"Me too!" I tell him, a little shocked he's also a nerd.

A few more people walk into the kitchen, talking loudly and laughing, our little chat about to be interrupted. Mitch must feel the same way because he comes half a step closer and leans in so slightly if I wasn't fixated on him, I wouldn't have noticed.

"Maybe we could go to the history museum together some-time." He suggests quietly.

My heart starts pounding again and I dig deep for Bitchy Dana to set it straight but she's nowhere to be found. I still think going out with Mitch is like playing with fire after you've just been burned. You're either stupid or crazy, and I like to think that I'm neither, but I can't deny how this man affects me.

Biting the side of my lip, I reply. "Maybe."

We don't really talk much after that but for the rest of the evening, I'm hyperaware of Mitch's location at all times. I feel drawn to him, in a constant battle with my feet to stay where they are, fighting the urge to rub against him like a cat claiming its person.

It's getting harder and harder to remember why I shouldn't go out with him, but I need to stay strong. I'm not getting burned again.

Chapter Sixteen

MITCH

Since Sunday dinner, I've been feeling pretty good about things with Dana. We didn't really talk much more after I suggested we go to the history museum sometime but her maybe was encouraging. I'm trying to follow Liv's advice to be patient while still making my interest known. I took her maybe as a win and then keep my distance for the rest of the night.

I caught her looking at me more than a few times and every single time she quickly averted her eyes. She may need more time to get past my thing with Jessica, but it doesn't stop her from wanting me.

Yeah, that sounds like I'm egotistical and full of myself, but there's no mistaking the chemistry between us or the appreciative looks she gives me when she thinks I'm not looking.

Oh, Dana, I'm always looking at you.

I rode that high all week, letting it propel me through the long days of work and home repair until I could see her again. This morning couldn't come fast enough but finally, I'm at the park, waiting for her to show up for our Saturday morning run. She doesn't keep me waiting long and now it's me giving her the appreciative looks as she bends over to stretch.

We set off at a comfortable pace which means I can't lag behind her to check out her ass without it being obvious. Her arm brushes against mine and fire erupts under my skin at the contact. All my blood starts rushing away from my brain, and I swallow, fighting against the sensation. Running in the well populated park is not the time or place to have that kind of physical reaction. Running shorts don't hide anything.

"Did you watch the Ancient Aliens marathon last night?" She asks me.

Right now, I can't remember my own name much less what I watched on TV last night or if I even turned the TV on. My mind is solely focused on her or more accurately, what she's doing to me.

I pound out a few more steps before I can get my voice to work. "Nope, missed it."

She doesn't say anything for several paces, and I realize I probably came off a little short and pissy. Not what I was going for.

"What season was it?" I ask in hopefully a more pleasant tone.

"Season three. I thought of you when the episode about secret messages in D.C. came on."

She thought about me? That's a good sign, right?

Dana gives me a summary of the show and even if I wasn't into it, the fascination in her voice makes me wish I had watched it again.

"I remember seeing that episode before, but it's been a while. I'll have to rewatch it."

We jog a few more steps and I search for something else to say. I don't usually have a problem making conversation with women, but it's always been for one of two reasons. Networking or to get laid. Talking to a woman I actually like and want to know better is a new experience for me and I'm coming up empty on interesting things to say.

I blurt out the first thing I think of. Do you believe in aliens?"

Dana stops short and turns to me. "Of course. Don't you?"

I almost slam into her and end up grabbing both of her arms, spinning her around me, breathing hard from the effort of not flattening her to the trail.

We're standing so close I can feel her chest rising with each inhale and once again I'm fighting my body's reaction.

Tilting my head to the trail in front of us, I indicate we should continue and reluctantly let her go. "I think it would be naive to assume we're the only inhabitants of the universe," I answer as we start to run again.

I hear her say, "Good answer," but I'm pretty sure she was talking to herself which puts a big stupid smile on my face.

"I mean, the very first episode of Ancient Aliens has some pretty convincing stuff with all the ancient texts talking about aircraft and the maps showing Antarctica hundreds of years before it was discovered. If we had that knowledge and technology, how did we lose it? It leads you to believe someone either gave it to us or wiped it from our memory." I tell her, reciting the episode that got me hooked on the show.

"I don't know about having it wiped from our memory." She says with a little laugh because honestly, it does sound absurd. "But I have wondered why we had to rediscover things people thousands of years ago apparently already knew."

"Some people argue they didn't know it and we're just reading into it because we want aliens to exist."

From the corner of my eye, I see Dana wipe the sweat from her brow and nod in agreement. It doesn't get past me I've never enjoyed a Sunday morning run as much as I am right now. It's a beautiful day. A gorgeous woman is beside me. She likes the same dorky things I do and I'm pretty damn sure soon she's going to be mine.

We keep up the conversation as we finish our jog and slow down to a walk the last quarter mile. Heading across the parking lot, I follow her to her car, not yet ready to end our morning together. We're steps away from that happening when my patience just up and disappears.

"Will you have dinner with me?" The words are out before I knew I was going to say them but now that I have, I don't regret it at all. Not when I see the blush creeping across Dana's cheeks.

Her eyes meet mine and she pauses for half a beat. "Maybe."

My big stupid grin returns and I'm helpless to hide it which earns me a full smile from Dana in return.

As she opens her car door, I'm unwilling to let her go just yet. My hand reaches out, but I stop myself just in time and take a step back.

Be patient, dumbass. I tell myself and plunge my hands in my pockets.

"So, same time next Saturday?"

Dana slides into her seat and starts her car. Grabbing onto the door, she looks up at me and the instant our eyes connect, a missing puzzle piece clicks into place inside me.

"Of course. We have to see if you can turn that maybe into a yes." She says, holding my gaze a beat longer than necessary.

I catch her flirty smile right before the door closes and cheering erupts in my head again.

Very soon, Dana Tolliver, you are going to be mine.

CHAPTER SEVENTEEN

DANA

I've never wanted a weekend to be over so badly. I've been counting down the hours to six pm Sunday night and now that it's here, I'm a strange mix of nervous and excited with a little bit of self-consciousness thrown in. I changed clothes five times and reapplied my makeup twice after an unfortunate incident with a mascara wand. If I wasn't helping Liv make the side dishes, I probably would've already downed three glasses of wine and be looking for a fourth.

He's just another guy, get a hold of yourself.

Every time there's a knock on the door, I jump like someone just scared me and Liv has snickered every single time. All of the guests are here, Brent and Emily, Jake and Suzette, Nick and Hannah and Dave with a new woman named Marissa. The only person missing is Mitch and now I know the next time someone's at the door it's going to be him.

I've never played hard to get. I always know what I want and take it but these last few weeks, having Mitch chase me, I see the appeal in not giving in so easily. Every time I see him, a little thrill runs through me, and I secretly wonder how far he'll get, how far I'll let him get this time. I really had no intention of going out with him after the non-girlfriend appearance, but Mitch set that straight and made his interest very known.

Since then, the anticipation has built deliciously. Add to that my insane attraction to him plus our shared love of history and Mitch has become very hard to resist.

I almost gave in last Sunday when I heard him telling the guys about the new exhibit at the museum. He sounded like a kid with a new toy, spouting off all its features with pride and wonderment. I felt a little mushy inside along with a few other pleasant things and those feelings only grew yesterday while we were running and talking.

Yep, that's right. Dana Tolliver is waving the white flag.

"I think that's good."

I hear Liv's voice, but her words don't make it through the chaos inside my head. "What?"

She pointedly looks at the cutting board in front of me and repeats herself. "I think that's good."

Looking down, I see the lettuce I've been cutting for the burgers now resembles a pile of grass instead of the bun sized pieces I was assigned.

"I'm sorry, Liv. I guess I'm just distracted."

She slowly slides the cutting board away from me. "I never would have guessed from the way you slaughtered the lettuce."

Reed steps into the kitchen, halting our conversation. He and Liv exchange a look and suddenly I have a bad feeling in the pit of my stomach. I'm looking back and forth between the two of them like it's a freaking tennis match and finally, Reed speaks up.

Shoving one hand in his pocket, the other holding a long metal spatula, he clears his throat and looks at me instead of Liv. "Mitch just text and said he couldn't make it. Something came up at work and he needs to handle it before tomorrow morning."

Liv comes around the island, a look of pity on her face and I work hard to keep my expression neutral. I will not show the disappointment I'm definitely not feeling.

With a carefree shrug, I try to make my voice as light as possible. "Ok." It doesn't come out light or carefree, but instead of trying again, I shove my face in the open refrigerator frantically searching for a reason to be looking in here.

Milk. No, no one's drinking milk tonight.

Leftovers. That's not going to work either since we're cooking at this very minute.

Zucchini. Maybe. What are we making again? Oh right, hamburgers. Nope, zucchini isn't needed either.

I hear whispers across the room and... you know that thing when people are whispering and you can't hear what they're saying but you know, I mean you really know, they're talking about you? Yeah, they're talking about me.

Still scouring the fridge for a valid reason to be scouring the fridge, my vision clears, and I see them.

Condiments.

Grabbing every condiment bottle known to man, I load up my arms and back out of the fridge. My eyes see the back door and I walk that direction without a glance at the two people I have to pass to get there.

"Just going to set these out here." I toss over my shoulder and walk outside.

The fall air helps cool my heated skin down but the happy couples surrounding me makes me feel weird. Not really because I'm the third, or eleventh, wheel but more because they all seem really happy and in love. Well, maybe not Dave and his flavor of the month but the rest of them do.

And I want that.

Unconsciously, I heave a sigh and look down at my condiment laden arms. Oh yeah, that's what I was doing.

"You ok?" Hannah asks coming up beside me. Taking some of the bottles out of my hand, she helps me spread them across the table.

"Yeah. I'm fine." I put enough positivity into my voice, she won't suspect the truth.

Hannah scoffs. "Sure." *Ok, maybe I didn't use enough positivity.* "Maybe fine works on men, which if they're smart it doesn't, but fine doesn't work on other women. There are only two reasons we say we're fine. Either everything's going along without any problems, but we're bored as hell."

Hannah stops and I find myself prodding her for more. "Or?"

"Or. Something is not fine, but we don't want to get into with the person asking."

I try to find fault in Hannah's logic but there isn't any. She's spot on. And from the look on her face, she knows it.

A voice behind me butts into our private conversation. "Mitch isn't coming."

I want to glare at my best friend, but did I really expect her to not bring it up?

Hannah's eyes squint like she's trying to do calculus. "What the hell is wrong with him?"

I appreciate she's upset on my behalf, but I end up speaking on Mitch's. "He had an emergency at work," I tell her.

She suddenly looks downright delighted. "Oh, you talked to him? So, are you two...?" She's moving her finger back and forth in what I assume means 'together' and I blush for no good reason at all.

"No. He texted Reed."

"But. They have run into each other a few times so..." Liv supplies, letting her optimism show. Optimism I'm no longer feeling.

It's a good thing you didn't already give in. He's skipping dinner to work on the weekend. Sounds like a workaholic. After Chris, you swore you wouldn't date another one.

"He doesn't miss dinner very often. I think it's like only the third or fourth time since we started doing this last year." Liv tells me, accurately reading my thoughts.

Ok, maybe I'm being a little too harsh. Emergencies do come up. I reason with Bitchy Dana.

Hannah jumps back on Team Mitch. "He really is a good guy. You should give him a chance."

"I was thinking about it." I mumble.

"What was that?" Liv asks, poking me in the arm.

I look between the two of them, both with encouraging and expectant looks on their faces. They're right, I should give him a chance. So, he was maybe kind of seeing someone else when we met. It obviously wasn't serious since none of his friends knew about her and he ended it right after he met me.

This working on the weekend thing is a bit concerning but Liv just said he doesn't miss Sunday dinner very often, so he makes time to see his friends. And he runs at the lake every day before going to the office and Saturday mornings. He seems to have a good handle on what's important in life and balancing it all with work. Hopefully, he's ready to add me to that list of important things.

If I just give him another chance.

"Ok, I will," I say with confidence.

Hannah's eyes get wide, and Liv's jaw goes slack for two seconds before they both unfreeze and start a mini celebration. I shush them but not before everyone else notices.

"What's going on over there?" Dave asks jovially, slinging his arm around.... what's her name?

"Dana and Mitch!" Liv is practically jumping up and down, happiness radiating off her which I find a bit excessive since I only agreed to give him another shot not spend the rest of my life with him.

"You're going to put him out of his misery and say yes?" Reed asks, smiling at me and I shrug, smiling back.

"Well, he's persistent. And persistence should pay off."

I just hope he doesn't make me regret it.

Chapter Eighteen

MITCH

This week was one of those that makes me rethink my career choice. I'm used to being busy, really busy, but I've barely had time to eat for the past five days with all the sudden issues demanding my attention on top of my usual workload and overseeing the renovation at my house. I've been running back and forth from the office to home and back again every day and I'm beat. The only thing that helped get through the week was knowing I would see Dana Saturday morning.

By Friday, I was certain I would have to work through the weekend to get everything done for my last-minute meeting with the Attorney General Monday morning, but I pushed myself to work late into the night so I could have today off. I'll still have to do some meeting prep tomorrow, but today I'm not thinking about work or the construction zone I'm living in, only Dana.

She should be here any minute. If I can finally convince her to say yes to dinner, my plans for tonight will be set too.

A bird flies overhead and caws, grabbing my attention. I watch it swoop down towards the lake and effortlessly glide across, inches above the water. This is why I run here every day. You don't see that kind of thing running on a treadmill or inside a gym with music blaring from the speakers.

"Hey!"

Dana's voice comes from the parking lot, cutting through my appreciation of the outdoors and I turn to see her coming my way. It's not a hardship to change the scenery, she looks good, hell, fantastic, in those tight athletic pants and tank top.

"Good morning," I say when she's closer and we both stretch then start off on our run.

"You weren't at Sunday dinner." She comments but I hear the question she's not asking. Why wasn't I at Sunday dinner?

"I had an emergency meeting get set for Monday morning and needed to go over everything. I was knee deep in proposed agriculture policies about the time Reed fired up the grill."

"How did you know he grilled?"

"Are you kidding? Reed grills almost every Sunday. He loves that thing."

We share a laugh, still running our way around the lake.

"Well, you were missed." She says, not breaking stride or looking my way. I want to ask if she, specifically, missed me but I know she won't admit to that.

Fuck it, I'm going to ask anyway.

"Did you miss me?" I put emphasis on the word you.

I don't expect her to answer. When she does, I'm surprised. "Yes."

Pleasantly surprised. My big stupid grin is back, and I can't make my face stop smiling so I fall back half a step putting her in front of me. Big mistake. Have I mentioned her ass?

Dana is focused on the path in front of us, probably hoping I won't dig more into her missing me last weekend. It's fine with me, I got all the information I need to convince me she's ready to accept my dinner invitation.

"Do you work on the weekends a lot?" She asks, flicking her eyes over her shoulder in my direction.

"When I need to," I tell her honestly, I just leave out that I need to most weekends. No woman wants to hear that. "What about you? The life of a paralegal can be pretty hectic too. You must work some long hours."

"Yes, I do." She says hesitantly and I think maybe I offended her by asking.

"Should I not have asked that?"

When she glances my way again, I see her brows are pulled together and I wonder how that question could be taken the wrong way. She doesn't leave me in suspense very long.

"I've never heard an attorney acknowledge that paralegals work long hours too." She says, almost sadly.

"That's because most attorneys are pompous assholes." I quip, knowing I've been considered an asshole but hopefully not pompous.

"That's true." She agrees with me, her brunette hair swishing behind her, and I have the sudden need to know more about her.

"Have you worked with a lot of attorneys?" I don't like the thought of her working for people who don't appreciate her and how hard she works. You don't have to share an office with Dana to know she goes out of her way to get the job done quickly and efficiently. She has a no-nonsense way about her but she's also fiercely loyal and a dependable friend.

Not many people fit that description and I never even noticed until I had a group of friends who did.

"The office I was at in Dallas had twenty-six attorneys, but I only worked with a few. The place I started out at, right after college, was small, just a father and son team, but it was awful. Almost every Friday, they'd drop a stack of files on our desk at four thirty and say it needed to be done by the time they came in Monday morning. And if we asked for time off, they would say something shitty like how hard it was to find reliable help." Dana says in a neutral tone.

It pisses me off, the way some people get a little bit of power then think they have the right to treat other people poorly. It's something I've always tried not to do. If you treat your employees well, they will work harder for you. It's simple really, but some people get off on being mean.

"Is your job here better?"

She takes a moment before answering with a nod. "Yes. So far."

At our usual place, we slow down to a walk, and I know the moment I've been waiting for all week is finally here. Taking a deep breath, I ask the question before I can chicken out. "Will you have dinner with me?"

She doesn't turn my way, but I see her smile. "Yes."

"Tonight."

She still doesn't look at me, just counters my offer. "I was thinking next weekend."

"Not gonna happen, babe. I'm not giving you time to talk yourself out of it. I'll pick you up tonight at seven."

Dana stops walking and looks at me. She's trying to make me relent, but I meant what I said, we're having dinner tonight. A full minute passes before she finally, finally accepts. She doesn't do it vocally, instead just rolls her eyes and smiles. There was a head shake in there too but I'm telling myself it wasn't a no, just part of the eye roll.

We start walking again and get almost to the parking lot when she starts to ask a question.

"About dinner..." She pauses to move a stray piece of hair blowing into her eyes, so I try to reassure her.

"Don't worry, it's casual."

By the look on her face, I don't think that's what she wanted to hear. I'm just about to cave and tell her it doesn't have to be when she stops walking again and starts talking a bit defensively.

"I'm not looking for something casual. I've done that in the past, but it's not what I want now. If you're just interested in sex or having a dinner date, you should probably look somewhere else. I want more than that." Her eyes look over my shoulder then tentatively find their way back to mine. "I want someone I can be all-in with."

She's not looking for something casual.

I'm not ashamed to say hearing this makes me very happy. This beautiful sexy woman is looking for someone to be all-in with and it sounds like she may want that with me. I puff out my chest a little, even though relationships weren't what I was talking about.

Dana's looking around nervously, a side of her I haven't seen before, and I find it totally endearing. Her fingers tap against her leg and she's biting the inside of her lip. I know she's freaking out in her head.

I wait until she finally looks at me to clarify.

"I meant to dress casual."

I watch my words sink in and the blush spread across her face.

"Oh, ok."

CHAPTER NINETEEN

DANA

When Mitch said dinner would be casual, I didn't really know what to expect. Usually, first dates follow an unspoken set of rules.

Date #1- Dinner at a nice restaurant, somewhere she can dress up and wow you with her tight, but not over the top sexy dress and heels.

Date #2- Usually dinner again. Sometimes it's more casual but still nice because you both want to impress each other and get to the next date.

Date #3- This is not dinner. This date involves something physical. Depending on who you are, it can be dancing, mini golf, bowling... you get the picture. This date is one that potentially leads to sex so anything he can "teach" you or has you pressed against him is acceptable.

Based on those rules, casual doesn't come first and it's never really casual. It just means girls can wear pants and flats instead of the dress and heels. So, when Mitch guided me, in my favorite skinny jeans and red wedges, to the National Archives Museum, I was both surprised and delighted.

This guy gets me.

We started slowly wandering around, looking at the various items on display. In the car, we made small talk about the weather, our jobs and our mutual friends but since walking into the museum our conversation stayed on the exhibits.

I point to the 1297 Magna Carta and open my mouth to ask if he really thought it inspired the Founding Fathers, but his voice cuts me off.

"So, Dana, did you grow up in Texas?"

It seems like an odd question. Even though it is technically our first date, we've seen each other several times and it feels like we should be past the basic background stuff.

"Yes, I did. San Antonio."

Before he can ask another question, I plead my case. "We can talk about the usual stuff, where we grew up, our families, why we both went into law, blah, blah, blah. But there's always time to learn about that."

His lips hitch up on the side. "Ok, what do you want to talk about then?"

Knowing we're both big nerds who spend their evenings watching history documentaries and believe in aliens, I wonder what other ridiculous things we have in common. "I think we ask each other the most ridiculous questions we can think of."

"Only if we both have to answer all the questions."

"Deal. Should I go first?"

"By all means," Mitch says gesturing with his hand like he's a model on The Price is Right. Of course, picturing that makes me giggle and I have my first question.

"What's your favorite game show?"

"Of all time?" He asks for clarification.

I give an exaggerated nod. "Of all time."

He doesn't have to think about it, responding automatically. "The Legends of the Hidden Temple."

"I forgot all about that show, I used to love it!" I tell him. "Mine is Double Dare."

We shared a look that is flirty and silly at the same time. "Two kid shows. What does that say about us?" He muses.

"Ok, your turn."

He scrunches up his face like he's thinking hard. "What TV family did you want to be part of?"

Instantly, I'm taken back to my early years. "The Tanners on Full House."

Mitch has a weird smile on his face. "Why?"

"Because even though their mom died, they seemed to have this great family. They were loud and sometimes they fought but they loved each other and were surrounded by people that loved them back."

"Did you not feel that way as a kid?"

"I was an only child. My dad was an artist, always in the garage painting and my mom worked a lot so most of the time, I was on my own. We always had dinner together in the evenings, but it was so quiet. Not at all like the Tanner house." We take a few quiet steps looking around and then I ask him a question. "Do you have any siblings?"

Mitch nods, sticking his hands in his pockets. "Two younger brothers."

"Are you close?"

"Not really. They were twins so they always had this bond I wasn't part of." He says it like it's not a big deal, but I sense that it is. Things feel a little too serious at the moment and I want to lighten it up.

"What TV family would you pick?" I ask him.

Mitch smirks, raising a brow. "The Tanners. But I wanted to be the neighbor. I had a crush on DJ."

I laugh because of course he had a crush on her, but it doesn't escape me we both choose the same family. He could be just saying the same answer as me, but I don't think he is. Continuing our ridiculous question game, I ask another. "If you could add anyone to Mount Rushmore, who would it be?"

"I need to think about that for a minute."

"It's a very important decision." I deadpan.

"Exactly. You're really asking who I think is a good representative of America. Does it have to be another president?"

"It can be anyone you want."

"Chuck Norris," Mitch states immediately.

My steps falter and I wrinkle my eyebrows. "Chuck Norris?"

"You said it could be anyone I want and is there a better representative of America than Chuck? He's a badass and everyone loves him." He says, defending his answer with a shrug.

"Ok, Chuck Norris it is." I concede tempering the grin wanting to bust out. I've never dated anyone who was such a contradiction. Most business professionals are kind of stuffy, but Mitch isn't fitting that description at all.

"Who would you put up there?" He asks.

"I was thinking someone like Susan B. Anthony. She's a well-known symbol for women's rights and collected anti-slavery petitions when she was just a teenager. She played a part in America recognizing all people deserve the same rights despite skin color or gender."

"Well, when you put it that way, I guess Chuck could go on a smaller mountain over to the side," Mitch comments drily. "But it would need to be a full body sculpture, not just his head."

"Of course." I agree and we both smile.

"My turn again," Mitch says. "If you had your own late night talk show, who would you invite as your first guest?"

"Oh. Good one."

He pretends to dust his shoulder and I burst out laughing at his dorkiness which makes him laugh too. Other patrons in the museum are staring, some even pointing at us, but we don't care. Let them stare.

"Ok. Ok," I say, composing myself. Once I make sure the last giggle is out, I think about his question.

"Do they have to still be living?"

Mitch gives an immediate no.

That's easy. "Martha Washington."

"Why?"

"Because you always hear about George and how great he was. I bet his wife would love to tell everyone all about what he was really like. Leaving dirty socks on the floor and singing in the shower, or bath, even though he sounded like a dying cat. And what if he liked to pass gas while they were in bed and then pull the covers over her head?!"

At that, Mitch starts laughing again hard. "Can you imagine George Washington, the father of our country, pulling a Dutch oven on his wife?!"

I start laughing too and lean into Mitch to hide from the growing number of people watching us. One or two was fine but now almost everyone in this room is focused solely on us.

We're both still laughing and wiping tears away when a museum security guard comes over and asks us to keep it down. Mitch and I manage to quiet ourselves enough so we're not making a spectacle anymore and decide to move into a different part of the museum. One that's far from the security guard still giving us the evil eye.

We make it to the room where the Declaration of Independence is held, and I tell him it's his turn to answer the same question.

Without missing a beat, Mitch answers. "George Washington."

I make a curious face at him and ask why.

"You have to give the man a chance to defend himself."

And that's how we get kicked out of the National Archive Museum.

Chapter Twenty

MITCH

When we left the museum, we walked over to a little Spanish bistro for dinner. The food was good, the margaritas were great, but the conversation was even better. We continued the ridiculous question game, and I don't think I've ever laughed that much in my life. We threw in a few more serious questions too, deciding they still fit the ridiculous theme because who admits their biggest flaw (me-working way too much, her-holding people to really high standards) on their first official date?

But seeing Dana so relaxed and happy was the best part. She let her guard down with me tonight and the woman I've found so mesmerizing became the woman I'm falling for. I won't say I'm ready for the L word yet, but I can see myself moving in that direction.

Pulling up to her house, I tell her, once again, to stay in her seat so I can get the door for her. She just laughs at me, shaking her head like she did earlier and tells me again she's perfectly capable of opening her own door.

"I know you are, but I want to do it for you."

She stops halfway out of her seat and gives me a look, one I can't decipher, then sits back down and closes the door.

Victory floods through me. It may seem silly but every little win with Dana feels like a gold medal.

I open her door and extend my hand to help her out. Taking a small step back, I give her space to clear the open door but not too much space. She has to step close to me, so close we're almost touching before I take another step back and close the door.

Disappointment flashes across her face before she looks away. Pushing down the smug feeling of another victory, I try to put a smile back on her face as we head to her front door.

"I've never been thrown out of a museum before."

"We didn't technically get thrown out. We were asked to leave." Dana states indignantly.

"Told to leave." I correct her.

"Same thing." She says with a straight face.

When she's not able to contain her smile any longer, she ducks her head to hide it from me. Damn, she's cute. And so fucking sexy. I thought her ass looked good in those tight pants she runs in but in these jeans and wearing those high heel shoes... fucking perfection.

I want this woman so bad, more than I've ever wanted a woman before, but it's not going to happen tonight.

Yes, I want some hot, naked time with Dana but for the first time in my life I want more than that, so I'll wait.

We're at her door, but she hasn't reached for her keys yet, stalling us here. I know if I leaned in right now, she would let me kiss her. Pretty sure she would be kissing me back with gusto but I'm not letting that happen tonight either.

In the few weeks I've known Dana, I've figured some things out about her. She needs things between us to move slowly. It may be partly due to her thinking I was just in a relationship, a term I am using loosely, and her wanting to put some time between that one and my relationship with her. The term not used loosely when it comes to Dana.

But something tells me it also has to do with her past and that's a much bigger obstacle than her thinking I need a palate cleanse between women.

Another thing I've learned is if things go faster than she's ready for, she's going to throw up walls quicker than a farmer at a barn raising. She did it after the ill-fated dinner with Jessica, which I don't blame her for at all. It just showed me how fiercely she'll protect herself if she's uncomfortable or feeling hurt and I don't want to have to break those walls down again. I mean, I will because she's totally worth it, but I don't want to if I can help it.

I also learned today, that when she's ready for things to move forward, those walls come down and she jumps right in. I want her to keep jumping with me, I just don't want her to wake up tomorrow and regret it. For that very reason, I am not kissing her tonight. I want her to want that kiss and even though I'm pretty sure she does right now, I want to know she's just as desperate for our first kiss as I am. So, I'll wait.

"I had a good time tonight." She says quietly.

I lean in and match her tone. "I did too."

"I've never been to a museum on a date before."

"Neither have I." I admit and we both smile at each other.

"Ummm... will you be at dinner tomorrow?" She asks and all I hear is she wants to see me again. Another gold medal settles around my neck.

"Yeah, I'll be there. As long as you'll be there too?"

Her smile lights up even brighter with pleasure and my heart makes a hard thump.

"I'll be there." She confirms.

I know she's waiting for that kiss now and as much I want to wait, it's just too damn hard. My hand reaches up to rest against her neck, my thumb caressing her cheek and we both take a breath. I see it in her eyes, she wants this kiss. The question is, will she still want it in the morning when she's gone over her feelings with a microscope?

Screw it. I can't just walk away without kissing her. The perfect date needs the perfect ending.

My thumb brushes lightly over her skin and I lean in the last few inches.

Her eyes drift closed a second before my lips touch down.

I press a kiss, soft and gently, to her cheek. I want to linger but now I've felt her skin under my lips, my resolve is weakening. If I don't move away now, I won't go at all and that isn't part of the plan to be patient.

Pulling back, I watch her eyelids flutter open, her own lips still so close to mine.

"Thank you for having dinner with me," I tell her sincerely.

"Thank you for not giving up." She says with just as much sincerity. Her eyes flick down to my lips, and I pry myself back a step, letting my hand drop.

Dana's brows draw in with confusion and the last thing I want is to leave but I have to. There will be plenty of time for kissing once she's mine for good.

"Good night," I say barely above a whisper, hesitating to walk away. "I'll see you tomorrow night."

Her expression changes from confusion to curiosity, like she's not sure what to make of me but she's not going to question it.

"Good night." She finally whispers back.

I take a step backward then another and she's still just watching me.

"You should go inside now," I tell her, knowing I won't make it to my car if she doesn't.

She's completely still at first then finally gives a slight nod and turns around. I stay there, two feet away from this enchanting creature, and wait for her to go inside. We make eye contact one more time as she closes the door behind her, and something sifts into place inside me.

Is this what falling in love feels like?

CHAPTER TWENTY-ONE

DANA

The door is barely open when Liv starts talking. "You were supposed to call me when you got in last night. Oh! Did you not call because he stayed all night?" She asks, her voice going from perturbed to eager, causing doubt to run through me again.

"What happened? Was the date bad?" She asks, reading my face as I walk inside.

"No, the date was great. The best first date I've ever had!" I say in a borderline wail.

"Then what's the problem?"

"That's what I want to know!" I yell.

Liv is clearly confused but the feeling is mutual. Pulling me into Reed's office she closes the door behind us as I exhale loudly.

"Mitch is already here, and he seems really happy. What happened?" She hisses.

At the mention of his name, my blood runs hot. I start fanning myself and shift my hair off my neck to cool it down. "He didn't kiss me," I whisper shout back to her.

Her head jerks back like she was slapped, and her eyes grow wide. "You're upset because he didn't kiss you?"

"Well, he did actually, but it was a kiss on the cheek." My own eyes get large with alarm, and I emphasize. "On the cheek!"

Liv doesn't say anything just stares at me like I've lost my mind which from the lack of sleep I got last night, and the continuous loop of Mitch induced questions, I probably have lost my mind.

"What does that mean, Liv?"

She grabs my hands and pulls me down onto the small sofa under the big picture window. A smile has replaced the WTF look that was previously on her face, and she squeezes my hands.

"I think it means he really likes you and he's trying to take things slow."

I like the part where she said he really likes me, but I don't get the other part. "Why would he want to take things slow?"

"Ummm, hello! You said he needed distance from his last relationship."

"I did, but..." I try to cut in, but she keeps talking.

"And you've been reluctant to go on a date with him."

"Yes, but..."

"So, when you finally said yes and the date was awesome, he didn't want to screw it up by moving too fast."

Her words finally get through to me. It's one of the scenarios I quickly tossed aside last night when I was replaying every minute of our date over in my head, trying to figure out why he didn't want to kiss me. He did kiss me. Just not the way I was expecting.

I stare over Liv's shoulder, silently working through the problem in my head, then look back at her. "So, you think he really likes me?"

"Yes, I think he really likes you." She says smirking. "Maybe he'll even ask you to the prom."

We both laugh at the silliness of my question until I remember something else from last night's date.

Liv gives me a quizzical look. "What?"

I have the fleeting thought to just deny it, but we've been friends way too long for her not to notice there's still something on my mind. I give in, letting my shoulders sag dramatically while I look at the ceiling for answers.

"He admitted his biggest flaw is he works way too much."

I don't have to say anything more, Liv gets me.

"Dana, that man is crazy about you. He's been chasing you for weeks now with very little encouragement from you." I look at her petulantly, something I'm not proud of, and she keeps going. "Yes, he may work a lot, but he's made an effort to see you every Saturday morning at the lake and most Sundays here."

Liv is making sense, knocking down the wall I've been trying to rebuild. Knowing it, she goes in for the final blow. "And if he recognizes he works a lot and tells you this up front, then he's aware it could be an issue. One he's maybe willing to work on it if he found the right woman."

"I guess you're right," I tell her. "This time."

Liv squeezes my hands again but doesn't let them go and I return her quizzical look.

"I have something to tell you." She confesses. "I wanted you to be the first to know. Well, not the first, that was me and Reed, but the first other person to know."

I already know what she's going to say, and tears fill my eyes.

"I'm pregnant!"

Dropping her hands instantly, I throw my arms around her for a long hug and we're both crying when we pull away.

"I'm so happy for you. When did you find out? You better not have been keeping this a secret from me." I mock scold her.

Liv wipes under her eyes. "I just found out today and I almost called you as soon as I saw the test was positive, but I figured my husband, the father of my baby, should get the news first."

"Ok, he gets this one, but the next time you find out you're pregnant, I want to know first!"

"Deal!" She says and we laugh again.

"Have you thought of any names yet?"

"It's still early." Liv tries to contain her happy grin, but she can't. I just wait. I know her too well.

"Ok, so we maybe already started talking about names." She concedes, rolling her eyes. "If it's a boy, we like Liam, but we haven't decided on a girl name yet. I really like Sophie but Reed said that's Dave's ex-wife's name so it may be weird for him."

"Dave was married?" I ask. This is news to me. I've known Dave for a few years now and no one has ever mentioned he was married.

"Yeah, they've been divorced for years so it shouldn't matter but..." her voice trails off.

"Apparently it does still matter. Is he not over her?" That would explain a lot, actually.

"He's never mentioned her to me. I had no idea until I brought up the name Sophie and Reed told me. I mean, Dave dates a lot, but I don't know if that has anything to do with her."

"Hmmmmm, interesting," I murmur.

"So, anyway, Sophie's out."

There's a knock on the office door and we both turn as Reed sticks his head in and sees the tear stains on our faces. "I figured you were in here telling her." He says lovingly to his wife.

Her smile back to him is filled with so much love and joy I can't help but feel a little jealous. I want to love someone that much and know he loves me the same way.

"Well, everyone's here." He tells us.

Liv jumps up and drags me to the door with her. "Ok, let's go share the news."

As soon as we get to the back door, my eyes find Mitch. He dressed comfortably, in faded jeans and a t-shirt and holy hell, he looks good. Walking toward me, he's completely at ease with who he is, and I feel like everything is falling into place.

His hand lightly lands against my neck, his thumb on my cheek, just like last night and I instantly close my eyes. I feel his lips caress my other cheek.

Liv was right. He does like me.

When he moves away, I slowly open my eyes. I don't see my best friend standing three feet away with a huge smile on her face. I don't see her husband grabbing her hand while trying to hide his own big smile. I don't even see the other eight people surrounding us, all with matching expressions on their faces.

I only see Mitch.

"Hi."

His thumb is still stroking my cheek and it's so distracting, I struggle to get out a reply. "Hi."

He doesn't move but his gaze goes over my head and sweeps to the side before returning to mine. "Before all the questions start, tell me you'll have dinner with me again."

Dinner. Lunch. Breakfast. As long as it's with Mitch, I'm in. Like I told him, I want someone I can be all in with and I've decided it's him.

"Yes, I'll have dinner with you again," I say a little bit flirty. His fingers gently squeeze my neck and I know he's happy with my answer.

"Good. Now let's hear Reed and Liv's big news."

Chapter Twenty-Two

MITCH

I've been flying pretty high since Sunday night. No, that's not true. I've been on this high since Saturday morning when Dana agreed to go out with me. It was one of the best weekends of my life and I've had some really good weekends.

Dana agreed to have dinner with me again, but we didn't make plans for when that would happen. Yesterday, I looked at my phone at least a hundred times wondering if it was too soon to call her and set our next date. I'm not trying to play any games with her, that wasn't what stopped me from calling. I'm trying to be patient, not push too hard too fast, Liv's advice, so I've been taking my time and moving slow.

Kissing her on the cheek Saturday night and again Sunday after dinner, was sweet torture. I finally got my lips on her skin but not in the way I wanted to. Don't get me wrong, kissing Dana in any way was well worth the wait and the effort but the chaste cheek kiss has only fueled my desire for her.

You remember those intimate times with my right hand I mentioned before? Yeah, well, it's gotten the job done the last two nights, but it hasn't really helped.

Only one thing will help but that has to wait until I know she's ready to be mine.

It's weird, this wanting to be with someone, to share my life with a woman and wanting her to feel the same way about me. It's not something I've ever wanted before, ever really even thought about. Sure, I planned on getting married and having a family someday but someday was always in the distant future.

Until Dana.

Now, the previously dreaded word, commitment, doesn't make me want to run and hide. Hell, she's not even saying it, I'm the one wanting to put a label on us and use terms like always and forever.

I'm turning into a woman.

"Hey, you busy?"

I'm jerked out of my musings to see Nick standing at my door.

"Hey. Not too bad. Come in, sit down."

Nick walks across the plush beige carpet and drops his bag onto the chair next to him.

"You fixing up everyone's computers today?" I ask. He doesn't usually stop by my office unless he's here for an IT issue so I'm a little curious what he's doing here today.

Crossing one ankle over his other knee, I see he's trying to put his thoughts into words. Pretty good thoughts based on the smile he's trying to hide.

"Come on. Out with it." I nudge.

"I'm going to propose to Hannah."

I'm out of my chair and circling my desk within a second and pull Nick into a hug. Not a bro hug, an actual hug with both arms around him.

"That's great, man! I'm happy for you!" I tell him with a few slaps on his back. I move over to lean on my desk, and he retakes his seat, huge smiles on both our faces.

"Thanks. I haven't told anyone else yet, but I couldn't keep it in any longer." He tells me and I feel honored to be the first to know.

"Did you get the ring yet?"

He nods and reaches into his bag. Withdrawing a little velvet box, he flips the top and turns it to me. The round diamond is sizable, and a circle of smaller diamonds surrounds it. It's beautiful and I tell him so.

"Thanks. I hope she likes it." He says and I hear the nerves he's fighting back.

"She will," I reassure him. "Hannah loves you. You could probably give her a ring pop and she'd still say yes."

Nick laughs and nods his head. "Yeah, she probably would. She hasn't pushed for a ring, but I know she loves me, and we've talked about our future together so..."

He lets his statement trail off, but I know what he's saying. All of our friends know these two love each other, it's just been a matter of time before they made it official.

"So. What's going on with you and Dana?" Nick asks like he already knows the answer.

I try to contain my full-on smile but it's no use, that sucker wants to be seen.

"Things are going well. We've been running together every Saturday for a few weeks, and we finally went out Saturday night."

His grin is now what you would call shit-eating.

"We were wondering. You two seemed pretty chummy Sunday night."

I roll my eyes and step back around my desk to sit in my chair.

"When are you going to see her again?"

"That's a good question. I was thinking about texting her when you walked in."

Nick puts his hands on the chair's armrest and pushes himself up. "Well, don't let me stop you." He says, grabbing his bag and slinging it over his shoulder.

I stand back up and reach out to shake his hand, telling him congratulations.

"Don't congratulate me yet." He says walking backward toward the door. "She hasn't said yes yet."

"She will." I declare and wave as he leaves.

Picking up my phone, I decide if Nick can ask Hannah to marry him today, I can ask Dana to have dinner with me again so soon after our first date.

Me: Are you free for dinner tonight?

I only have to wait a few minutes before her reply shows.

Dana: Maybe.

She adds a winking face after, and I vividly remember a similar conversation just over a week ago.

Me: What can I do to turn that maybe into a yes?
Dana: Promise me some good food and wine.
Me: Done. I'll pick you up at 7.
Dana: Great, see you then.

I set my phone down, not expecting any more messages from her and am halfway through reading a proposal when my phone signals I have a new text.

Dana: Can you give me a clue where we're going?

Shit, I guess I need to figure that out.
Quickly, I send back a reply that buys me some time.

Me: Someplace nice.

I open my web browser and search for restaurants.

Dana: So, dress and heels?

An image of Dana in a dress and high heels instantly pops into my head and my blood starts running south. I wanted our first date to be casual to try to take some of the pressure off but now I want to see Dana all dressed up.

For me.

That thought has me adjusting myself discreetly behind my desk, my office door still standing open from when Nick left. I look down to see my phone is still in my other hand and that I owe Dana a response. Good thing it's only one word because I can't think beyond that right now.

Me: Yes

CHAPTER TWENTY-THREE

DANA

"Ok, show me what you've got," Liv tells me over our video chat.

When I told her about our first date, she was disappointed it was going to be casual, and I wouldn't get to "dress super sexy for Mitch" as she put it. She made me promise when I finally got the opportunity, I would let her help me get ready. Unfortunately, my best friend and newly pregnant schoolteacher had a pretty rough day due to morning sickness, so I convinced her to stay at home and let technology do as it was intended.

Help with fashion choices.

"I'm thinking one of these," I say, turning the phone to show the three dresses I have hanging on the closet door.

"Hmmmmm..." I can see her tapping her finger against her lips on the little screen.

"Maybe it will help if I hold each one up to me in the mirror," I suggest and she quickly agrees.

Grabbing dress number one, I walk to the full-length mirror and hold the black dress in front of me. I angle the phone in my left hand showing Liv the whole mirror.

"That one's nice but I don't think it's the one." She says. "Grab the red one."

"Coming right up." I toss the black dress on my bed and pull the red one down. Posing with it, I make sure Liv can see my reflection.

"What about this one?" I ask looking at myself in the mirror.

"Red is a great color on you. It reminds me of the dress you let me wear the night I met Reed." She reminisces with a blissful look on her face.

"That's because it is the same dress. I had the stained part at the bottom cut off, making it shorter." I tell her then toss it on the bed too. "Feels weird to wear that dress now. You should keep it."

"Oh, I couldn't." She says without meaning it. I'll bring it over on Sunday and forget to take it home with me.

"So, that just leaves the blue dress," I tell her, once again positioning myself, the dress and the phone so she can see.

"I know you have more dresses than that." She scoffs. "But it doesn't matter, that's definitely the dress."

I check myself out more thoroughly. "Are you sure?"

"Yes. Absolutely."

"Ok." Hanging the dress back up, I turn the phone camera back on me. "How should I do my hair?" I know I want to curl it and wear it down but Liv wants to be part of this, so I let her give me her opinion.

"Curl it and wear it down." She says and I smile big.

"Just what I was thinking."

"That's why we're best friends."

I move into my bathroom and prop my phone up so she can see me and get my makeup laid out.

"Smokey eye, nude lip." She instructs and I mock salute her.

"Yes, ma'am."

I start applying my makeup, having washed off my day makeup when I showered after work. No, I wasn't sweaty and gross after sitting in my cubicle all day, but I wanted to be fresh for our date.

"What shoes are you going to wear?" Liv asks and I hold up the gold strappy heels for her approval.

"He's not going to be able to think straight once he sees you in that dress and those shoes." She replies giddily.

"That's the plan."

We talk while I finish my makeup and do my hair. It's getting close to 7 so I slip into my dress and shoes and show Liv the final result.

"Wow. I want to date you." She says with raised eyebrows.

"Too bad. You're mine." I hear Reed's voice through the speaker.

"Don't worry, Reed. I'll share with you." I tease him and Liv laughs as he suddenly wraps his arms around her on my phone's screen.

Reed looks at me and shakes his head. "Not gonna happen." He gives her a kiss that makes me a little envious until I remember why I'm getting dressed up.

If I'm lucky, I'll be getting kissed like that before the night's over.

Liv makes me promise to call her first thing the following morning to give her the rundown before she lets me go. I put on my jewelry and put my phone, keys and wallet in my gold clutch. Checking my reflection from all angles again, I give myself a stamp of approval when the doorbell rings. My stomach flutters and I tell myself to calm down as I'm walking to the front door.

With my hand on the knob, I take a deep breath and pull open the door.

Holy...

My eyes rake up and down Mitch's body, taking in the sexiness that is Mitch Ainsley in a suit. I know he wears a suit every day to work, and I've seen him dressed like this before but somehow this is different. This suit seems to showcase all the right places and knowing he probably changed into this suit just for me makes it even better.

I'm still unabashedly checking him out looking at his perfect face and see he's doing the same thing to me. He has a look of sheer wonder and knowing I could make Mitch, literally the sexiest man I've ever seen, look at me that way makes me more than a little happy.

I'm pretty damn pleased about it if I'm being completely honest.

Slowly, Mitch reaches out and takes my hand, pulling me through the door.

"Are we ready to go?" He asks huskily and I almost tell him no, that I want to stay in tonight, but I nod in reply.

He reaches around me to lock the door from the inside and pulls it closed. I haven't moved an inch, putting us very close and I catch the scent of him, something subtle but spicy. For a moment, neither of us move and I know he's having the same internal war.

His hand slides down my arm, our fingers intertwining, and I think the decision to go back inside has been made.

"Let's go before I take you back inside and stop being a gentleman." He winks and softly tugs on my hand to follow him.

Damn those gentlemanly manners.

Chapter Twenty-Four

MITCH

I almost choked on my own tongue when I saw Dana. The woman is gorgeous, and she knows how to highlight every sexy thing about herself.

That dress, it looks like it was made for her. It gently hugs her curves showing off her small waist and flaring over her chest and hips making her a perfect hourglass. I've never cared if a woman had the traditionally sexy body type of an hourglass but seeing Dana's shape on display is making me a believer.

And those shoes. Gold high heels with straps across her toes and around her ankle. They make her legs look amazing and I want them wrapped around me, shoes included.

Her hair has this wildness to it that makes her look like she's been rolling around in bed. My bed. I can picture her dark hair spread across my pillow as I watch her eyes close from pleasure. Or the way it would sway over me when she...

Dammit. I need to control myself. I can't get hard right now, there's no way to hide that although, she seemed open to taking me inside her house and...

Nope. There I go again. I promised myself and Dana, even if she doesn't know it, that we would take this slow and only move to the next step when I knew she was beyond ready for it. I don't want any regrets on her part. I couldn't take it if she regretted me.

Reaching out, I turn the radio up, desperately trying to focus on something other than the woman beside me. I know I should try to make conversation, but my brain has been consumed with dirty thoughts and animal noises since she opened the door. I'm frantically searching for something to say but nothing is coming to mind except random history facts. I blurt one out before I even realize I've opened my mouth.

"George Washington never lived in the White House."

I cringe, literally and mentally. From the corner of my eye, I see Dana turn to me and prepare for the polite dismissal I usually get from people when I talk about history.

"I know, John Adams was the first President to live there with his wife, Abigail." She says softly.

I blink a few times trying to determine if she really just said that or if I'm still fantasizing about her sexy ass and equally sexy mind.

Briefly, I glance at her and she's still looking at me, a smug little smile on her face.

"So, we're back to George Washington. Are you trying to add on to the list of places we've been kicked out of for inappropriate behavior?"

My eyes flick back and forth between her and the road a few times and her smile turns into a laugh, the little minx. It helps relieve some of my tension and I start to relax.

Reaching over, I grab her hand. "I wasn't planning on getting kicked out of the restaurant tonight but for you, I can make an exception."

"We'll just have to see what happens when we get there." She says squeezing my hand back.

We arrive at the restaurant, a pricey place I've never been to before but since our first date was casual and... cheap, alright, it was cheap, I wanted to show Dana I also think she deserves more. I want to spoil her if she'll let me, something I'm looking forward to doing. I've never wanted to spoil or pamper a woman before, but Dana is bringing out all these new feelings in me.

As we follow the hostess to our table, I notice heads turn our way. Men and women alike are checking us out and I want to yell "Hell yeah, she's with me!" but I refrain. This is a classy place after all.

We order drinks and when they're delivered, we give our dinner order too and hand back the leather-bound menus. Now that the distractions are out of the way, it's just her and me.

"You really do look beautiful tonight," I tell her and am rewarded with a blush.

"Thank you. You look great too."

Her eyes sparkle with the candlelight and I'm helpless to look away. We both are. Reaching out across the table, I take her hand in mine. I have to touch her, to be connected to her in some way. We're both quiet but this time the silence is comforting. I don't have any history facts running through my mind, I'm able to just enjoy being in her presence.

Dana takes a sip of her wine and scans the room. Setting her glass down, she leans across the table conspiratorially. In a whisper she asks, "I think we could get kicked out of here pretty easily, but can it wait until after we eat? I'm starving and this wine is so good."

I mimic her and whisper back. "Before or after dessert?"

Dana thinks for a second then replies. "Before. I didn't see anything on the menu that I wanted for dessert."

"Probably because dessert wasn't on that menu."

She holds my stare a few seconds longer then shakes her head and laughs quietly.

"You really don't want to get kicked out just yet, do you?" I say and she looks at me quizzically.

"You forget I've heard you laugh, really laugh, and I know it's a sound somewhere between what a goose and a sheep make with a cute little snort thrown in."

A loud noise, something between what a donkey and a sheep make, bursts out of Dana and she slaps a hand over her mouth. I erupt in laughter myself not caring in the least that heads are once again turning in our direction, this time not in appreciation.

Dana ducks her hand and fans her face, her eyes shining with moisture, as she shushes me.

"I do not sound like a goose or a sheep!" She hisses.

"You're right. It's more like a donkey mixed with a sheep. I stand corrected." I agree. The look on her face is priceless and I laugh out loud again causing her to do the same thing. his time she hears it.

"Ok, maybe I do, but I don't snort!"

I tilt my head and raise an eyebrow until she concedes, covering her eyes in horror. "Oh god, this is so embarrassing!"

I'm still holding her other hand and tug until she looks back at me. "It's endearing."

"No, it's not." She grumbles and I tug again, trying to restrain the laughter I always seem to have around Dana.

"Fine. Be endeared by it but it's still embarrassing." She tries to say with irritation but can't fight her own smile.

"So is blurting out random history facts," I tell her but she doesn't agree.

"I like history facts. That's not embarrassing."

Some people say they like history, but they like it the same way they like hearing about someone else's vacation. It's nice to get the highlights and a picture or two but anything more than that and you lose them. I've never had a woman tell me she liked history before and knowing Dana isn't just saying it to be nice fills my chest with a pleasant tightness.

"Agree to disagree." I rumble, holding her gaze, my thumb stroking over her fingers.

"Ahem." The waiter makes his presence known. "Would you care to move to the patio? Our louder guests tend to sit out there." He says with a chiding scowl.

The guy's kind of a dick but I remind myself he's just doing his job and trying to make this an enjoyable dining experience for all the guests.

"We're good here but we'll keep it down," I tell him while Dana ducks her head and presses her lips together tightly.

The waiter gives us a questioning look before setting our plates down and walking away.

Dana and I look at each other and a second later we both start laughing again. We're quieter this time, the food looks way too good, we can't get kicked out yet.

CHAPTER TWENTY-FIVE

DANA

"**D**inner was great. I'm glad we didn't get kicked out." I tease Mitch.

"Yeah, even the dessert." He replies with a wink.

We shared a Molten Lava Chocolate Cake and I'm pretty sure he's referring to my audible response to the first bite, I've been hanging around Liv too long, and not the cake itself.

The night has been as close to perfect as possible and now we're steps away from my door. I admit I'm a little bit nervous.

I want him to kiss me. I want him to grab me, one hand in my hair, the other wrapped around my hip, and press me up against the door. I want his lips on my skin, skirting across my jaw and down my neck.

I want his teeth nibbling on my throat and biting into my shoulder. I want his tongue slicking over my heated skin and plunging past my own restless lips.

I want his hand trailing down my stomach and climbing up my thigh. I want his ...

"Dana?"

Mitch's voice jolts me out of the vivid fantasy and back to my front porch, inches from my door. The front door I was just picturing us against doing things not suitable for public.

My face is flaming but I can't fan myself, that would be a dead giveaway to my lusty thoughts although from the look on his face Mitch knows exactly what I was thinking about.

His lips, the ones I was dreaming about on my eager body, are turned up in a knowing smile with just a hint of cockiness showing through but his eyes... There's fire smoldering behind that heated gaze and I desperately want to fan the flames.

Mitch steps closer to me, so close I can feel the heat coming off him and I have to tilt my chin up high to look him in those fiery eyes. His hand reaches up and slides around my neck, weaving into my hair just like I imagined. Next is the hand gripping my hip.

"I was asking if you want to have dinner again on Friday."

This wasn't part of the fantasy.

Swallowing hard, I push the naughty images away and will my body to stop throbbing. I'm still only able to get one word out. "Yes."

Mitch doesn't smile, doesn't give any indication he's happy with my answer, he just bores into me with those intense eyes.

"I don't want to wait that long to see you." It's barely more than a whisper but spoken with such force it takes my breath away. I sway into him, drawing air deep into my lungs causing my chest to rise. We're so close I'm brushing against him with each ragged breath. His other hand finally grips my hip and my eyes flutter with the surge of want racing through me.

"I don't want to wait that long to see you either," I murmur into the shrinking space between us.

I watch as he descends, slowly closing the distance to my waiting lips, giving in to his desire.

His hand, still cradling the back of my head, guides it to perfectly align for the barest of kisses. I'm not positive our lips even touch before he leans back a fraction to look into my slowly opening eyes.

This moment, embracing each other, our lips barely apart, our eyes locked together feels more intimate than every sexual encounter from my past. Combined.

Mitch is in complete agreement. I can feel it as his fingers gently soften and caress me. In the way his eyes gaze tenderly into mine and contentment settles over us both like a warm blanket fresh from the dryer.

I know we're not going to have sex tonight. It would almost spoil this perfect moment. One I'm going to remember for the rest of my life as the moment I knew I was falling in love with Mitch Ainsley.

Sex can wait. It's not that the desire has gone away, not for either of us. I can feel Mitch's hunger for me pressing into my stomach, inches from where my own body is craving to be filled but we're not going to trample over what's happening right now. Letting ourselves fall slowly and completely in love.

Mitch must see it in my eyes. He brings his lips back to mine and this time I feel them touch. I feel them graze over one another, sipping, tasting, savoring.

Years later, Mitch leans his forehead against mine pivoting his lips to the side then kissing my cheek. When he did that last time, I was confused and, I admit, a little bit offended but now it feels like the sweetest of gestures, something I with cherish every time he does it.

We both pull back, knowing it's time to call it a night but still reluctant to let go.

"I don't want to wait until Friday to see you again," Mitch repeats.

"I don't either. Are you free for lunch tomorrow?" I ask and watch disappointment flash across his features.

"No, I'm having lunch with my old mentor."

"How about the next day?" I ask, not wanting him to feel bad he already has plans.

He cringes so I save him the trouble of answering.

"Lunch on Friday?"

"We're back to Friday again." He says, neither of us bothering to hide our disappointment this time.

"I have a work thing tomorrow night, so I'll be there pretty late," I tell him.

"And I have basketball with the guys on Thursday. We usually have dinner after."

"I'm having dinner with Liv and the other girls that night too."

"So, we're back to Friday." He states again. He looks like a sad puppy, and I giggle, thankful it's not my goose/sheep/snort laugh and make an affectionate aw sound.

Mitch's lips quirk up and he nuzzles my temple. "I guess I just have to wait until Friday."

"I guess so." I breathe out turning my head to brush my lips over his again.

His hand slides from the back of my neck to my jaw, his thumb grazing my bottom lip.

"Until Friday." The words are more of a growl, but I hear them just fine.

"Until Friday."

Chapter Twenty-Six

MITCH

"Rick, get that to me tomorrow morning so I have time to review it before the meeting."

"Sure thing, Mitch."

Looking around the conference room, I see everyone poised and ready to go, their folders, notebooks and various other items already stacked so it's easy to grab and bolt. I can't blame them.

Before most of them arrived, I sent an email instructing them to come straight into the conference room. My own email had a message telling me to be ready for a meeting tomorrow afternoon with some of the big dogs in town. You would think being Assistant Attorney General would give me a little bit of sway in this city but when certain people have their people tell you to be in their office tomorrow at one pm, you show up tomorrow at one prepped and ready to go like you had two weeks' notice.

Once everyone was here, I promised them lunch if this meeting went past noon, which got me a few grumbles but not as many as I expected. It's eleven forty-five now and we've pretty much covered everything, just a few minor items remain.

Out of the corner of my eye, I see Lisa and Jason both checking their watches.

"Ok, guys. Great work. I'll connect with a few of you later on the remaining items."

The last word is barely out of my mouth when the stampede barrels through the door. I don't take it personally. They all have other things they were supposed to work on this morning and calls that had to be rescheduled or missed. Our days are pretty busy around here and adding a last-minute four-hour meeting doesn't work with anyone's schedule. Most of them will work late to make up some of the lost time. Hell, most of them work late every day anyway.

I pick up my things and head to the door. At least I didn't have to cancel lunch with Thomas.

My phone rings in my pocket and I scoop it out and look at the screen. "Speak of the devil."

Accepting the call, there's already a smile on my face when I start talking.

"Thomas! I was just thinking about you."

His jovial laugh fills my ears and reminds me of my dad. My father and I may not have the same priorities but he's still my dad and that means something to me. Homesickness runs through me, and I try to remember the last time I was home. It's been a while since I've seen my family and calls with my brothers are usually kept short since we're all so busy. Hell, work is always busy. If I don't have time for a call, I sure as hell don't have time for a trip to New Hampshire. I know I was there for the holidays and then...

Have I really not been home since Christmas?

"Mitch, my boy!" Thomas' voice shakes me out of my thoughts. "Sorry to do this, but I won't be able to make it to lunch. My grandkids just showed up and surprised us. They're making sandwiches so we can go on a picnic."

It's hard to be disappointed when Thomas sounds so happy to be spending time with his family. After our last talk, I realized that while he was a great mentor and friend, I never saw him as relaxed and upbeat as he was the day he visited my office. He deserves this time with his grandkids after all the years of sacrifice he made for his career.

I wonder if my dad will be like that with my kids?

When did I start thinking about having kids?

About two seconds after I met Dana.

Shaking that thought off, I reassure Thomas. "No worries. I completely understand."

There's a shriek on his end of the call followed by children's laughter and then Thomas' robust laugh.

"Mitch. Remember what I told you. Remember what's really important."

An image of me and Dana standing in a kitchen with laughing children instantly fills my head and I smile bigger which is strange. Just a few months ago that picture would have had me running for the hills but now it kind of sounds nice.

"I will Thomas. Enjoy your picnic."

"I will. Let's try to catch up next week."

There's so much background noise on his end, I'm not sure if Thomas hears me agree and say goodbye before I end the call.

"Well, there goes my lunch plans," I say to myself and stop mid-stride in the hall. Pulling my phone back out, I text Dana.

Me: Do you have lunch plans?

I'm not sure how long it will take for her to respond or if she's already at lunch. I can wait a while, there's always more work to do to keep me busy.

Luckily, she replies just a few minutes later.

Dana: No. I thought you did.

Me: Cancelled. When can you leave?

Dana: 12:30 I get an hour.

Me: No problem. I'll come to you.

I give her the name of a deli close to her office. With lunch hour traffic it will take me twenty minutes to get there so I drop my meeting notes and folders in my office and head to the elevators. If traffic's not bad, I should get there before she does and can grab us a table so she doesn't have to waste any of her lunch break waiting for one.

Walking down the main hall to the bank of elevators, people passing me are giving me strange looks and I hear a few whispers after I pass.

After the third time, I know it's not a coincidence and quickly look down to see if I spilled coffee on myself or maybe left my fly unzipped. Nope. No stains I can see, and my zipper is in the upright and fully closed position.

Maybe it's something else.

Getting in the half full elevator, I turn around, standing front and center of the tight space. There's another whisper behind me followed by giggles.

What the hell is going on? Is there something on my face?

As the shiny doors close in front of me, I see that yes, there is indeed something on my face.

One big ass grin.

No wonder my cheeks were starting to hurt. I guess I never did smile this much before Dana.

CHAPTER TWENTY-SEVEN

DANA

"**I** can top that." I insist and immediately kick myself.

"By all means, proceed," Mitch says with a wave of his hand.

I glance away, ignoring the blush I already feel rising.

"Ok, so everything was fine up until I went to the restroom."

I can't believe I'm telling him this.

"We had finished dinner and just ordered dessert." I pause, stalling a little, but he doesn't let me stall for long.

"What happened?"

Meeting Mitch's eyes, I quickly look away, rolling my own and momentarily hide my face behind my hand. When I look back, I see Mitch squash his lips together, choking back a laugh. He's so going to laugh at me. Why did I start telling this story?

"Did you go into the Men's restroom?" He asks trying to guess.

Pressing my lips together tightly, I shake my head no.

"But I have done that before," I admit quickly, trying to keep the goose snort laugh at bay.

Mitch suppresses a chuckle and reaches across the table to wrap his hand around mine, giving me his support. It's sweet and a sudden rush of emotion runs through me bringing back those feelings from last night. Affection. Intimacy. Falling in love.

Ok, I can do this.

"I come back from the restroom which was on the other side of the restaurant from our table. So, I had to walk in front of just about every person there that night."

He's nodding encouragingly, and it helps bolster me on. I lean in conspiratorially like I'm about to tell him a secret and look into Mitch's eyes. I'm pausing for dramatic effect but also because this story is embarrassing, and I need to work up a little more courage.

"When I get back to our table and sit down, he's just sitting there, looking like a deer in headlights, completely frozen. He's not moving at all except he's blinking, rapidly and it kind of freaks me out. I ask him what's wrong, but he doesn't say anything. He just keeps blinking at me, not moving and color is rising up his neck and face. I'm starting to think he had a stroke or something while I was in the restroom, and I need to call 911. I'm really getting worried and reaching for my purse to grab my phone when the lady at the table next to us leans toward me. She whispers just loud enough for me to hear. 'Excuse me dear. But you have something sticking out of the back of your shirt.'"

Mitch's hand is over his mouth, but I can still hear him start laughing, the bastard.

I can't really blame him though. It is pretty funny.

Now.

Years later.

"So, I reach back and sure enough there's something hanging from the back of my shirt or more accurately, the top of my pants. I pull it out, frantically trying to figure out how toilet paper could be sticking out of my pants, and I have to keep pulling. It's much bigger than just a few squares of toilet paper. Now, I'm really starting to freak out over how much toilet paper I just trailed through the restaurant when I realize it's not toilet paper." Am I really about to admit this?

"It's the paper ring that you lay down to cover the toilet seat."

I barely get the last words out before unleashing my own obnoxious laugh. I've never told anyone about that incident, not even Liv, but when Mitch shared his most embarrassing date story, there was no way I couldn't share mine. Please, toilet paper ring accessory beats forgetting your date's name and spilling a drink on them, hands down.

Seating in a deli on my lunch hour, laughing over embarrassing shit from our past, I realize I'm more comfortable with Mitch than I've ever been with anyone before. Even my best friend.

In past relationships, I've always felt like I had to keep part of myself hidden so I'm not judged for my quirks, but Mitch seems to like those quirks. He finds them endearing.

This man likes me. All of me, not just the smart, dignified woman I present to the rest of the world but also the history loving nerd girl who has found herself in more than a few embarrassing situations.

Ok, dignified woman may be pushing it, but you know what I'm saying.

"You win." Mitch concedes after a good long laugh on both our parts.

He leaves a few bills on the table since my lunch hour is almost over and walks me to my car. It's a beautiful sunny day and I wish we could take the afternoon off. Maybe go for a walk, hand in hand, around our lake, taking the time to enjoy this day instead of just running through it.

Maybe this weekend...

I pull my keys out of my purse, getting ready to unlock my car, when Mitch slides his hand down my back turning me towards him. I expect another chaste kiss, we are in public, but I am very mistaken.

He draws me in, closing the distance between us, then oh so slowly, he leans me back against my car. My heart is thundering in my chest before his lips even meet mine but once they do, I have a brief thought that I may need to see a cardiologist. The way he always gets my pulse pounding can't be good for my heart.

His tongue traces my bottom lip and I open for him on command. That naughty tongue of his slides against mine then curls back as he retreats, grazing the roof of my mouth like it's an ice cream cone and I melt a little more with each lick. Mitch devours me over and over, his body pressed tightly to mine, holding me in place. The solid metal behind me and the firm, muscled body in front, are a delicious contrast to my senses and with the way his hips press harder into me, and his tongue is fucking my mouth, my nerves are overloaded.

An ache is blooming between my legs, and I shift, seeking desperately to relieve it.

Mitch slides his hand down my side, over my hip and around to my ass. He grips me hard, his fingers digging into my cheek then moves his hand down further to guide my leg up. In my heels, I'm tall enough he's easily able to hook my leg over his hip and I squeeze him closer to me. Adjusting his angle, he places his leg against my core and a moan rolls out of me as I squeeze him even closer. Mitch growls in return, and I feel it quake through my body.

I have never been this turned on in my life.

I don't just want him, I need him inside me. If he unzipped his pants right now, I wouldn't hesitate to stop him, even if we are outside.

Oh shit! We're outside!

I jerk to attention and Mitch draws back. He's confused for exactly one second before he realizes the same thing I did, but instead of ducking his head like I'm trying to do, he gives me a cocky smirk and rolls his hips into me again.

"I should get back to work." He whispers huskily against my temple. I never thought my temple was an erogenous zone before Mitch.

"You have that work thing tonight?" He asks.

Finding my voice is shaky, I answer. "Yes. And you have basketball with the guys, tomorrow."

"I'll cancel." He says, lazily running his hands up my sides.

"I'm supposed to have dinner with the girls," I say, grazing my cheek across his jaw.

"Do you want to have dinner with the girls?"

At this moment, that is a big, fat no but it's the first time I'll be hanging out with just them and I don't want to bail. Sighing, I lean back, resisting the urge to rub against him like a kitten.

"No. But I don't want us to ditch our friends."

Mitch lets out his own sigh then nods his agreement. Stepping back, he reaches down to adjust himself discreetly and arousal pools in my core again.

Maybe we can ditch our friends this once.

Before I can say it out loud, he exhales loudly and takes a small step back. "What are you doing Friday night?"

I raise my eyebrow as my own naughty smirk comes out to play. "You tell me."

Chapter Twenty-Eight

MITCH

I pass the ball to Nick and he shoots. We all stop and watch the ball swoosh through the net, winning our team the game. Nick, Dave and I high-five while Brent, Jake and Reed groan and we all head for the bench.

I'm just starting to take a drink when Reed nonchalantly comments, "So, things are heating up with you and Dana."

I'm so caught off guard I spit out my water in a misty spray that falls on my legs. How did he already hear about the parking lot kiss that went a little too far?

All five of my friends are looking at me like I just sprouted another head. I guess it is unusual for me, who is normally un-rufflable, to react with a spit take. Wiping the back of my hand over my chin, I set my water bottle down before responding.

"They are. What did you hear?"

I'm not sure I want to know the answer to that but I'm curious as hell.

"That you two went to dinner again the other night."

"Oh, that. Yeah, we did. It was nice." I say trying to play it off as no big deal, but I hear my mistake.

So does Dave.

"Oh, that? Did you think he was talking about something else?" He asks. I avoid eye contact and Dave, the son of a bitch, catches that too.

"Did something else happen?" The curiosity quickly fades from his voice and is replaced with a knowing grin. Bastard.

I'm not sure what to tell them or more actually, how much to tell them. We don't really talk about women since Dave and I are the only ones not married or engaged.

That's not true. They talk about their wives and fiancé all the time but not about having sex with them or anything leading up to it. X-rated details aren't something you want to brag about when you love a woman and want to spend the rest of your life with her. Or so I've been told.

I've never been one to brag about that stuff anyway but it hasn't stopped these guys from giving me or Dave a hard time about it. Lately, though, they've been making comments to both of us about finding a good woman, someone to spend quiet nights with, not just a few hours of fun. I need to tread carefully here.

"We had lunch yesterday," I tell them, keeping my tone as neutral as possible.

"Two dinners and lunch in less than a week. Sounds like things are moving along." Jake comments but I hear the underlying question.

So does Reed.

"Lunch isn't a reason for 'Oh, that.'"

Damn it.

Kissing Dana against her car has played on a constant loop in my head since she drove away. I've thought of little else except the taste of her skin, the feel of her curves, the way I almost lost control with her pressed so tightly against me. I've been amped and ready to explode since then.

Last night, every time I closed my eyes, I was back in that moment. I could smell her perfume, hear her low sighs and moans of pleasure, feel her body respond to each grasp, lick and nudge. It ratcheted up my discomfort to alarming levels and I knew I wouldn't be able to sleep until I relieved some tension.

Three times in a row, and it barely helped.

The last time finally took the edge off, but I was nowhere near satisfied and only dozed off and on until the sun came up. I dragged my tired, irritable ass to the lake and ran around twice, glad there wasn't a single person there to witness the tent pole in my shorts. Then I went home and took a cold shower only to manhandle myself again out of frustration.

I couldn't tell them all of that, but I could give them the basics.

"After lunch, I walked her to her car and... kissed her."

Their lack of responses tells me they heard my hesitation before I said I kissed her. Here we go.

3

2

1

"You kissed her? Or you kissed the hell out of her?" Dave asks.

"The latter," I confirm and I hear their smiles without having to see them.

"So, I guess that means things are going very well with you two," Brent says, sounding happy for me.

I nod my agreement, trying to keep the big stupid grin off my face. Not my polite business smile, the full-on grin. It's been right under the surface ready to take center stage since I meet Dana and it makes frequent appearances. I don't think I've ever smiled this much in my life.

"You look happy," Nick says and Jake tags on.

"I know that look."

They start chuckling like he just told a joke and a bit defensively, I set my shoulders back and ask, "What look?"

The chuckling gets louder and now all five of them are in on it. Dave, the son of a bitch, shakes his head.

"Another one down." He mutters and takes a gulp of his water.

Another one down? Me? As in, I'm off the market?

Huh. I guess he's right. Dana's it for me.

Now I just need to convince her of that.

Using my sleeve, I wipe sweat off my forehead and stand back up for another game. Grabbing the ball from Jake, I point to Dave. "That just leaves you." I tease and start dribbling the ball across the court to take a practice shot.

From the bench, I hear Dave mutter. "That's never happening again."

We'll see, my friend. We will see.

If I could find Dana, there has to be someone out there for Dave.

CHAPTER TWENTY-NINE

DANA

I haven't seen Mitch since the R-rated kiss in the parking lot on Wednesday. We've talked and texted every day since then and that alone has fed my erotic fantasies keeping me more aroused and frustrated than I have ever been in my entire life.

Last night, I dreamed about him.

Again. I seem to dream about him a lot which tells me he has even my subconscious worked up and raring to go. By the dirty deeds we were doing in my dream, my subconscious is horny as hell and needs a lot more than just dreaming about naked Mitch touching me.

Licking me.

Pushing inside me.

I woke up so damn turned on, I was in pain. The ache in my core consumed me and I had no choice but to make it go away. It was easy to imagine it was Mitch's hand skimming down my stomach. Sliding into my satiny underwear, his fingers grazing over the throbbing tender flesh and slowly dipping inside.

Two little flicks of Mitch's, my, fingers and I was crying out in relief and agony. The orgasm crashed through me so hard, I felt it in my toes, all my nerve endings lighting up to the point of pleasure filled pain.

I laid there, trying to catch my breath, only to realize I needed more. My body wasn't satisfied, and I craved something I couldn't give myself. It didn't stop me from repeating the scene, this time groaning out Mitch's name when I came again.

After suffering through a cold shower, I spent the eight hours of work, equally loving and hating the slide of my lacy underwear against my still throbbing skin. Most of the day my legs were crossed tightly under my desk while I chewed on a pen cap. I was still so turned on from my dreams and constant thoughts of Mitch, I clenched my thighs tighter, almost orgasming at my desk, in the middle of the paralegal bullpen, twice.

But now he's here, standing at my front door, looking more delicious than ever.

"Hi, Gorgeous."

I want to lick every inch of you.

"Hi." I purr not capable of better conversational skills in my current state.

His eyes trace my body as he reaches out for my hand. "Let's go while we still can."

I let him lead me to his car and miss his touch the instant he lets go to close the door. My eyes feast on him through the windshield, watching him quickly round the car and drop into the seat next to me. As soon as we're on our way, he reaches over and grabs my hand again.

"I've thought of you all day." He tells me, his voice the only sound in the car.

Hearing the man you're falling for admit you've been on his mind does phenomenal things to your self-esteem and your hormones. Not that they needed any help. I'm ready to have him pull over so we can defile his car right here on the side of the road but a body like Mitch's deserves to be appreciated and I can't do that in these close quarters. Car sex will have to wait until I've spent a few weeks up close and personal with everything under his suit.

Well, maybe not weeks...

Thinking about car sex, or any sex, with Mitch hikes up my arousal even more. I can't look at him or I won't be held liable for my reaction.

"I've thought about you all day too," I tell him, keeping my eyes on the passing scenery.

Mitch gives my hand a little squeeze and then he's lifting it and placing a light kiss on the back. No one ever mentions how sensitive the skin on the back of your hand is. I melt a little more and a breathy sigh leaves me.

"Let's pick that back up after dinner." He says and I grind my teeth together but agree.

"Where are we going?"

"It's a surprise." He tells me with a wink. I've always hated when men wink but when Mitch does it, I find it adorable and endearing.

Funny, that's the same thing he said about my laugh. Not the adorable part but endearing.

I sneak another peek at him and warmth floods me. Yep, I'm falling in love with this man and I'm pretty sure he feels the same way about me.

"What are you smiling about?"

I'm not ready to say the words just yet and I doubt he is too, so I cover everything I'm feeling with a playful shrug and give him a quick once over with my eyes.

Mitch reacts the way I want him to and growls a little while adjusting his position in the seat.

"Stop looking at me like that." He says with more heat than his words imply, and I drag my eyes away to see what exit we're taking.

"Until we're on our way home." He finishes and a hot flash rolls over me, stopping in my core.

I squirm in my seat, hearing Mitch chuckle before he says, "Serves you right."

Oh, he'll pay for that.

Right after we play a few rounds of Naked Naughty Time and I am declared the winner.

Over and over and over...

"Dana. I'm serious. You have to stop, or we won't make it to dinner." He almost pleads, reading my mind.

"Maybe, if you tell me where we're going?" I say coyly.

Mitch groans, good naturedly I think, and shakes his head. "You'll like it, that's all that matters."

He told me to dress casually again but I really liked the way he couldn't stop checking out my legs during our last dinner date, so I opted for a flirty little wrap dress tonight with a pair of red heels. I haven't missed the discreet looks he thinks he's given them, telling me my plan was a success.

Minutes later we're pulling into the parking lot of a bar and grill, not what I was expecting, and Mitch sees the confusion on my face.

"Just wait until we get inside." He coaxes when he opens my door.

"I'm not opposed to eating here, I'm just surprised."

He stops and turns to me, putting his hands on my waist. Leaning in I inhale his cologne causing my body temperature to rise again. Everything about this man turns me on.

"If you want to go somewhere else, we can." He says quietly.

My brain is mush with him this close to me, I can't really process what he said. My only coherent thought is that his voice is so nice. When I don't answer, Mitch turns back towards the entrance and tugs my hand to follow.

"I just thought you would enjoy it." He throws over his shoulder to me.

Now I'm curious about the place. If it's a chain restaurant, I've never heard of it, but it must be pretty good. It looks crowded, like you would expect for a place like this on a Friday night, and something appetizing is floating in the air.

We walk in and wait as the hostess seats another couple in the mostly full dining room. When she returns, Mitch tells her we need a table for two.

"Are you here for Trivia Night or just dinner?" She asks and I give a little squeal inside when Mitch tells her we're here for trivia.

As soon as she shows us to our table and leaves, I confess. "This is great, I love trivia!"

Mitch tries to keep the smugness to a minimum, but he isn't successful and the smirk that I swoon over makes its appearance.

"I thought you might." He tells me. "Let's kick some ass."

Chapter Thirty

MITCH

I know trivia night at a bar and grill isn't sexy, but I thought Dana would like it and I was right. She was so excited, she was vibrating with energy and joy. Once the game started, we got caught up in it, our focus shifted to winning and all the sexual tension that's been building took a back seat.

We did win, by the way, earning us a free dessert and half off our next meal there.

Throughout the game, the tension was still there, it just wasn't all consuming. We were distracted by our quest to become the champs, enabling us to relax and enjoy dinner. Both of us letting the stress from work fall away and putting ourselves at ease.

I wanted this woman so badly I could get off in two seconds flat and I didn't want our first time to be rushed. More importantly, I didn't want to disappoint her with my lack of finesse or stamina. I had hoped trivia night would force me to think about other things and just enjoy Dana's company without fighting the urge to rip her clothes off the whole time and it worked. For the most part.

Dana seemed just as explosive as I felt when she answered her door and that was fucking hard to walk away from. It was torture to walk away from her house, but I wanted to take my time exploring her exquisite body and that wasn't going to happen if we skipped dinner and went straight to dessert. It would have been over in minutes, and I can't have her thinking that's how I operate.

Besides, she deserves more than that.

So, my distraction plan was a success but dinner's over now and the air around us is crackling in suspense.

Our drive back to her house is quiet. We haven't said a word since we left the bar, not even allowing ourselves to look at each other. We both know what's going to happen when we get back to Dana's but neither of us wants to break the spell by saying it out loud.

Her hand grazes over mine and I weave my fingers through hers. I feel, more than see, Dana take a deep breath and wiggle just a bit in her seat. My own pulse is racing.

Almost there.

Four excruciating minutes later, I park in front of her house and turn off the engine. For a moment, neither of us move, our breaths the only sound, and the tension thickens around us. Slowly, I turn and meet Dana's molten gaze. A spark jolts between us and in seconds we're out of the car and at her front door.

My hands rake up her sides, slowing to enjoy the dangerous curves and she fumbles with her keys, dropping them. Placing my palm on her lower back, I firmly press her to the door while my other hand travels down the length of her leg to pluck the keys off the ground.

I'm inches away from her perfect legs and her satiny skin calls out to me. My lips skim from her calf to her thigh where I place a kiss just under the edge of her dress.

Using the tip of a key, I lightly scrape up from her ankle, trailing up the back of her leg. A shiver runs through her body, passing through my hands and straight to the part of me begging for her touch. My fingers dig into her back, my head dropping forward to graze across her delectable ass. I nuzzle my nose over the sweet curve and Dana lets out a soft moan.

Rising, I drag the key further up the back of her thigh, sliding under her dress, inch by excruciating inch. My chest is flat to her back, my body molding itself to hers, our heat fusing us together. I find the curve of her neck and scrape my own teeth over it.

A whimper escapes Dana and I roll my hips into her ass earning me a lusty moan.

The key reaches the top of her leg and I linger there, sliding the key inward then up the curve of her ass. When I reach her panties, I plan to skim the key along the seam, over her hip to her front.

Are they lace? Or satin? Maybe both.

My blood pumps harder.

Any second now I should reach them.

The key continues its journey up. Any second now.

Nothing stops it.

Holy shit! Is she not wearing any?

A straggled sound comes out of me, and I try to cover it with a growl.

My other hand has found its way to her stomach and glides up to palm her full, unrestrained breast.

No bra either!

My lips meet the shell of her ear and I whisper harshly. "Do you have anything on under this dress?"

I pull on her nipple as I ask, and another moan greets me as her head falls back, landing on my shoulder.

I bite down on the sensitive flesh just below her ear then demand, "Answer me."

She grinds her hips into me then rolls her body an inch away, her hands reaching down to cover each of mine. One on her breast, the other on her ass.

Looking over her shoulder, Dana only says one word. "No." But the dare in her eyes asks what am I going to do about it.

This woman sat in my car, was across the table from me for dinner and trivia, the whole time not wearing a damn thing except this black dress. She planned on sexing me tonight whether I seduced her or not.

Well, honey, no seduction needed. Getting you naked and fucking you senseless has been my only dream for weeks and it's finally going to happen.

Yanking our hands out from under her dress, I reach around her and unlock the door. She's distracting as hell, running her hand up the side of my leg, her other still clamped down on mine plying and pleasuring her breast.

As soon as the door opens, we fall in. The keys hit the floor, but I don't care. My foot reaches back to slam the door shut, not wanting to take my hands off of her, but she has other things in mind.

Stepping out of my grasp, Dana turns around.

"Stay." She commands and my body halts unwillingly.

Please don't change your mind, I beg in my head but soon it's very clear that's not happening.

Transfixed, I watch her hands skim over her curves, her hips swaying to a song only she can hear but I am enjoying the hell out of. One hand glides down from her shoulder, over her perfect tit and smooths across her stomach. The other hand starts on her leg, her fingertips skating over her skin and drawing up her dress towards her sweet spot.

I'm mesmerized and focused on that hand, waiting for my first glimpse.

The black material rises until it's just her hand hiding the treasure. I watch as one by one she lifts each finger revealing more to me. My heart is pounding in my chest, I may die but this show is totally worth it.

Her last finger begins to lift away but she shifts her hand, and the material falls back into place.

A frustrated growl rips out of me. "Don't tease me, Dana. I can't take it." I fiercely beg, watching those damn hands again.

They reach for the knot on the side of her dress and time slows with each tug of the fabric. The material falls open, but she catches it before it bares her to me. Her other hand snakes inside the dress and I stop breathing when she moves painstakingly slowly to unwrap herself like the gorgeous little present that she is.

The dress is forgotten as I take in the sight before me. Her body is sheer perfection, just like I knew it would be but better. My eyes roam over each curve, each dip, each inch of her and I finally take a breath and meet her eyes.

She answers my unspoken question, dropping the dress to the floor leaving her standing there in nothing but her sexy ass red heels.

"Now you can touch."

CHAPTER THIRTY-ONE

DANA

"Mmmmm"

I wake up from the best sleep ever and feel my body start to come alive. A large hand flexes on my hip then slides over my naked skin up my stomach and molds to my breast.

A smile takes over my face and grows when Mitch's nose glides over my ear.

"Good morning, Gorgeous."

His husky morning voice melts my insides, reminding me of all the things we did last night. Of the many times he made my body shatter into tiny highly satisfied pieces only to do it all over again.

"Good morning," I murmur, letting myself be pulled closer to him.

Mitch lightly pinches my nipple and I bite down on my lower lip to keep in the erotic sounds only he has been able to entice out of me.

"Let me hear you." He says gruffly, pinching a little harder.

"Mitch." His name comes out raspy, needy.

"That's it. Say my name." He quietly demands, teasing my other nipple now.

My next orgasm is so close, rushing at me with lightning speed.

How can I already be there? With just a few pinches and flicks, he has my body trembling on the edge ready to jump. I grind against his hardness, desperate for relief and amazed I can come again. I lost count of last night's orgasms after the fourth one.

The first one was minutes after I stripped off my dress. As soon as I gave him the green light, Mitch grabbed me and set me on the edge of my dining room table. He was inside me almost instantly. It was hard, fast, frenzied and I loved it. We both cried out in ecstasy, our fevered brows meeting while we tried to catch our breath.

When I realized I was completely naked and Mitch was still fully clothed, I started giggling. Mitch muttered something like, "You won't be laughing next time," and whisked me to my room where he proceeded to "do it right". His words, not mine. I wasn't complaining about round one, but his doing it right made my body explode like the fourth of July.

Twice. So, I chose not to argue with him.

We passed out for a few hours until a wandering hand woke me up. That time it was slow and gentle and pushed me over the edge then brought me back and did it all over again a few times. Like I said, I lost count. It was the middle of the night, and my brain wasn't really working anymore.

"Dana." He rumbles and I feel it all the way to my core.

Mitch's hand grazes down my stomach, just missing the place I want it to stop and wraps around my inner thigh. He pulls my leg over his own and soon we're lost in the pleasure.

When our bodies are finally satisfied and we've both caught our breath, Mitch turns me to him. Tenderly, he swipes my hair back from my eyes and gazes at me.

"I've never said this to a woman before but..."

Whatever he's going to say, this feels like a big moment. My skin tingles with anticipation and my chest tightens.

"Dana. I'm falling in love with you."

Tears spring to my eyes and my throat clogs with sheer happiness but Mitch takes it the wrong way.

"I'm not saying this because I'm in a sex haze. I've felt this way for a while now, I just didn't want to scare you if you didn't feel the same way. But now, I can't keep it to myself anymore." He finishes in a whisper.

The tears roll down my face and Mitch reaches to brush them away with his thumb. My hand slides up his arm and I twine our fingers together, never looking away from his eyes.

"I'm falling in love with you, too," I confess. "I knew it Tuesday night, after dinner when you kissed me."

The barest of smiles is his response. I can see the emotion in his eyes, feel it in his touch and I do my best to show it back.

We don't speak for long minutes, choosing to relish in the moment, letting ourselves soak in the emotion.

Unfortunately, my bladder forces me up but not before I kiss this man one more time.

"Do you want to go run?" He calls out to me as I walk away.

"Of course. It's our thing." Looking over my shoulder, I see his attention on my naked ass and I give him a little shimmy. Mitch's eyes light up like he's a kid and it's Christmas morning.

I better get dressed fast or we're not making it out of this room anytime soon.

"I guess we need to stop by your house so you can change," I call out to him when I'm done in the bathroom.

"Yes, we do." He says only inches away from me and I shriek, making him laugh.

I swat at him with one hand, the other over my heart. "You scared me!"

Mitch wraps his arms around my waist, pulling me flush to his naked body. "Sorry." He mumbles into my neck, still laughing.

"It doesn't feel like you're sorry," I say trying not to give into his roaming hands but the nibbles on my neck are too much for me. Reaching down, I slide my fingertips over him, and he hisses in a breath before pushing himself into my grasp.

"I thought we were going to your house." I tease grazing my lips over his collarbone.

"We are." He murmurs grabbing the back of my head in one hand and kissing me hard. Not too gently, I bite down on his bottom lip, stroking my hand up then down.

Mitch has me in his arms, stalking back to the bed in seconds and this time it's me laughing.

"I guess we're not going running." I get out right before he throws me on the bed and settles over me.

"Later."

Chapter Thirty-Two

MITCH

Dana and I stopped by my house so I could change clothes and show her my newly renovated bedroom and bath then we headed for the lake. It's weird pulling up to the park and having her with me. Usually, I'm doing this alone, anxious to see her but today, her fingers are drawing up my forearm and it's distracting as hell.

We should've just stayed in bed.

Last night with Dana, and this morning, was incredible. Better than I imagined, and I imaged it pretty damn good. I've heard people say that sex is better with someone you love but I never got it.

Now I do.

What I previously thought was good sex isn't even in the same ballpark, the same league as what it was like with Dana. Every time was better than the time before and that first time almost killed me.

Seriously. I think my heart stopped beating for a second there.

Parking the car, Dana hops out and strolls to the spot where we always stretch, with me following behind.

"Come on, slow poke. Or are you too worn out?" She teases me with a sexy ass smirk.

This woman is perfect.

Rushing up to her, I smack her ass. "Just enjoying the view," I whisper in her ear then leave her frozen as I move away to stretch.

But she doesn't stay frozen for long. Moving in front of me, she folds in half, stretching her calves and hamstrings, putting that ass on full display. I reach for her but she's inches beyond my grasp and I know she did that on purpose. The little vixen turns around to face me and dips to the side. The sports bra she's wearing frames her tits perfectly for eye fucking and she knows it.

My eyes are glued to her cleavage and memories from last night assault me.

Shit. Now, I'm getting hard at the park.

I avert my gaze and start thinking about baseball but that doesn't work so I go over one of the pending files waiting on my desk. Dana sees my predicament and giggles, the woman giggles! Then she takes off on the trail.

Like a puppy, I follow her.

We jog in silence for a few minutes and the world seems right. It's a beautiful Saturday morning. The woman of my dreams is beside me. Last night was the best night of my life and I get to spend the entire weekend with her.

Life is good.

"What are you smiling about over there?" She asks her dark ponytail swinging.

"Just enjoying the view," I say again and she rolls her eyes at me. This woman has no idea what the sight of her does to me. "I was thinking we see if we can get kicked out of another museum today."

Her smile tells me she loves that idea before she ever says a word. "I think I could be ok with that. What museum did you have in mind?"

"How about the Museum of American History? Since you weren't able to go with me last time."

She tosses me a dirty smile over her shoulder. "You still jealous about that?"

I scoff. "No."

Maybe.

Pretending not to hear her "Mmmmmmhmmmm" I have to bite down on my back teeth hard to keep the smile off my face. It doesn't matter if she turned me down and went on a date with someone else that night, she's mine now.

We finish our run, chatting about the museums in town she wants to visit, and walk to the car with me stealing a few kisses along the way. As soon as I open Dana's door, I hear my phone ding with an incoming email. It dings again before Dana sits down.

And again.

By the time I round the car and pull my phone out of the console, there are twenty-three emails, twelve texts and four missed calls and voicemails.

What the hell happened?

Quickly scanning the texts, I move to the emails and let out a string of profanity.

"What's wrong?" Dana asks beside me.

I wanted to spend the whole weekend with her, holding her close, stealing more kisses, taking my time with others, and falling more in love with her. But now I have to leave her, after our first night together, to put out fires at work.

Swiping my sweating hair back from my face, I turn to look at her fully. "Something we thought was handled on Friday just turned to shit. I have to go fix it before the meeting Monday."

I feel like shit about it, and see she's disappointed too, but she fights it back and does some pretending herself. "It's ok."

I know it's not, but Dana's in the legal field. She knows sometimes things come up at inopportune times and can't be ignored.

It happens more than it should.

Grabbing my hand, she squeezes. "Mitch, really. It's ok. I understand if you have to go in to work. And it's not like we haven't spent any time together this week." She says with a smile that has me picturing her under me, naked.

"It will probably take most of the weekend to sort this out, but I should be done in time for us to have dinner tomorrow."

"Do you want to skip Liv and Reed's? Have dinner, just the two of us?"

How did I forget about Sunday dinner? It's become tradition but one I'm willing to skip if I need to.

I lift her hand to my lips and place a light kiss on her fingers. "I want to be with you. Wherever you are, I'll be there."

Her cheeks pinken, something she doesn't do a lot, and she leans over to kiss me back. It's not a lusty kiss or a demanding one. This kiss is one of caring and understanding. Of knowing we'll both do our best to make the other happy.

I'm grateful she isn't pissed I have to work all weekend. I just hope that stays the case when this happens again.

Because it will.

CHAPTER THIRTY-THREE

DANA

I didn't want to make plans in case Mitch finished his work early and could get back to me. Instead, I made some lunch, watched a little TV then unpacked the last few boxes I had tucked away in the garage. That only took about an hour, so I decided to tackle the overgrown flower beds in my yard.

After several hours, the flower beds look much better but I'm filthy, my back is aching and there's more dirt under my fingernails than I left outside.

Taking a hot shower, my second for today only this time alone, I scrub until my skin is red and my nails are clean. The rest of the evening, I binge watch the History Channel and check my phone for messages from Mitch. I know he's working, I guess I'm just hoping for a quick "I miss you" or "I'm thinking about you" text but by eleven pm I still don't have any and haul myself to bed.

It's raining when I wake up Sunday morning and I lay there listening to it hit the roof and stretch luxuriously thinking about Mitch.

Did he call?

I grab for my phone, wondering how I didn't hear the phone ring or even ding with a text until I see the screen.

No missed calls or texts.

Disappointment instantly hits me, and I drop the phone on the bed.

He's busy. He told you he'd be working until later today. Rational Dana tells me.

"Yeah, but is he so busy he can't even send a text?" I mutter out loud to the empty room.

The rational part of me defends Mitch again, reminding me of what I told him yesterday. We did spend a lot of time together this week and I do understand if he has to work extra hours.

Sometimes. Bitchy Dana grumbles.

Then Rational Dana brings out the big guns. *He's not Chris.*

She's right. Mitch isn't Chris. I can't assume he's going to treat me the same way Chris did. It's not fair to Mitch or to me to expect that he will.

Deciding to attack the day, I fling the covers back with gusto and know it's a mistake as soon as I do it but it's already too late.

My phone goes flying across the room, slamming into the wall. A crunching sound tells me it's not good before I see the damage. The screen is shattered, the picture from my last vacation distorted.

"Looks like I'm getting a new phone today," I mumble to myself.

After getting dressed and drugging myself with coffee, I leave for the nearest phone store which I had to google it on my laptop since I can't search for one in the Maps app on my phone.

While the sales lady is helping me, my phone lets out a pathetic beep and I get excited it's Mitch finally calling me, but the screen's so busted we're unable to answer it. She transfers all my data to the new phone, and I hurry to my car to call Mitch back.

Only, it wasn't Mitch, it was Liv, telling me to bring a dessert tonight.

Shit. I forgot to tell her we weren't coming.

Well, I guess we'll go there for dinner but he's coming home with me after. Thoughts of what I'll do to him have me singing and dancing around my kitchen for the next few hours while I make cookies and a cheesecake.

Have I mentioned Liv and Reed have a thing for cheesecake?

It's late afternoon when my new phone plays a weird tone and I hit the accept button. "Hey! I've been thinking about you all day."

"I've been thinking about you too, Gorgeous." Mitch's voice is smooth and deep, but I hear something else behind that.

"Is everything ok?" The oven timer beeps, and I reach over to crack it open it so the cheesecake can cool down but his sigh stops me, and I straighten with concern and a little dread.

"I'm not going to make it to dinner. This was worse than I thought. I still have at least four more hours of work before I'm even close to being ready for tomorrow's meeting."

Well, that sucks. But it's ok, it's just one weekend.

Putting a smile on my face, because you can hear a smile, I try to set him at ease. "I'm sorry you've had to work all weekend, but don't worry about dinner. Hey, do you want me to bring you something? Maybe you can take a break for a few minutes?"

"Aw, honey. I would love that, but I've got six other people here with me. We'll just order something in." My shoulders slump with the rejection. "I'll call you tomorrow."

I try to inject some cheer into my voice. "Ok. Don't work too hard."

Mitch forces a chuckle because we both know he's got a lot more work to do then in a more serious tone, he starts to say something else. "Dana, I..."

He doesn't have to finish that sentence, I know exactly what he's wanting to say, and those words go straight to my heart, putting a real smile on my face.

"I know. I feel the same way about you."

Chapter Thirty-Four

MITCH

"**N**o! You can't do that. Not unless you want to open yourself up to a lawsuit!" I yell.

The suit across the table from me snorts. "A civil lawsuit." He says dismissively.

My fist pounds the table as the words erupt from me. "It doesn't matter! Any lawsuit against a government agency is bad, period!" My voice echoes in the room. "Even a civil one!" I add to prove my point.

The blowhard thunders back. "We wouldn't have to open ourselves up to any lawsuit if you would've just done your fucking job in the first place!"

Fury clouds my vision, my lungs heave in my chest. This asshole wants to blame me for the shitstorm he's currently in! Un-fucking-believable.

With deadly calm, I respond. "Everyone in this room knows you went against my advice because you thought you knew better. And now you're fighting me on how to fix it. If you're not going to listen to me, then get the hell out of my office. I've wasted enough time on you already."

I don't think I've ever sounded more like my dad.

Rising from my chair, I stalk out of the conference room and down to my office. I want to slam the door but despite what just went down, what's been going down for days, I'm a professional. Throwing a temper tantrum isn't acceptable.

Yelling isn't either but we've been over and over this. Hell, we've been going over this since Saturday and it's Wednesday morning. I think I'm entitled to a little yelling at this point.

Roughly running my hands through my hair, I take a deep breath and close my eyes. I need to calm down before going back in there. I'd rather not since I have lunch plans, but this job is hell on your social calendar, which never bothered me until recently.

I love this job and not just because I've worked my whole life to get here. Knowing I'm having an impact on legal matters for this country is profoundly fulfilling.

Or it used to be. It didn't matter I worked through lunch and most weekends, or that I didn't leave the office until I was ready to crash from exhaustion. I didn't make plans or engage in relationships that required much from me and it suited me just fine. I happily traded a social life for a career where I was leaving my mark on the world.

Until last year.

I knew Nick since he handles our IT, but we never talked outside of the office. One day we end up by ourselves at the same café down the street and decided to sit together. I recognized one of the guys at the next table over and we all struck up a conversation. By the time we left, we had plans to play basketball with Reed and Dave that night and meet for lunch again the next week.

After that, they started inviting me to things and I realized something I'm a little embarrassed to admit. I'd never had any real friends, only acquaintances or co-workers much like my parents. Sure, there were people I could call to grab a drink with after work or some I would run into occasionally and hang out with, but no one I considered a close friend. An inner circle.

I started making an effort to show up when they invited me, and I found out that I like having friends.

Then I met Dana.

For the first time in my life, I'm really happy. Not that fake social media happy bullshit but honest to God, "I wake up with a smile on my face and feel happy down to my bones" happy. And I LOVE it.

I have an amazing woman and a great group of friends that I would do just about anything for so, what I'm about to do sucks ass.

But I don't have a choice. Sometimes your personal life has to take a backseat to your career, especially when legalities of government agencies are concerned.

Me: I can't make it to lunch. Serious shit hitting the fan.

Barely two seconds pass before I start getting replies.

Dave: You're bailing on us? Come on, you have to eat lunch.

Reed: Work shit or Dana shit?

Me: I'll eat lunch here.

Nick: Dude, you skipped Sunday, now lunch too? Must be bad.

Me: Work shit

Dave: No one wants to eat lunch in their office.

Reed: So things are good with Dana? Liv said they are but...

Nick: Work shit? Should I cut the wifi? Would that help?

Dave: We'll bring lunch to you. Tacos?

Reed: She seemed fine on Sunday. Better than fine.

Me: Things are good with Dana. Really good.

Me: I don't think cutting the wifi would help.

Reed: So you two...?

Me: Tacos sound awesome but no, I really don't have time.

Nick: I can give them a computer virus... just saying.

Me: We're together.

Reed: Good. Liv will be happy.
Nick: Go to Bergman Jewelers for the ring.
Dave: Another one down

I smirk at that last one. This is what I was missing before I met these guys. Friends who would have lunch in my office if I was too busy to get away or give someone a computer virus to help me out. People who care if I'm happy and have a life beyond my career.

They're the kind of friends everyone needs. I hate bailing on them, but it can't be helped.

Which reminds me, I haven't talked to Dana since I called her on Sunday.

Shit. I haven't even responded to her text. She's probably pissed.

Every time I've started to call or text her back, it's been late at night or someone has interrupted me. It's a shitty excuse, I know, but it's the truth. I should have just called or texted anyway, just to say hi, but I didn't.

I have to now.

The ringtone plays in my ear and I'm preparing to apologize, grovel if I have to. I care about this woman and the day after we finally take things to the next level, physically and emotionally, I pretty much ghost her. I'm such a dumbass.

There's a click and I wait to hear her voice, the words 'I'm sorry' already on my tongue.

"This is Dana. I can't come to the phone right now. Leave me a message."

Great, her voicemail.

"Hey, Gorgeous. I'm so sorry I haven't called or returned your messages. Things have been bad, fucking terrible actually, and I..." *I'm making excuses.* "That's no excuse. I should have called." I admit with a heavy sigh.

"I don't know when I'll wrap this up, we still have a lot to do, but I'll try to call you later tonight or tomorrow. I miss you."

Disconnecting, I let out a harsh breath and rub my eyes. I'm such a dumbass.

CHAPTER THIRTY-FIVE

DANA

"**I** worked on it for three days and when I give him all the research, he doesn't even bother to look at me, just waves his hand and says there's been a new development and it's all useless now," Gina says and we all nod our heads in sympathy.

"We've all been there." Leslie commiserates.

"What pisses me off is when they don't tell you about it until days later when you could have been working with the new information the whole time," Allison adds.

"That happened to me last week," I say. "Fields had me chasing down similar cases and when I asked if there were any specifics I needed to look for, he said no. Three days later, when I gave him the list, he was like, "What's this? There can't be that many cases where the contract includes this specific phrasing in the distribution plan."

"No!"

"He didn't!"

I just raise my eyebrows and nod.

"What an ass."

Their outrage on my behalf proves we're kindred paralegal souls.

"Well, enough about work," Allison says, taking a sip of her soda. "Is everything ready for the wedding, Leslie?"

Leslie lights up with that bright smile only a future bride or mommy-to-be can truly deliver. "Yes, everything is done, down to the last detail."

The rest of us start to Awwww when Leslie practically shouts. "Oh, Dana!"

"Leslie! I almost poked myself in the eye with my straw." Gina playfully scolds her.

"Sorry, it's just that I almost forgot," Leslie mumbles to her open purse she's digging around in.

"Found it!" She says triumphantly, holding up an envelope.

"You want me to put that in the mail for you?" I ask her as she hands it over.

Leslie tinkles out a tiny little laugh I'm super envious of and shakes her head. "No. It's an invite to the wedding. I didn't have your address to mail it and I didn't want to give it to you at work since most of those people aren't invited. I know it's late notice since the wedding is less than two weeks away but please say you'll come. We haven't known you very long but you're one of us now. You have to be there."

"And bring that sexy man with you," Gina says.

"Yes, absolutely!" Leslie agrees.

I open the envelope and pull out the invitation to stall. I haven't known Leslie, Gina and Allison very long, but they are quickly becoming good friends and them wanting me to be part of Leslie's big day is touching. You don't always make real friends in the workplace, but these ladies are already so much more than co-workers.

I swallow my emotions and slide the invitation back in. "On one condition," I say then look directly at Leslie. "It better be an open bar."

She shrinks back, looking offended. "Do I look cheap?!"

We all laugh and grab our purses so we can get back to work. All morning I've managed to not check my phone for any missed calls or texts from Mitch but once I'm back in my cubicle the urge is too strong, and I dig my phone out.

My heart jumps up and down when I see I do have a missed call and a voicemail from him. I'm disappointed I missed it but glad he finally called. I know he's swamped at work and is probably spending eighteen hours a day at the office but a little part of me is ticked off he hasn't even returned any of my texts.

Ok, maybe that part isn't so little. It started small the first day, but it's grown every day I didn't hear from him. It's getting harder to believe Mitch isn't the workaholic he appears to be, but seeing he called today erases those feelings completely.

I press the icon to play his voicemail, already smiling to myself.

"Hey, Gorgeous. I'm so sorry I haven't called or returned your messages. Things have been bad, fucking terrible actually, and I... That's no excuse. I should have called."

His sigh comes through loud and clear, and I feel bad for being ticked off. It's not his fault he has to work so much right now, and I know from experience the long hours everyone on a difficult case has to put in. He's probably exhausted.

I realize I missed the last part of what he said, and I replay the message to hear it again.

"I don't know when I'll wrap this up, we still have a lot to do, but I'll try to call you later tonight or tomorrow. I miss you."

Hmmmm. Hearing the last part kind of ruins the beginning. Not the I miss you part. Hearing Mitch say those words does things to my heart and my lady parts.

No, it was what he said before that. He'll try to call me later tonight or tomorrow.

I get having to work crazy hours but he can't even stop for two minutes to call and tell me good morning or good night?

I know he just did, but it's been days since I heard from him and that last call was just to tell me he wouldn't make it to dinner.

I mean we finally have sex, he tells me he's falling in love with me and then radio silence for three days!

What the hell is that?!

I don't think I'm asking for much, just thirty seconds out of his entire day to send me a text.

Chucking my phone back into my purse, I close it in the drawer with a slam before Rational Dana starts pleading her case.

You're being overly dramatic.

He didn't go radio silent. He's called you twice in the four days.

Mitch is falling in love with you and you are with him too.

"But why hasn't he returned any of my texts?" I ask her.

She responds with my favorite piece of wisdom. I remember telling Liv this same exact thing about her and Reed when they were first dating. *If this is something that bothers you, talk to him.*

I huff in irritation, ticked off that Rational Dana is right.

Ok, fine. I'll talk to him.

Chapter Thirty-Six

MITCH

It's been a really shitty week. I'm exhausted. I've barely seen the outside of my office since last Saturday and I've eaten so much takeout the thought of another deli sandwich makes my stomach roll. On top of all that, I haven't seen Dana since I dropped her off after our run last weekend and I've only been able to talk to her a handful of times.

We played phone tag Wednesday afternoon and her final message said to call her no matter what time it was, so I did. I could hear in her voice she wasn't happy, and she didn't waste time before calling me out on my shitty communication skills. I wasn't angry because she was totally right and I could return a text or give her a call just to say hi on my way to or from the restroom or on my way to work in the morning.

My only defense was I've never been in a serious relationship before so things like that don't come naturally to me, hell, they didn't even occur to me but yeah, that excuse is bullshit too.

I should have made more of an effort, and I told her I would, starting then. I've made it a point to text her in the morning and before I hit the bed every night and I've managed to get in a short phone call every day since then.

It's not much but Dana seems happy with it, and I can admit, it's the least I should be doing for the woman I'm falling for.

The woman I'm about to see in 3.

2

1

The door opens and I freeze.

She's so beautiful, my mind hasn't done her justice. It didn't put the way she looks with the scent of her perfume and the magnetic pull of our attraction together. It didn't remember the sparkle in her eyes or way her hair frames her face or the light blush rising in her cheeks.

With one look, I'm breathless trying to take it all in.

Then she says my name and it's like a prayer, it's reverence telling me she feels the same way.

Our bodies meet of their own accord and then my hands are in her hair and she's pressing her lips to mine in a sensuous kiss that blanks my brain. I want nothing more than to take her inside and spend the next few hours worshipping her body, but I promised to be at Sunday dinner after bailing on lunch with the guys.

"We leave as soon as we're done eating," I say against her neck, breathing her in.

"Not a minute later." She agrees before I drag her to the car so we can get this dinner over with.

"My friend Leslie is getting married next weekend. Do you want to go with me?" Dana asks after we've both grumbled about the long week and not seeing each other enough.

Do I want to go to a wedding? Hell no. But I will if it's with her I will. I'm realizing I'll do a lot of things I otherwise wouldn't if it's with her.

Treading my fingers through hers, I give her a quick glance and a smile. "Sure. Can you text me the details? So, I don't forget."

Her face lights up and damn, that makes me happy.

"Absolutely." She says and I know I would do just about anything to keep seeing that smile.

We're the last ones to arrive for dinner. There's razzing about me being a long-lost stranger but I know it's all in good nature.

Grabbing drinks for us, I take them out to her on the back porch. Just as I'm tasting my first drink of a much-needed beer, the doorbell rings. Everyone looks around and you can see us all counting heads and trying to figure out who could be at the door. No one's missing.

Reed heads off to find out and the rest of us return to our conversations. Brent's telling the guys about his new golf clubs and the new woman with Dave is asking the girls if they've had eye lasering. Weird. He can do so much better.

I don't notice the footsteps until they're just inside the patio door. That's when it hits me I'm hearing high heels clicking on the tile. Everyone else must have heard it too because we all turn as a group and watch Reed step outside.

Followed by Jessica.

Dana stiffens beside me, and I automatically pull her closer to me.

"What is she doing her?" Suzette whispers under her breath.

My eyes find Dana's and I try to relay all the things in my head with a single look. We must be getting good at this relationship thing because she nods her head and smiles, showing her understanding that I have no idea what Jessica's doing here but I'll get rid of her. Now.

Reluctantly I leave Dana's side and motion for Jessica to follow me back into the house. As soon as we clear the door, hushed voices fill the silence behind us.

Moving out of view, I turn on her. "What are you doing here?" I'm not angry, just confused. Ok, maybe I'm a little angry. This woman already almost made me blow it with Dana. I'm not letting her do that again.

"I wanted to see you and you haven't returned my calls."

Oh, yeah. She left me a few messages I just deleted. Maybe I should have listened to them first, but I didn't think it was anything serious. The last time we talked I thought I made it clear we were over. No more sex, no more dinner dates, we were done.

Taking a step closer to me, Jessica's subtle perfume I used to enjoy now gives me a headache. She reaches out, touching her fingers to my chest before I take another step back out of harm's reach.

"I went by your house, but you didn't answer. Then I re-membered it's Sunday and last time your friends said you always come here for Sunday dinner. So..."

She says this with a nonchalant shrug and reaches for me again, but I catch her hand in the air. Jessica takes this as a good sign, not what I was intending, and comes a step closer, invading my personal space.

"I've missed you, Mitch." She purrs and rolls her body to rub against me.

For the second time tonight I'm frozen, but this time it's not in a good way. What the hell does she think she's doing?

"I know you don't want a relationship and I'm ok with that. Really. I think we should pick up where we left off. Just enjoying each other when we can. No strings attached."

Her last words knock me out of my trance, and I grip her shoulders setting her back from me. I can't let her get too close again, I don't want Dana to think I'm encouraging or welcoming it.

"No."

Jessica tilts her head patronizingly and gives me a flirty smile. "Why not? You know you miss me too."

Did this woman not see Dana standing right next to me? Did she not notice my arm around another woman's waist only sixty seconds ago?

"Jessica. We're not going to happen again." I tell her sternly, but she doesn't listen.

"We could," She starts to say but I cut her off.

Again, I tell her no then take a steadying breath before being completely honest with her.

"It was just sex, that's all it was. I didn't want anything more and you were ok with that, so it worked. But things changed."

"They can go back." She tries to reason but I talk over her.

"I've met someone." I pause to let that sink in and the way her face falls tells me when it does.

"You're dating someone?" She asks, confused. "Really dating someone?"

In a firm but gentle tone, I tell her yes. For what has to be a full minute, she just looks at me like I'm a math problem she can't figure out. The whole time, I'm ready to shove her into her car and get back to the woman I want to be with.

Nodding sadly, Jessica finally speaks. "Ok, then."

Grabbing my hand and giving it a squeeze, she turns to leave then stops and looks at me over her right shoulder. "But if that ever changes, let me know."

The flirtatious smile is back along with the sway of her hips.

"Let me walk you out," I tell her but she throws up her hand.

"I can find my way to the door."

Good, I'd rather be outside anyway, so that's where I go, leaving her to find the front door herself.

Chapter Thirty-Seven

DANA

When Mitch walks back outside, I release a sigh of relief.

He puts his arms around me, pulling me into him once more, and whispers against my ear. "Problem solved." He says then places a kiss on my temple.

Good.

Later, I'll ask him for the details but right now I'm just glad she's gone. It's bad enough I have to share Mitch with our friends tonight, I really didn't want to share him with his ex too.

With that taken care of, I excuse myself to the bathroom.

The door is closed when I get there and when I grab the knob and turn, it's locked. I don't remember anyone else going inside but I probably didn't notice since I was so focused on what was happening with Mitch and Jessica.

Just as I'm turning to go wait in the kitchen, the door opens, stopping me immediately.

Jessica.

"Oh. Hi. Dana, right?" She says with a friendly smile.

I'm instantly on edge.

What does she want? Even Rational Dana is feeling defensive.

"Yes, Dana," I confirm because of my southern manners, which is the only reason I can come up with for why I ask the next question.

"How have you been?" Southern manners dictate I'm polite, however, it doesn't say I have to like it and Jessica can hear the displeasure loud and clear. Her face goes from slightly confused to full understanding in seconds.

"Look, I didn't know he was seeing you or I wouldn't have come. I'm sorry about that."

Yeah, right.

"But there's something I think you should know." She says, leaning in conspiratorially.

"Mitch is a textbook workaholic. Always working late hours. Not wanting to make plans because he knows he'll have to cancel them. Just generally so focused on his job nothing else really matters."

A sinking feeling grows in my stomach as she tells me my biggest fear.

"Mitch's career is the most important thing in the world to him and nothing is ever going to change that. He's never going to be the guy who's home for dinner every night or even the one who bothers to let you know if he's not going to make it to dinner."

Please stop.

"He's not real relationship material. If you're looking for someone to have fun with when he happens to be available, then you won't be disappointed."

Hearing her talk about Mitch this way feels like a knife to my heart, but I'm hooked, hanging on every word she says, and she knows it.

Jessica flicks a glance down the hall towards the kitchen then back at me. In a lower voice, she continues. "But if you're looking for a serious relationship. Someone you can build a future with," she pauses again to make sure I'm listening, "then you should probably look somewhere else. Mitch isn't that guy. He doesn't want to be that guy."

Bringing her hand up to her chest, she gestures to herself.

"I knew that, and I thought I was ok with it but then ... then I wasn't. And when I told Mitch I wanted more, he just ended it. Completely."

She reaches out and puts her hand on my shoulder in a comforting grasp.

I hate it.

"You seem nice, and I don't want that to happen to you too." She says, giving me a sad smile and squeezing my shoulder before walking away.

I watch her close the front door behind her and hear a car start in the distance, the whole time wondering if I can believe anything she said. Jessica obviously wants Mitch back, she could be lying about everything just to get in my head and make me break up with him.

Much of what she said doesn't line up with the Mitch I know. He did make plans with me. Before we were even dating, every Saturday morning he asked if I would be there the next Saturday. Ok, maybe that's not really making plans, but he did make plans for us to have dinner a few times and didn't cancel. And she was wrong about him not calling and just not showing for dinner plans. He did call when he couldn't make it to dinner last weekend.

As for him not wanting a serious relationship, well, telling someone you're falling in love with them sounds pretty damn serious to me.

I hold on to that triumph briefly until my brain forces me to think about everything else Jessica said.

Some of it also rings true of the Mitch I know. He has been working long hours and his career is very important to him, something I simultaneously love and despise. He even admitted his workaholic tendencies to me on our first date. At the time, I brushed away the concern remembering our friends said he rarely misses Sunday dinner or their weekly lunches but over the past week he's missed both.

This jumbled mess of thoughts is still running through my head when Mitch finds me, standing alone in the hall.

He cups the back of my neck with his big hand, his thumb stroking my cheek.

"Is everything ok?" He asks, his concern evident in his tone.

Is everything ok? I don't know if it is, if he's really the man Jessica says he is. The man I fear he is, one who will always put work before me. Will I ever be the most important thing in his life? I search for the answer in his eyes.

"Did Jessica say something to you?" Now there's heat and suspicion in his voice.

I'm not going to lie to him so I might as well go with the truth. But how much of the truth? I don't want to rehash the whole conversation. How much do I say?

"Dana?"

"Yes, she did..."

"What?" He tries to interrupt but I cut him off.

"But it doesn't matter. She's wrong." I say with conviction.

I really hope she's wrong.

CHAPTER THIRTY-EIGHT

MITCH

T his week should have been better.

I woke up Monday morning in Dana's bed and was almost late to work but I didn't care. No one can accuse me of slacking off when I put in almost a hundred hours last week. I deserved the extra hour in bed with Dana wrapped around me.

I knew work was going to be hectic for a few days. We had backburnered so much to put out the colossal fire we'd now have a shit ton of little fires if we didn't play catch up fast. I worked late Monday and Tuesday to clear some of it out and Dana was fine with the extra hours. She completely understood.

Then Wednesday I get a call from the White House, the President's Chief of Staff to be exact. The President has a policy proposal we needed to review, and he wanted it back by Monday morning.

This happens on a fairly regular basis and it's the part of the job I live for. The President of the United States needs my opinion on something before he can give his approval. Talk about boosting your ego.

In the past, I would work day and night to get this finished early and I'd love every minute of it. I wouldn't care if I had already worked an insane amount of hours the week before or if I was willingly giving up another weekend for my job.

But now...

Now, I'm tired. I want to take a few days off so I can rest and enjoy the life I finally have. I don't want to go another seven days before I see Dana.

Maybe I need a vacation.

Or maybe my priorities are changing.

Either way, I can't say no to the President and from the look of this file, it's going to take every minute I have from now until Monday to get it done. Which means I have to cancel on dinner tonight.

Dana's going to be pissed and I don't blame her.

Feeling like I'm walking into a firing squad, I hit send and listen to the rings.

"Hey. I was just thinking about you." Her voice soothes the raw edge of my frustration.

"Were you? Did I have any clothes on?" I flirt and get her hushed giggle back.

God, I love that sound. I love her loud honking laugh too but this one, it touches a place deep inside me I didn't know existed before her.

And I'm about to smash her happiness to pieces.

I clear my thought. Here goes...

"Listen, Gorgeous. I just got a file I need to review for the President so I'm going to have to cancel on dinner tonight."

I hesitate before going on because I know she's really going to be pissed about this next part.

"And I'm probably going to have to work through the week-end to get it done for Monday."

No sound comes through my phone for so long that I pull it away from my ear to make sure I didn't lose the call.

Nope, still connected.

Tentatively, I place it back to my ear and test the waters. "Dana? You still there?"

"Yes."

Yep. She's pissed.

"Look," I let out a harsh breath and squirm in my chair like I did as a kid when I knew I was about to be scolded. "I know I said things would be returning to normal, but this just came up."

"I get it, Mitch. I really do."

It doesn't sound like she does...

"I understand you'll have to work late a lot or sometimes things will come up at the last minute and you'll have to cancel plans so you can get it done. I work in a law office too and I see what it's like with the big cases."

It's not really the same when it's the President...

"Last week couldn't have been avoided and this can't be either. I know that." She stops abruptly and I sit up straight. It feels like she's about to drop a bomb on me.

When she speaks again, it's slow and deliberate. "It just seems like this is a pattern for you and I question where I fit in. What your priorities are?"

"Dana." I plead her name, begging her, with that one word, to know I would do anything for her. "You are my priority."

"It doesn't feel like it when you cancel on me. When you work late every night and through the weekends." There's no anger or heat in her words, just the sad truth.

"Am I always going to come second to your job?"

"No," I reply vehemently. "You are not second to my job. Right now, is just a crazy time, there's so much going on."

"When is it not a crazy time for you?"

When is it not a crazy time for me? Most weeks, I eat lunch and dinner in my office while reviewing files, only taking an hour each morning for myself to fit in a run. Most weekends, I take the time to run on Saturday mornings then spend the rest of the day and most of Sunday working until I go to Reed's for dinner. I've worked like this for years and never saw anything wrong with it.

Until I met Dana.

I finally have someone I want to spend time with. More than just the time it takes for both of us to get off. The only problem is I've created this life that requires me to work almost every minute I'm awake. It doesn't leave much time for Dana.

"Ok. Let's make a deal. I will work late for the next few nights to get this done before Saturday so you and I can spend the weekend together." I don't know how I'm going to get this done by Saturday but I'm damn well going to try.

"You in?" I ask her. I know it's not a great deal, but it's all I can give right now. Hopefully, she's willing to compromise.

"I'm in." She says and I feel like I just dodged a bullet.

Now I just need to make sure I can deliver on my end of the bargain.

Chapter Thirty-Nine

DANA

When Mitch offered his deal, I knew it was the best I was going to get. His work requires a lot of his time, more than I would like, but if we're going to make this work, then I have to compromise.

I just don't want to be the only one doing the compromising like in my past relationships. But, unlike Chris, Mitch seems willing to make some changes too. It may take us a while to get to smooth sailing but we're working on it. Together.

I try to give Mitch space over the next few days, only sending him a text each morning and at night. I don't expect replies to any of them, knowing he's up against a tight schedule made even tighter by our deal, but the man surprises me by replying to every text I send. It may only be a simple 'good morning' or 'good night' but it's enough. He heard my complaint last week about him not taking the time to respond to me and he's trying to do better.

What more can I really ask for?

My phone rings in my bag as I'm leaving work Friday. Seeing Mitch's name on the screen lights me up like a Christmas tree and I feel ridiculously giddy.

"Hi! How's it going?"

"Hi, Gorgeous. It's going good." I hear the smile in his voice. "That's actually why I called."

Intrigue tilts my head. "Go on."

Mitch chuckles and certain parts of me start screaming for his undivided attention.

"Well. I'm closing in on the finish line." I'll pardon the sports metaphor since I like where this is going. "I mean, I still have a lot left but if I stay late and work on it first thing in the morning instead of running, then I can catch up with you for lunch."

I thought I liked where this was going but my brain sticks on him saying he's going to skip running with me Saturday morning so he can keep working. Am I supposed to be happy about this?

My lack of a response doesn't go unnoticed.

"Dana. Then I'll have the rest of the weekend to spend with you." He says slowly and I perk back up.

"Oh! So just you and me? No work?"

"Yes, just you and me. No work." He confirms in his smooth voice. Oh, the things I'm going to do to this man. We better not get interrupted.

Teasingly, I ask, "What did you have in mind?" Please say forty hours of naked fun time.

"I'd like us to get away for the weekend, but we won't have time for that. Maybe we can plan something for a few weeks from now."

I like the way he's thinking.

"For this weekend, I think we just stay in and... enjoy being together." He says, lowering his voice suggestively.

My body is humming in anticipation, and I bite my lower lip. "Exactly what I was thinking. Do you want me to pick up a few things, so we don't have to go out?" Like wine. Sexy lingerie. Anything lickable.

His growl rumbles in my ear and straight to my core. A throb hits me so hard I stumble before leaning against a random car.

"Yes, to all three but especially the lickable thing."

I guess I said that out loud. Good thing I'm not shy about what I want to do to him. Or with him. Or have him do to me.

God, I need to get home to my vibrator. Just enough to take the edge off until Mitch can fuck me five ways to Tuesday and leave me blissfully spent.

The thought of that alone has me clenching in need.

Damn it! Home, now.

Straightening, I spot my car a few spots over and make a beeline for it. I'm so turned on, the friction from my lace thong has me pausing to ride out a burst of pleasure. My eyes slam shut, and I bite down hard on my lip, but the moan makes it out anyway.

"Dana." He rasps my name, and I can barely open my eyes, much less respond.

"Did you just..."

"Yes." I cut him off and sprint the last few steps to my car.

Safely inside, my body falls into my seat. Distantly, I hear a door shut but my brain can't compute any more than the unbearable pulsing between my legs and my nipples rubbing against the fabric of my bra.

I have no idea how I'm going to drive home like this.

"Dana. Are you alone?" I faintly hear what sounds like a zipper and instantly clench my legs together.

"I'm in my car now." I breathe out. "In the parking garage."

"Are there people around you?" He asks.

Breathing deeply, I take a look around. "No, it's mostly empty now."

"Good. Lock your doors first."

"Why?" He can't be about to suggest...

"So, no one jumps in your car while you're doing exactly as I say."

Oh! He did! And I am so down for that. My pulse is racing with anticipation of what's about to happen. Glancing around again, I make sure no one is nearby to question why I'm just sitting in my car instead of driving home as I lock the car doors. The click of the locks moving in place must be loud enough for Mitch to hear.

"I like that you follow my orders so well." He says calmly but his words mixed with the wild beating of my heart makes this feel dangerous. Illicit. Indecent in the best possible way.

"Are you wearing pants or a dress?" His voice drops lower, striking a cord deep inside me and my eyes fall closed again savoring the sensation.

God, all Mitch did was ask me what I'm wearing and I'm already so close.

"Dress," I say on an exhale.

"Is it tight?"

"No."

"Perfect." He says with satisfaction. "Place your hand above your knee."

Silently I obey, softly laying my hand down and heat blooms across the skin beneath it.

"Is it there?" He asks.

"Yes."

"You have to tell me, Gorgeous. I can't see for myself."

"My hand's on my leg," I reply softly, my chest rising with my breaths.

"Over your dress or touching your skin?" His voice asking if I'm touching my own skin sounds dirty and my nipples harden painfully.

"Touching my skin."

"Good. Raise your hand until just your fingertips are still touching you."

The palm of my hand raises until my fingertips are grazing my skin. "Just the tips of my fingers are touching me."

"Slowly slide them in and to the bottom of your dress."

My hand obeys, sliding across my skin until it rests just below the edge of my dress on my inner thigh. So far, I haven't done anything sexual but my body disagrees, tightening deliciously with need and I let out a hum of pleasure.

Mitch makes a similar sound but his is more of a growl and I almost explode right then.

"Dana. Are you ready to continue?"

Oh God, am I? "Yes." I breathe out.

My pulse pounds through my body as I wait for his next command.

"Spread your knees for me, baby and relax." He says, giving me a moment to do as I'm told before he continues.

"Very slowly, draw your hand up under your dress, lightly gliding over your skin."

I don't hesitate, caressing my way up my thigh.

"How does it feel?" Mitch rumbles and I bite my lip, sucking in a breath.

"So good," I murmur.

He lets out a groan and my back arches as my fingers come to rest next to my heat.

"Ms. Tolliver. Are you wearing anything under that dress?"

"Yes." My breaths are coming harder, faster now, I'm seconds away.

"Tell me." He demands.

"Black lace thong." I pant as the scrap of lace brushes against me.

Mitch lets out a harsh exhale. "Skim your fingers over the lace."

My fingers do as they're told, floating over the lace and tingles rush through my core. It constricts hotly, desperate for more and I whimper with need.

"Do you like that?"

I shutter out a single word. "Yes."

"Slip your fingers inside the lace."

It's not my fingers that slide under the fabric and across the swollen skin. Jolts of ecstasy zip in my core. My mouth drops open with a silent cry.

"Tell me how wet you are, Gorgeous." He commands in a strained voice.

I can't even speak as I feel myself, fighting the moans trying to escape me.

"Let me hear you, Dana." Mitch orders roughly and I let out a moan that turns into his name.

"That's it." I hear him grumble and every muscle in my body tenses. Another swipe across, another dip inside and spikes of pleasure shoot through me, curling my toes. I burst, shattering with bliss and screaming his name as his voice grunts out mine.

Panting and still trembling with aftershocks, I manage to open my eyes and remember where I am. Having phone sex in my car, in the parking garage at work. It's not something I ever thought I would do but HOLY SHIT!

"That was..." I can't even put it into words and neither can he.

"I know." Mitch agrees between heavy breaths. "Look, I have to go but I'll call you later, Gorgeous." He tells me and I'm too spent to even be disappointed.

"Don't work too hard, Mr. Ainsley," I whisper before ending the call. It takes a few minutes for my legs to stop shaking enough before I can drive home.

After changing clothes, I make a list of things we'll need this weekend. Once Mitch walks through my door, we're not leaving until Monday morning, so I need to stock up.

The first stop I make is at a lingerie store. Yes, I have some nice pieces already, but I want this weekend to be special. And nothing says special to a man better than buying new scraps of fabric for him to take off of you.

Well, blowjobs probably do but this way, I'll be in new lacy lingerie when I do it.

It doesn't take me long to pick out a lacy bra and panty set in bold red and the matching chemise. I also buy another one in black that's a satiny material with a little red bow under the cups. If you tug on the ribbon, the cups open up and fall to the sides, baring your breast. I can't wait to see Mitch's face when I perform this little magic trick.

Since it's still early, I drive to the liquor store next so tomorrow I only have to pick up groceries. I want us to have plenty of food and alcohol to keep us fueled for certain strenuous activities. Just as I walk in, my phone rings.

"Hey, how was school today?" I ask Liv cheerfully, grabbing a shopping cart and moving to the back of the store where the beer is. I'll start there and work my way up.

"You just had sex!" She yells in my ear.

I glance around to see if anyone else heard her since her voice rattled my phone but no one's looking my way.

"No, I didn't," I tell her, dodging a guy in the aisle.

"Liar." She says smugly and I laugh.

"I promise you I did not just have sex." I whisper yell into my phone so that guy doesn't hear.

"Huh. That's your just had sex voice."

"I don't have a just had sex voice." I scoff at her.

"Yes, you do. It sounds all cheerful but relaxed. The only time you sound like that is when you've just had sex." She informs me.

I roll my eyes, not that she can see me, and blurt out my confession. "Fine! I had phone sex with Mitch while I was in my car! In the parking garage at work!"

"I KNEW IT!" She yells triumphantly at the same time I feel compelled to check my surroundings and see if anyone has overheard me. One by one, I make eye contact with the three random men standing near me, all of them with a leery smirk on their faces as they scan up and down my body. The only other woman grimaces at me, then yanks on her man's arm to pull his attention back to her.

I guess I did say that a little loudly. Oh, well. Men aren't the only ones allowed to enjoy sex.

Grabbing the beer Mitch always drinks at Liv's house, I quickly move to the wine section. Liv asks questions about me and Mitch that most people would consider inappropriate but we're best friends. We talk about everything.

And we do for the next two hours until Reed's pulling her out the door for dinner. By that time, I'm heating up leftovers and finishing my grocery list for the morning. After tidying up, I go to bed early, ready to get tomorrow started.

Waking up early Saturday morning, I throw on clothes and go to the store then spend the next hour washing, shaving and lotioning my entire body before moving on to my hair and makeup.

By the time Mitch knocks on my door twenty-one minutes after noon, I'm ready in nothing but the black chemise with the red bow and my sexy red heels.

CHAPTER FORTY

MITCH

This woman knows how to rock my world.

I'm laying on the floor in her bedroom, trying to catch my breath after our sexathon that moved through three rooms, four if you count what we did in the hallway, and had us in more positions than a yoga session.

My skin is damp, my muscles are aching and at one point, I think my heart stopped.

This amazing woman of my dreams stretches lazily then rolls halfway on top of me. Her lips press a kiss to my pec before she bites my nipple. I swat her ass hard, and she lets out a little yelp.

"Give me a minute, Gorgeous. That last time almost killed me." I grumble good naturedly and she smiles sweetly before biting my nipple again.

The little vixen.

Dana giggles at me then hops up. Instantly, I miss her body on mine and vow to up my cardio.

Opening a drawer, she pulls out a shirt and I stop her. "No. This is a clothing free weekend."

She eyes me like she's sizing me up then drops the shirt back in the drawer and slams it shut. I crook my finger at her, and she leans over me, putting her luscious tits right in my face.

I'm not sure I'll survive the weekend, but I'm prepared to give my life for the cause.

Slowly, she moves away and stands. With a little shimmy, she turns and walks out the bedroom door and I'm helpless to follow.

We walk past our clothes on the living room and kitchen floor where she starts pulling things out of the fridge to make us dinner. Bending over, her naked ass is so damn tempting I don't hear what she's saying.

"What was that?"

Dana looks over her shoulder at me, still bent over, and the memory of her in the same position over the kitchen table two hours ago makes me hard again.

"I said that my friend, Leslie, is getting married next Saturday." She says standing up, her eyes going right to my dick, and she inhales quickly. In less than five minutes, I'm going to be inside her again. I guarantee it.

"Do you still want to go with me?"

I'm watching her tits sway with each movement. "Where?"

"To the wedding." She says but my eyes are on her naked skin so it's not getting through.

Dana smacks the food on the counter and props her hands on her hips making everything jiggle perfectly. A growl escapes me and my hands clench with the need to touch her.

"Mitch, if you can't stop eye fucking me long enough to answer a question then I'm putting clothes on." She threatens.

She's jokingly serious and I can't have her getting dressed so I force my eyes up to hers. Crossing my arms over my chest, I assume a serious face.

"Sorry. What were we talking about?"

Her stern façade cracks and she can't hold back her smile anymore. "I asked if you can still make it to my friend, Leslie's, wedding next Saturday."

"Of course. Just text me the info so I don't forget."

I fleetingly wonder where my phone is, but lust overshadows that thought when Dana rounds the corner and hugs me. Naked.

"I already did. I watched you add it to your calendar." She reminds me then slides her hands down my body as she kneels in front of me.

Her tongue slides down the length of me before her lips wrap around my most prized possession.

The last thought I have before I turn my brain shuts off completely is that I was right.

Less than five minutes. Hell, probably less than one,

Dana blows my mind with her wickedly talented little tongue and after I return the favor, we make dinner together. Moving back to the bedroom, we eat in bed with The History Channel playing Modern Marvels in the background. The scene is so damn domestic, I shake my head at how much I love it.

"What are you smiling about?" Dana asks me with a little smile of her own.

"How much I like being here with you," I reply honestly. Her smile grows brighter, and I find myself telling her more. "I've never done this before."

"Done what?"

"Spent an entire weekend with someone."

A strange mix of things crosses Dana's face before she looks back at the TV. "Why is that, you think?"

She asks it quietly, with no emotion behind the words but I sense my answer is important. I just don't know what it is she's looking for, so I go with the truth.

"I've never met anyone I wanted to spend this much time with."

She slowly turns back to me, her eyes traveling up my bare chest, my neck and jaw, and finally meeting mine. "Me neither."

"You've never been in a serious relationship?" I ask, thinking it's a damn shame no other man has appreciated this woman the way she should be.

"There have been a few." She admits hesitantly. "But none of them felt like this. Not even..." Dana stops abruptly and shoves a forkful of food in her mouth. I watch her chew very carefully and when she's done, I ask the question that's looming between us.

"Not even who?"

Her face scrunches for half a second like she can't believe she has to answer this question, then she smooths it out and answers, still looking at the TV. "Chris."

I wait for more, but nothing comes. The attorney in me wants to question her further and the man in me is feeling the same way. "Chris?" Not really a profound question but it gets the job done.

Dana sighs in defeat. "Chris Foster. We dated a few years ago. I thought it was serious, he... I guess he did too."

My heart is pounding, and my hands are sweaty. I hate hearing Dana talk about being with another man but there's more to this than she's saying. More than I think I want to hear. But I have to. "But?"

She doesn't answer right away and when she does, I feel like she's censuring her words. "But other things were more important to him."

Dana still won't look at me, telling me there's more to this story, but I do the only thing I can. Setting my own plate aside, I wrap her in my arms, snuggling her into my chest. My lips lightly slide along her neck, moving up to press a kiss to her temple. Breathing her in, I say the words I believe with all my heart.

"Nothing is more important to me than you."

Slowly, she turns in my arms, her hands skirting around me to hold me closer to her. Her eyes shine as she smiles tenderly. "No one's ever said that to me before."

"It's true, Gorgeous," I say, running my hand up her back to cup her neck and I know I'm ready to say the words I've never spoken to a woman before.

"I love you."

"I love you too." She whispers right before our lips meet.

Hours later, Dana's asleep next to me, my arm holding her against my side. I don't know why no other man saw how amazing the woman next to me is, but it's their loss. Dana is mine and I'm going to make sure she never questions how important she is to me.

Putting someone else first doesn't come naturally to me but since I met Dana, I've been doing a lot of things I've never done before. Like setting some boundaries at work.

Nothing in this world could ever compare to Dana. Now I just need to show her that I mean it.

CHAPTER FORTY-ONE

MITCH

We skipped dinner at Reed's last night, neither of us wanting to put clothes on long enough to be around other people.

Dana had stocked up the fridge, so we didn't even have to order takeout. That would have been interesting since I haven't worn a stitch of clothing the entire time I've been here. I meant to grab my phone from the living room last night so I would have my alarm, but we were already in bed by the time I thought of it and Dana set her alarm to go off earlier for me.

Prewarning my friends, co-workers and family, I told everyone I was unplugging this weekend and anything barring an emergency would have to wait until Monday. I received everything from 'enjoy your weekend' to 'don't forget protection' but all responses were saying the same thing. I deserved this time off. No questions asked.

Giving in, I did check my phone yesterday afternoon, just to make sure there hadn't been any emergencies and for the first time I can remember, I didn't have a single missed call or text. Then Dana handed me a beer, while completely naked, and my phone landed on the floor as I pulled her into my lap.

I assume my phone is still on the living room floor since that's the last time I saw it.

Monday morning comes too early, and a foghorn jars me awake. Dana's arm reaches out from under the blanket and slaps her phone until it's blessedly silent again. That same arm snakes around my waist when I roll her over to me. I can smell her floral shampoo from our shower last night and I breathe it in deeply.

"Good morning." She mumbles and nuzzles my chest.

I stroke my hand down her silky skin. My fingers graze the curve of her hip before sliding to rest on her ass, eliciting a breathy moan from her.

"Good morning."

"Do you have to leave right away?"

I'm moving before she gets the last word out. Reaching up, I weave my fingers in her hair, angling her face up to receive my kiss, as I roll her under me. "No."

Taking my time, I kiss down her body, knowing it's still early and I don't have to go to the office before my eight-thirty meeting at the White House. Normally, I would be heading to the park for a run right now but some things are more important than physical fitness.

Skimming my lips down the outside of her leg, my tongue darts out occasionally to join in the fun. My hands are having fun on their own. Touching. Exploring. Circling.

When I reach her ankle, I swirl my tongue around the bone then start nibbling my way back up, this time on the inside of her leg.

When I reach her calf, Dana's fisting the sheets, a hum escorting each breath she takes.

When I get to her knee, she's moved her hands to my hair and rolls her hips in a silent cry for attention.

I bite her inner thigh and she wraps her legs around my neck, pulling me higher.

When I clamp down where she wants, Dana screams my name.

I spend a good portion of my morning feasting on her, pulling away to indulge on other enticing parts of her body, then teasingly working my way back to her sweet spot. I've never heard my name spoken so many times in a row or with such passion, desire and need.

At some point, her alarm went off again but it didn't distract me from my mission. I just adjusted my hold on her as she shifted to reach it. I have no idea how long ago that was, so caught up in my objective to see how many times I could make Dana come.

Eventually, we're both so spent, our bodies physically exhausted from the turbulence of arousal to sensation then beautiful bliss, that we lie wasted and winded side by side. Dana's arm is thrown over her head as she breathes deeply.

"What time is your meeting again?" She asks.

"Eight-thirty," I answer and sit up. "What time is it?"

She looks to the side table that only holds a darkened lamp then heaves herself over the side of the bed. Her naked ass once again begs for my attention, as she grabs for something on the floor. I've just slid my hand over the roundness when her voice floats up to me.

"Seven oh five."

I don't process the words right away, caressing her flesh until she rolls over trapping my hand underneath her.

"Isn't your meeting in an hour?"

"Hmmmm?" The softness of her skin is so damn distracting. Wait. Did she just say it's after seven?

"Shit!" I yell, jumping out of bed and searching the floor wildly.

"Your clothes are in the living room." She says calmly, sliding off the bed behind me.

Storming through the house, I find my pants and jam my legs in. Immediately, I hear something vibrating nearby. I ignore it in favor of pulling on my shirt, but the vibrations only stop for a few seconds then start back up again.

Frazzled, I mutter to myself, "I'm going to be late," and reach over to pick up my socks and shoes catching a glimpse of my phone a few feet away. The screen is lit up and a constant flow of notifications are popping up one after another.

My body freezes and my blood runs cold.

This can't be good.

I hear Dana walk into the room behind me as I slowly reach over to grab the offending device and read the last message.

"FUCK!" I roar with the frustration that's desperate to get out.

"What's wrong?" The woman I love asks and I round on her.

"What's wrong? WHAT'S WRONG?! I'll tell you what's wrong!" I yell at her, causing her to lean away from me and pull the belt tighter on her robe.

"My meeting with the President was moved up to seven today. Do you know what time it is right now?" She grimaces when I say seven fully aware I missed the meeting, but I don't stop.

"It's seven oh seven, Dana. I should already be at the White House and be shaking the President's hand right now. Instead, I'm here trying to find my clothes after screwing around all morning. I should have already been up and starting my day, not making you come for the hundredth time this weekend!"

"Do you think this is my fault?" She asks but I'm too far gone to be rational now.

"Well, if I wasn't face down in you AGAIN then I would have seen the email that the meeting had been moved up!" I shout, directing all my anger at her.

A part of me knows this isn't Dana's fault, but I'm so pissed I need someone to blame and it's easier to blame her than admit I should have gotten out of bed last night to get my phone.

Dana doesn't respond but I can't seem to stop the tirade.

"You complained I had been working too much! You wanted me to take some time off! You made this plan that we wouldn't have to leave the house!"

I'm not even making much sense right now, but I don't care. I'm on a roll and helpless to stop it.

"This. This is why I don't do relationships. You women are all attracted to the fancy job title and the perks you think it can bring you. But then you start complaining. Making men out to be the bad guys because we have to work so much." I huff. Frustrated and angry doesn't begin to cover what I'm feeling right now, and I grip my hair and pull.

A guttural sound comes out of me and with it some of the steam, but I'm not finished. No, I'm too stupid to stop there.

"Really, it's my fault. I let you distract me with your tits and ass and blowjobs." I know I'm being crass but right now the only thing I want is to make her feel even a tenth of the rage I'm feeling coursing through me.

We face off, me with my arms at my sides ready for a fight, my chest heaving with each breath. Dana is as still as a stone, her face wiped of all expression. I'm just waiting for her to say something, anything, so I can rip it to shreds.

"I won't be a distraction for you anymore. You should leave." She says emotionlessly then turns and heads back down the hall.

I watch her walk away, still itching for a fight until I hear the quiet click of her bedroom door. Stiffly, I grab my shoes and walk out, slamming her front door behind me.

The second my car is on the road, I get on the phone to see if I can salvage this meeting and my professional relationship with the President. Since his office hasn't received a response from me or my assistant, who was blowing up my phone, they left my appointment at eight-thirty but let me know it will have to be cut short to accommodate the President's next meeting.

I go home, shower and dress in record time, and pull up to the White House at eight twenty-four. With six minutes to park and get to the Oval Office, I haul ass and skid to a stop just as Randall Simmons, the Chief of Staff, is asking the President's gatekeeper if I've arrived yet.

"I'm here." I blurt out, sticking my hand in the narrow space between us. "Sorry about..."

Randall grasps my hand and waves off the apology. "It's fine. I knew it was short notice, so I didn't expect to move the meeting. I just asked on the off chance you were up and available."

It fleetingly occurs to me that I just blew up my relationship with Dana for no reason as he motions for me to follow him into the Oval Office, and I dutifully obey but once I pass through the door, our fight is temporarily forgotten.

I've been in this office several times already but every time, I'm awestruck over the history that has taken place in this very room.

"Good morning, Mitch." The President greets me, and I hurry over to him for another handshake.

"Good morning, sir."

"I hope you had a good weekend." He says as we all take a seat and I stiffen at the image his words paint in my mind, before lowering myself to the chair.

Dana's naked body splayed out on her bed, touching herself as I watch, matching her rhythm as I stroke myself.

The President's voice snaps me out of the memory, and I tell myself to pay attention. I can think about Dana later.

So, I do. I focus on the meeting, giving the President my advice and suggestions on the policy. We're halfway through when Randall informs us we only have a few more minutes and we'll have to schedule another time to finish the conversation. Outside, the gatekeeper of the President's schedule tells me the only time he has available is the following Monday morning at eighty-thirty.

This sounds familiar.

It also doesn't escape me. I worked all those hours last week for a meeting that's now a week away.

At my office, there's already a stack of messages and new files to review but I ignore it all. Closing the door behind me, I drop into my chair and finally let myself think about the fight. It was bad. Really bad. Wincing, I recall my self-rage fueled rant. I said some shitty things. Things I didn't mean and should apologize for.

Did I mean them?

The question stops my hand's progress to my pocket, and I roll the words around in my head. Did I mean what I said?

A hard knock on my office door scares the shit out of me, jolting me in my chair. "Come in." I bark.

Susan, my assistant, walks in talking like we're already in the middle of a conversation. She's been with me since I started this job, and we work well together. It didn't take us long to work out our mind reading skills with each other. I only have to tell her basic information and she's able to read between the lines. When she leaves me somewhat cryptic messages, I know exactly what she's saying. I couldn't do my job without her.

But today, she's not making a damn bit of sense.

"Susan. Can you slow down? What was that about Abbott?" I ask her, rubbing my aching forehead.

She scrutinizes me like a science experiment before taking a 'God, help me' breath and repeating herself. "Abbott needs your sign off by the end of the day. The approval for the..."

I cut her off. "Didn't we just get the request from Abbott?"

Susan is not amused, and I receive a motherly look of disapproval. "We received it on Thursday." She states slowly then folds her hands together signally she's waiting for me to respond.

"Those requests take longer than two days. He knows that."

"Yes. Technically. But you agreed to move his items to the top of your list."

An impatient scowl sets up shop on my face as I wait for her to clarify what the hell she means.

Susan gives an audible sigh. "When you two came to that agreement last year."

Oh, that.

It wasn't really an agreement. He was sending me files to review that were only half finished. When I called him on it, Abbott said there was no point in 'polishing' the documents if I was just going to tear them apart after holding onto the file for weeks, so he was only sending me the basic information as he put it. I told him I would do my best to make his requests a priority if he would send me the complete and polished files.

Things seemed to get better after that but now I realize it's because of my own stupidity I work so many fucking hours a day. I make everyone a priority except myself.

I did better when I met Dana but eventually, the excessive working life I built for myself was going to ruin that. I was going to ruin that.

And I did.

Her last words from this morning drum in my ears.

I won't be a distraction for you anymore. You should leave.

The way she said it, the look in her eyes, can only mean one thing.

I did the exact opposite of what I said I would do. I made her feel second to my job, second to what really is most important to me, hurting her by showing her the truth.

My career will always come first, and Dana deserves more than a distant second place in someone's life.

Can I be the man she deserves? The one she needs me to be?

CHAPTER FORTY-TWO

DANA

I thought about calling in sick but made myself go to work even though I couldn't stop replaying our fight in my head. I was so angry with Mitch that I had gone from shaking with fury to the oddly calm one can only attain when they have resigned themselves to the rage.

I let it fuel me through the day, using it as motivation and making me more productive than ever before. The workday comes to an end too quickly and soon I'm back at the scene of the crime, my phone still buried in my purse. After hurling it in there this morning, I never pulled it back out, not allowing myself to see whether Mitch called to apologize.

His mean ass better call to apologize. I'm not accepting a text.

But now that I'm standing in the same place I was this morning, the anger is starting to fade, and my eyes begin to fill with unwanted tears. Sniffing them away, I stomp to my bedroom to change into running clothes. Since I missed my morning run, I'm doing it now and it doesn't hurt I have some emotions to burn through.

I usually just run around my block a few times before work but I need a longer run than that today. My car automatically heads to the lakeside park but when I see where I've ended up, I yank the car into reverse and drive away. There's another park down the street. One that doesn't make me think about Mitch.

Putting my earphones in, I crank my angry playlist then run until my legs are jelly and my head is empty. My phone dings with an incoming message but I make myself ignore it until I've run out the remaining feelings. After a shower and a glass of wine, I finally feel ready to see what he text. It should have been a call, but I'll take what I can get as long as it's an apology.

Liv: Was your weekend sextastic?

It's not from him.

So many emotions race through me, and I want to break down or lash out but I hold myself together. If I talk to Liv, I won't be able to keep the dam in place, so I send a vague response, promising to call her tomorrow.

Liv: I'll meet you for lunch.

Since she's a teacher, it's not often we have lunch together during the week so either she has more big news for me or she can tell something's up, and she plans to drag it out of me in person.

Me: I can't do lunch tomorrow but maybe some other time.

I know I should just tell her what happened, but I can't. Not yet. I'm still holding out hope Mitch will call me or better yet come by to apologize. I don't want to tell Liv about our fight and have her get all worked up over it if we're just going to work it all out and move on.

But what if he doesn't apologize? What if he really thinks I'm the one in the wrong? That I should be apologizing?

I stew on that for the rest of the night, replaying our fight over and over. Mitch said some awful things to me, and I can't see how any of it is my fault. If he's waiting for me to say I'm sorry, that's not happening. I don't have anything to be sorry for.

Standing firm on that, I sleep like crap and wake up in a terrible mood on Tuesday. By lunchtime, I've decided if Mitch doesn't apologize by tonight, then he probably has no intention to do so. I eat a tasteless sandwich in the breakroom and go back to my cubicle to prepare for a meeting, stowing my phone and purse back in my desk drawer.

The meeting lasts longer than I would like but it's a welcome distraction from the fight. A distraction that's history when I get back to my desk and check my phone again to see there's a missed text from Mitch. I almost feel nervous as I slide my finger across the screen to open the message.

Mitch: I'm sorry.

That's it? I'm sorry. Nothing else.

Well, you only said you wanted an apology and that's what you got. Rational Dana says.

But it's a shitty apology. Bitchy Dana argues. *He's not admitting he was wrong or even saying what he's sorry for. Just two words that don't mean anything if there's no remorse behind them.*

But it's still an apology. Rational Dana maintains and I decide to side with her.

Now my issue is, how do I respond?

The rules of fighting within a relationship dictate you start with a text and respond with one. Texting continues until things either cool down to the point you can have a sensible conversation or things heat up to the point texting just doesn't cut it anymore.

Calling Mitch back after the first text is breaking the rules but I do need to respond. His apology is lacking but maybe it was just his starting point, and he has more to say. The text did just come in ten minutes ago. He could be formulating a better, more in-depth apology and just waiting to hear if I'm ready to accept it. That would totally be following the rules.

I just need to respond in a way that says I'm acknowledging you and I'm open to hearing more.

Me: Ok

Does that sound mean? Like I don't care he said he's sorry?
I start to type out another message but stop myself from sending it. *Don't freak out and assume the worst, just wait. You responded the ball's in his court now. Let's see what he says next before going crazy girlfriend on him.*

It seems reasonable and I decide to embody Rational Dana for the rest of the day, waiting for a text that doesn't come. Dejected, I fall asleep thinking about how things were so perfect over the weekend and wishing we could just go back to then.

Wednesday passes slowly with me checking my phone every thirty minutes. By the time I leave work, I'm ready to cry but I don't know which emotion is fueling the waiting tears.

You said if he didn't respond to your OK reply, you would text him again.

Yeah, but he should have sent a better apology to begin with. He said he loved me, we had one fight and then all he can do is text I'm sorry!

He's never been in a real relationship before. Did you really expect him to send the perfect apology after your first fight?

No. But it doesn't take a genius to realize it was the mother of all fights and a two-word apology isn't going to cut it.

Rational Dana and Bitchy Dana argue with each other the whole drive home. Liv is parked in front of my house, and

I don't even have the energy to avoid her anymore. She's halfway across my yard by the time I get out of the car. I take one look at her, and all the emotions I've been bottling up since Monday morning come surging to the surface.

Pulling me down for a hug, not bothering with meaningless platitudes, Liv ushers me to the door. I let her settle me on the couch and pour me a glass of wine, grabbing a bottle of water for herself before tucking her legs under her in my blue and white overstuffed chair. I love that chair, it's my favorite place to curl up and watch TV but TV makes me think of the History Channel and the History Channel makes me think of Mitch.

Hot tears burn the back of my eyes and I swallow down the lump in my throat.

Handing me a tissue, Liv states the obvious. "I guess things didn't go well last weekend."

"What gave it away?" It was meant to be sarcastic but comes out watery and morose.

"Well. I didn't hear from you which I thought was a good sign."

It was a good sign, until it wasn't.

"You answered my text on Monday with a vague response."

Is she really going to list all the ways she knows something's wrong?

"You turned me down for lunch."

Signs point to yes. She is listing them all.

"And then you didn't answer my call this morning or bother to call me back all day."

I wince at that. She did call me this morning while I was getting ready for work, but I didn't want to get into it before I had to leave for the office.

"I meant to text you back but..." I trail off.

The chair creaks as Liv leans back trying to get comfortable.

"Tell me what happened." She says softly and like fragile glass, I break to pieces.

I let it all out, telling Liv exactly what Mitch said Monday morning between wiping away the tears that sneak out. Moving to sit next to me, Liv holds my hand and asks if I want to hear what she thinks.

Not really. "Sure," I mumble with a shrug.

"I think you need to call him."

See, I told you. Rational Dana agrees and I roll my eyes.

"Tell him you want to talk about what happened. Figure out if he really meant what he said or if it was just in the heat of the moment. Not that I agree with saying mean things because you're upset, but it happens."

Begrudgingly, I admit that's true but my voice gains heat when I think about what he said to me. "He said some really awful shit, even if he didn't mean it."

"You're right, and he should have called and apologized better but men are stubborn and prideful, you know that. Mitch might just need an opening, so he knows you're ready to hear his apology."

That's what I said. Rational Dana pipes up again.

"When did you get so mature and rational about this shit?" I ask Liv. "I recall giving you similar advice with Reed and you refused to take it."

Liv rolls her eyes like a champ. "Fine. You were right. Is that what you want to hear? Are you happy now?" She teases me and it does take the sting out of having my own advice handed back to me.

Heaving herself off the couch like she's much farther along in her pregnancy than she is, Liv bends to pick up her purse from the floor. "Call him, Dana." She commands and I give her a mock salute.

She laughs, waving goodbye, and I wait until her car is pulling away before putting on my big girl pants and grabbing my phone.

Me: Can we talk?

An hour goes by without a reply and any goodwill I was feeling towards Mitch dissolves a little more with each passing minute. It's almost completely gone when my phone rings and I see it's him. Relief has me sagging into my chair as I answer tentatively.

"Hi."

"Hi, Gorgeous." For a moment, there's silence as we both think about what needs to be said but Mitch breaks it in the best way possible. "I never should have said all of that to you. Missing those calls and emails and texts were on me, not you. But I was frustrated and... no, it doesn't matter. I shouldn't have said it and I'm sorry."

His words fill me with warmth, a smile spreading across my face.

That's a pretty damn perfect apology.

Doesn't get much better than that. Both sides of me agree for once.

"Thank you for apologizing," I say back softly not sure of what else to say besides the obvious. "I miss you."

"I miss you too."

"Do you want to come over? Have dinner?" I ask hopefully, already thinking about what I could make.

"Aww, honey. I wish I could, but I'm working late again tonight. The whole office is..." He trails off.

I'm disappointed he can't make it tonight, but I'm not going to let it show. "It's ok, how about tomorrow?"

Mitch hesitates and I know his answer before he speaks. "I can't tomorrow night either. I have a dinner meeting with my boss, and I can't cancel."

It's a little harder to keep my tone upbeat but I think I pull it off. "Ok. Well, why don't you stop by after."

"You drive a hard bargain, Ms. Tolliver." He drops his voice to a flirty tone.

"You haven't seen anything yet, Mr. Ainsley."

Chapter Forty-Three

MITCH

I buried myself in work at the beginning of the week to keep me from thinking about Dana and how I screwed things up. The long hours weren't much of an adjustment since work is my top priority regardless of telling her differently.

I'm no better than her ex and I'm pissed at myself for it. I wanted her to be the most important thing in my life and I thought I was doing a good job of showing her but looking back now I see I barely made an effort to cut back on my hours. I just fit Dana into the little time I was already taking for myself.

Our Saturday runs were a little later than I usually went to the lake but running there was already part of my schedule. Sunday dinners were something I had been doing for months before she was included so no change on my part for that either. The few dinners we had outside of that were on nights I didn't have a shit ton of work to do and had already planned on leaving early.

I never showed Dana she was more important than my job until last weekend. The weekend I almost ruined us.

Monday, I decided a clean break was needed, knowing Dana deserves better than me, better than the little bit of myself I can give her. I had no intention of ever contacting her again but after a sleepless night and spending most of Tuesday staring out my office window, the guilt was too much for me and I sent that shitty 'I'm sorry' text.

I knew it wasn't good enough but what was the point in getting into how sorry I was when she shouldn't be wasting her time on me anymore. When she replied back with just Ok, I figured she agreed.

Thankfully, I was wrong and seeing her ask if we could talk snapped my resolve. I was calling her before I finished reading her text and knew I had to give a sincere apology. I wanted nothing more than to go to her and make up in person but the avalanche of files on my desk blocked the door.

Unfortunately, it's two days later and I'm still waist deep in work.

I'm tired, the words are swimming on the page in front of me, and I lean back squeezing my eyes shut. Looking back at the page, the words are now a blur and I know I've reached my limit for today. A quick glance at my watch tells me it's hours past five pm and I should drag my ass home.

I should go to Dana's. I haven't seen her since...

Like a shotgun, I remember I was supposed to go there after dinner last night and regret explodes in my chest.

By the time the last drinks were gone, it was late, and I was too tired to think about anything other than crashing for a few hours before waking up and doing it all again. I didn't even text her after our call on Wednesday night. She's probably pissed.

Yanking my phone from under a file, I see I have a missed text from Dana.

Dana: Are you still going to the wedding with me tomorrow?

She texted me an hour ago, but it doesn't sound like she's mad.

She knows you had a ton of work to do.

But you did tell her you would come over last night and you didn't. You really are an asshole.

If she's asking if you're still going to the wedding, she can't be too mad.

Unless she's giving you an out because she doesn't want you to go with her.

That last thought jolts me into action. Opening the messaging app, I click her name, my hands shaking with a rush of adrenaline, but another message pops up before I finish typing.

Dana: I understand if you can't make it.

Does that sound like she's still pissed? Or like she doesn't care if I go or not?

I should call her.

And give her the chance to tell you not to go. To cut you out completely.

As fast as my fingers can move, I punch out a reply and hit send.

Me: I'll be there to pick you up at 5:30.

I exhale harshly and wait for her reply, hoping it's good and she wasn't implying I shouldn't go.

Dana: Ok

Well, that's better than a 'go to hell' so I'll take it as a win, but I need to make sure we're really ok. She could just be asking me about the wedding because she already RSVP'd that she was taking a plus one. But that's not something I can find out through text, I need to hear her voice. Better to do that in person.

Me: Sorry about last night, it was late. Do you want to have dinner tonight?

Dana: I already have plans with Liv and Emily. I'll see you tomorrow.

Yep, she's pissed and has every right to be. I've managed to screw this up again a day after fixing it. I really am bad at being in a relationship and Dana deserves better than me, than what I can give, her but I'm going to fix that too.

Me: Ok, see you then

I want to say I'll come earlier so we can talk but it's probably better to not give her a heads up on that. I'll show up early, with the biggest 'I'm Sorry I was a dumbass' bouquet of flowers she's ever seen. I'll beg for her forgiveness and tell her how much I love her and starting today, things are going to change.

She'll never doubt how much she means to me again.

Nothing is going to stop me from being there. From making this right.

Chapter Forty-Four

DANA

I told myself not to be so excited Mitch is still going to the wedding. It was already on his calendar from two weeks ago when he told me he would go, and I sent him the details. But seeing his reply, my heart did a crazy flip in my chest, and I suddenly felt lighter, like a weight had been lifted.

When he didn't show up Thursday night, I was ticked off but more than that, I was disappointed. We had just made up from our first fight, a really bad fight, and then he blew me off without even sending a text saying he couldn't make it. I knew he was having dinner with his boss, and it probably ran late but it still hurt when I finally accepted he wasn't coming.

Sounds like you're not much of a priority.

I shush Bitchy Dana and try to think positively. He was doing better before the fight and I really do understand he has an important job, one that requires long hours. It's going to take more time for him to figure out how to balance a relationship with his career.

Last night, I told Liv and Emily that Mitch and I had talked and we were going to Leslie's wedding together. Liv got all smug about it, saying she's a relationship guru and I should trust her to fix all my love related problems. I asked her if she wanted to be the pot or the kettle since I had been the voice of reason during her weeks of self-inflicted heartache after she thought Reed was cheating on her and refused to take his calls.

She happily replied that of course, she was the kettle in this scenario, so I immediately went online and ordered a custom tea kettle with her name on it. It should be here Thursday. I can't wait to see her face when she opens it.

I had a feeling he wouldn't be at the park this morning for his run so when he didn't show up, I wasn't too disappointed, reminding myself I would see him tonight. I've spent the past few hours, soaking, shaving and lotioning my body which feels eerily similar to last Saturday morning. Those hours of pampering were not in vain. It was the start of the work week that wrecked things.

Taking my time to get my makeup just right and styling my hair in a casual updo, I check the time on my phone and frown when I see it's a few minutes after five. I really thought he would show up early so we could talk first. He didn't say he would, it was just a feeling, but I guess I was wrong.

Mitch is very punctual, always arriving right on time, not too early or late.

"He'll be here at five-thirty." I remind myself in the mirror.

I step into my walk-in closet and pull out the deep burgundy dress I bought last year, when Nordstrom had a huge sale, and take it into the bedroom. Finally cutting off the tags gives me a little zing when I see the original price and remember how little I paid for it.

Sliding my robe off, I unzip the dress and slip into it. Slowly I raise the zipper and turn to my full-length mirror. It fits perfectly.

Back in the closet, I grab my strappy bronze heels and matching clutch. Next is jewelry. When it's all in place, I go back to the mirror to inspect the final product.

I look hot if I do say so myself and I shimmy just a little with satisfaction. Mitch is going to love it.

Speaking of Mitch, it's now five twenty-three, he should be here soon. Going to the living room, I stand there waiting for him to show up any minute.

And wait.

And wait.

Checking my phone again, I watch the time switch to five forty-two. He should be here by now. Knowing that he's always on time, I'm concerned something bad happened like he was in a car wreck or...

I do something I haven't done in over a week.

I call him.

The phone rings once, twice. Three times before his voice-mail kicks in and tells me he's not able to answer my call.

"Mitch. Call me when you get this. Let me know you're ok." I say, trying to keep the tremble out of my voice.

I wait another ten minutes then call Liv. She barely gets the word hello out.

"Can you ask Reed if he's talked to Mitch today?"

I hear her hesitate for half a second then she's yelling Reed's name. My eardrum may never be the same but that's a small price to pay for good friends.

Liv asks Reed and, in the distance, I hear him say the thing I was dreading.

The other thing I was dreading.

"Yeah, earlier. He was going into the office."

"Did you hear that?" Liv asks in her angry voice. She knows what that means and so do I.

He's not coming. He's working instead.

CHAPTER FORTY-FIVE

MITCH

I only planned on going into the office for a few hours, skipping my morning run to ensure I would have plenty of time and still be at Dana's house early. In my quest to catch up on all the work I had put off when focusing on the President's policy review, I had set the policy file aside. And forgot about it.

At two am, I woke from a dead sleep and remembered on Monday I had round two of meeting with the President to finish giving him my recommendations. I needed to review my notes again before the meeting and hopefully make up for missing last week's call to reschedule.

Any other weekend this wouldn't have been a problem, and it shouldn't have been a problem today. I had hours until I needed to be at Dana's, more than enough time for a final review. I didn't want to put this off until Sunday, hoping I could spend the day with Dana and zero interruptions.

So, there I was at the office at two in the afternoon just finishing up when I got a call from Randall, the President's Chief of Staff, asking if I could meet with the President today because Monday, he's now flying to Seattle.

I don't know if you realize this but when the President wants to see you today, you go see him today.

Randall insisted it would only take an hour tops so, in my stupidity, I didn't call Dana. I would make it to her house by five-thirty.

By the time I got to the outer chamber, his gatekeeper told me the President was on a call and I needed to wait. An hour later, Randall waved me into the office. I was the picture of calm as I checked the time on my watch. It was three-thirty but this wasn't supposed to take more than an hour, Randall insisted again.

So, I shook the President's hand again and sat down.

Three hours later, we were still going over the finer points of the policy.

At some point, I did recognize this was taking longer than it should but a good-natured debate with the leader of the free world ensued and everything outside of the Oval Office fell away.

We're finally wrapping up and Mr. President asks Randall and I to join him for a drink. I've been in his office several times, but never have I shared a scotch with POTUS. Hell yeah, I'll stay for a drink!

We're on our second round and laughing over the President's war stories when it hits me out of nowhere.

Dana! The wedding!

I almost spill my drink in my lap in my haste to see what time it is.

Seven-twenty. Shit!

"Everything ok, Mitch?"

"I'm late," I say, setting my glass down and grabbing my briefcase.

"She must be important." The President says and I pause, briefcase in hand, and look at him.

"She's the most important thing in my world," I confess.

"Tell her I'm sorry for keeping you so late." He replies sincerely.

My body is rigid, confusion over this strangely personal exchange, halting me.

POTUS and Randall share a look and both smirk at me.

"You really should go," Randall says and I quickly shake their hands again then speed walk out of the office.

Once, I'm past security, I haul ass to my car, pulling out my phone. I have a missed call from Dana and a voicemail. Hitting her name, I impatiently listen to the phone ring five times before her voicemail picks up.

"Dana, honey. I'm so sorry, but I'm on my way." I say into the phone before hanging up and opening the navigation app so I can find my way to the church. Hopefully, it's a long ceremony and I can catch Dana there. If they've already moved to the reception site, I'm screwed. Dana didn't tell me where it was since she was supposed to be riding with me.

Traffic is a bitch, but I finally see the steeple of the church. The sun is setting behind the giant cross, making it glow with a golden hue. It's beautiful and I want to take it as a good sign, almost convincing myself she will still be there until I round the corner of the building.

The parking lot is empty.

Empty except for a few lonely cars and a white van. The side of the van reads 'Enchanted Weddings, Making Your Happily Ever After Come True.'

Pretty sure I just annihilated my happily ever after.

I don't know what else to do so I go home and eat some possibly vomit-inducing leftovers, not even remembering when I ordered Chinese last. As I eat, I try to determine what time Dana will get home, but I have no clue. The only wedding I've gone to was my cousin's and we partied until two am, something I'm hoping isn't normal.

After wrestling with my decision, I finally get in my car and drive to her house calling her again on the way. The call, once again, goes to voicemail, and I hang up hoping to apologize in person this time.

It's after nine by the time I get to her house and all of the lights inside are dark. I knock on her door to see if she's already home, but she doesn't answer. She could be there and not opening the door for me, I wouldn't really blame her, but the house appears empty, so I get back in my car to wait.

And wait.

After an hour she's still not here.

Two of her neighbors have knocked on my window to "check" on what I'm doing. Fortunately, they both saw my car in Dana's driveway last weekend and deemed it ok that I'm sitting here.

Like a stalker.

I left my window down after the last neighbor and the cool breeze ruffs my hair. The radio is playing a pop station, something I hate, but I knew it would keep me agitated enough to stay awake. It's been a long ass day. A long ass week.

I want nothing more than to fall in bed with Dana and sleep until Monday morning.

No, I take that back.

I want us to take a vacation together, I don't care where. If it's tropical, then she'll be in a bikini. If it's in the mountains, it should be cool enough that she has to stay close to me for warmth. Either way, I want to leave my life behind for a few weeks and just be with Dana.

Just sleep next to her. Hold her in my arms. Cascade kisses down her body. Run my soapy hands over her slick skin in the shower. Dance with her in the dark.

Whatever I can do to show her how precious she is to me. How much I love her.

Headlights shine in my rear-view mirror, but I don't get my hopes up. I've done that too many times already and it's always been someone else. This is probably just another neighbor returning home from a Saturday night out.

Averting my eyes from the glare, I go back to my previous thoughts, but the car doesn't pass me. Glancing up in time to see Dana's car pull into her driveway behind me, I watch her headlights go dark.

I'm walking across her yard when her door opens, and a sexy bronze heel emerges. My mouth goes dry at the expanse of naked leg that follows, the slit in her dress exposing everything up to mid-thigh.

The wine-colored dress swirls around her feet as she rises, and I am so damn sorry I missed what's-her-name's wedding. Missed the chance to twirl my woman around a dance floor and drink champagne. Today was a celebration and that dress was made for the occasion.

Dana doesn't look my direction as she closes her car door and turns for the house but it's obvious she's seen me by the tense set of her shoulders and the stiff tilt of her chin.

"Dana," I call her name, trying to keep my voice even, keep my emotions at bay.

She continues her determined stride to the front door, and I think she's going to ignore me until she suddenly stops. Her head barely turning to the side as the rest of her stays stone still. She says one word.

"Don't."

Paralyzed, I watch her go to the door and unlock it. Watch the only woman I've ever loved, lock the door on us.

I want to believe there's still a chance but it's not looking good. I just blew my second, no make that third chance.

Dragging my ass home, I drink till I pass out.

A vibrating in my pocket wakes me up the next afternoon, still in my clothes from the day before. I can't make out the name on the screen but in my gut, I know it's not Dana.

"What?" I groan in greeting, the percussion section in my head, making it impossible for me to have any manners.

"How bad is it?" Reed's voice shouts and I groan again.

"Not so loud," I mutter and the asshole laughs.

These are my friends, people. "Asshole."

He laughs again, and I swallow down the urge to vomit. Getting serious, Reed quiets. "Look, it sounds like you screwed up."

"What gave you that impression?"

"You're hungover and whining like a little bitch. You wouldn't have done that to yourself if you weren't trying to drink your own stupidity away."

He's not wrong, folks.

"Liv is pissed. Dana told her you two are over."

The spinning in my head stops instantly but my chest feels like I've been stabbed. My hand tries to rub away the pain as those two words repeat in my head.

We're over?

I knew it was bad, knew last night was probably the end, but some part of me hoped I could maybe fix it once Dana's anger ran its course. It's not the first time I've screwed things up with her and had to wait for her to come around and give me another chance.

"You don't think I can fix it?"

"I don't know. But if you love her you should try." He says and I silently nod my agreement. "And probably sober up first. Maybe take a shower." Reed jokes but I hear the truth in his words.

"Ok. I just need to throw up first."

Chapter Forty-Six

DANA

M itch has called me twice a day since standing me up on Saturday. It's been almost a week and he's left nine voicemails, sent countless texts apologizing, all asking me to call him back. I've been expecting him to show up at my house again, but so far, he hasn't. Good. I don't want to be held responsible for my actions if he does.

I'm angry. Angry at Mitch for what he said during our fight, angry at him for not coming over after we made up and beyond angry at him for not showing up for the wedding. But mostly, I'm angry at myself for thinking he'd be there. I said I wouldn't let him fool me twice and now it's happened three times.

I'm holding onto this anger tightly, reminding myself of it every time he calls. If I don't, the sadness over what we could have had, what we did have for one week, consumes me and I'm not crying over someone who doesn't give a shit about me.

Mitch and I are over. He's never going to change, never going to put me first in his life and I refuse to be a distant second place.

My phone rings again, breaking me out of my stewing.

"It better not be Mitch again," I mutter, reaching for it.

It's not and I tell myself that's a good thing even though deep down it doesn't feel like it.

"Hi, Mom. How was the cruise?" I ask, trying to sound upbeat.

"Hi, baby! It was great! Frank and I had a lovely time." She says in a happy yet relaxed way you only get from taking a long vacation. I kind of feel bad for the giant eye roll I can't control.

"Of course, Frank had a wonderful time." I snip and immediately regret it. I've never expressed my feelings on my mom's gentleman friends before but I'm in a shitty mood tonight and can't stop the words from coming out of my mouth.

"Dana Nicole. What is your problem with Frank? I know he's not your father, no man is, but he's a very nice man and he treats me well."

"Mom, I don't have a problem with Frank. I was just saying I'm sure he did have a wonderful time since you paid for it all."

"I didn't pay for all of it." She defends.

"But you paid for most of it, right?" I know she did.

She doesn't try to deny it. "Yes, I paid for most of it, but it was my idea. I wanted us to go on the cruise, so I paid for it, and he paid for the extras. What's wrong with that?"

I let out a sigh. "Since Dad died, you've dated a string of losers," I confess begrudgingly.

"Losers?"

"Men that could never take care of you financially." Why am I having to explain this to her? She's a well-educated, successful woman, she should know what a loser is.

Mom let's out a sigh that says way more than my pathetic little one ever could.

"Dana, Sweetheart. First of all, I've dated six men in the almost twenty years since your father passed. I'd hardly call that a string." Really, only six? It seemed like so many more than that. "And just because they didn't make as much money as me doesn't mean they were losers."

"But..." I try to interrupt but Mom talks over me.

"I don't need a man to take care of me financially. I didn't need that when your father was alive, and I haven't needed it since." That's true. My dad was the best father and husband ever, but he was the epitome of a starving artist. My mom never seemed to mind that his paintings didn't bring in much money and she was the one providing for us but I figured it was because she really loved him and wanted to support his dreams.

After Dad died and Mom started dating again, every man she introduced me to had some crappy job and seemed so beneath my mom, I never understood what she saw in any of them.

"Dana, I haven't dated men because of what they could buy me. I dated men I enjoyed being with, men that made me laugh and made me feel special, the way Frank does. I don't care what he does for a living as long as it makes him happy. It doesn't matter to me how much money Frank makes as long as he can pay his own bills."

"But Frank lives with you, in your house!"

Patiently, she sets me straight. "And he pays for all the utilities and other household bills. He also does the yard work and any repairs that are needed. He isn't just sponging off of me."

"Huh. I didn't realize that." I admit.

"No, you just assumed it," Mom says back and I feel a little guilty.

Changing the subject, I ask for details from the cruise but only half listen, wondering how I misunderstood my mom's relationships so badly and how that has shaped my opinion of a worthy mate.

Maybe I've been too focused on a man's career to see past it. Maybe I've been dating the wrong men the whole time. I can't blame Mitch for being a workaholic when his job demands that of him. If I want a man who will put me before his job,

I need to find one whose job isn't so demanding and won't interfere with our lives.

The kind of man I never would have dated before.

I can't bring myself to say before Mitch but that's not the point. We were never going to work out even if we did love each other. Not when his job is the most important thing in his life, and I want to be at the top of that list.

But there's someone else whose job probably isn't so important to him.

Frantically, I start digging in my purse then turn it over, dumping the contents on the table. Wallet, keys, makeup, breath mints all tumble out landing in a heap and on top of it all lands the thing I'm looking for.

A crumpled napkin with a phone number written on it.

My phone rings again and Liv's name is showing on the screen. I called her Sunday and told her Mitch and I were over and I wasn't ready to talk about it but obviously, I wasn't going to dinner at her house in case he showed up. She wasn't happy with him and said he better not show up. I haven't talked to her since then.

"I have to go, Mom. I love you." I tell her, then answer the other call. "Hi, Liv."

"Oh, good. You're not avoiding me anymore." She says sarcastically.

Guilt has me ducking my head. "I... needed some time."

"And since you answered, I guess you got the time you needed?"

"I worked through some things," I confirm.

"Are you ready to give Mitch another chance?"

Looking back at the napkin, I decide to take a plunge. "No. I'm going to call Scott."

There's a pause before Liv's confused voice replies. "Who?"

"Scott. You know. The waiter from the restaurant."

Nothing. No response. She's either shocked, pissed or completely confused. Maybe all three.

"The one that left his number on a napkin when we had dinner right after I moved here," I explain further.

"Oh, Scott!" Liv says as it dawns on her. "Really? He's a waiter." Her voice is quieter when she adds this, but I hear what she's really saying. He's not up to your standards.

"Yes, really. Maybe you're right and I shouldn't be so hung up on a man's job." I expect her to ask about Mitch, push for me to give him another chance, tell me to talk to him, but Liv surprises me.

"My little girl is growing up." She says with a fake sniff.

"Funny," I reply drily but Liv gets serious.

"I just want you to be happy. If you don't think you can be happy with Mitch... I understand."

Tears threaten to burst out, but I blink them away and set my shoulders back. "Thank you."

I want to tell her how much I appreciate her support even if it means I don't end up with the man she was hoping for, but I can't get the words out. After telling her goodbye, I decide to call Scott before I lose the nerve. Typing his number into my phone, I hesitate to push the call button.

It feels wrong to go out with someone else, but if Mitch isn't going to show up for me, doesn't think I'm worth being with, what else am I going to do?

Chapter Forty-Seven

DANA

A day later, I'm on my way home from dinner with Scott and seeking comfort from Liv once again.

"His uncle owns the restaurant, so you were right, it's a family business."

"See! He probably wants to do something else but feels like he has to work there." She says with more enthusiasm than necessary.

I know she's not completely on board with me dating other guys so quickly but after I told her what Mitch said during our fight and then he stood me up for the wedding a week later, she agreed maybe I should explore my options.

"He has a degree in psychology but said it was too depressing and quit. He's working at the restaurant until he figures out what he wants to do next." I inform her.

"And you thought he lacked ambition."

"That was ten years ago." I deliver with punchline efficiency.

"Oh." Her voice falters but comes back stronger. "So, Mitch..."

"No." I cut her off, then lighten my voice. "The valet was sending some pretty strong signals so we're having lunch tomorrow."

Liv is stunned silent for a moment. When she speaks, her voice sounds strange, and I hold back a laugh. "You're going out with a valet?"

"Yes, and who knows. Maybe a tow truck driver after that." I joke, referring to the night her car broke down and she met Reed. Man, I really was a job snob back then.

"Wait. You were on a date with Scott and accepted another date with the valet?"

I cringe a little thinking about how bad that sounds. "When you put it that way, I sound terrible, but the date was over, and we had already said it was nice but not happening again."

"He said that, or you did?" She questions.

"Both. We were waiting for our cars, and I thanked him for dinner and said it was nice to meet him and he said it was nice to meet such an intellectual woman. But he hesitated before he said it, like it wasn't a good thing, and he was trying not to hurt my feelings. So, when Mike came up with my car and asked if I wanted to go out, I said yes."

"And you don't think Mike will find you too intellectual?" It almost sounds like she's telling me I shouldn't have lowered my dating standards. Or that I didn't have this problem with Mitch.

Too bad, Mitch and I had other problems. Problems I'm trying to avoid with this new outlook on dating.

"I guess I'll find out tomorrow," I say with optimism I don't feel because Liv's right. I didn't have that problem with Mitch. We actually had a lot in common and talked about things most people don't care about. Mitch never made me feel like a history nerd or like I needed to dumb myself down to be interesting. He liked me the way I was, and we always had a great time together.

When he showed up. Bitchy Dana grumbles and the crushing weight of losing Mitch shifts into determination to find someone else who treats me better.

Liv makes me promise to text her when my lunch date with Mike the valet is over, but the next day, I wait until I'm back at my desk before sending her the details.

Me: The food was good. The conversation was ok if you like cars.

Liv: What do you mean "if you like cars"?

Me: He really likes cars. Kept telling me about all the luxury cars he's parked at the restaurant.

Liv: You're lying!

Me: I wish. He said he always wanted to be either a mechanic or car salesman so he could be around cars all day, but both required too much work, his words, so he decided to be a valet.

Me: Professionally

Liv: Wow

Me: Exactly. But I do have dinner plans with someone else.

Liv: Did you meet a tow truck driver?

Me: Funny and no. The barista at the coffee place by my house asked me out this morning. His name is Ben and he makes the best macchiato.

Liv: At least you know you'll get good coffee out of it.

Me: Unless the date is awful and I have to find a new coffee place.

Liv: Minor inconvenience

Me: You haven't had his coffee!

Liv: HAHA! Are we still talking about coffee?

Me: Yes, I don't joke about coffee

Liv: Call me when it's over. I'm proud of you.

Thinking back over my lunch date, I realize my mom was right. It doesn't matter what someone does for a living as long as they're happy and don't expect someone else to take care of them.

However.

I think you need to have similar goals or, at the very least, similar interests and I didn't have either with Scott or Mike.

You did with Mitch. Rational Dana whispers and I slap her away.

"Dinner will be better." I insist but later that night I have to admit maybe I should listen to Rational Dana more.

"You're calling early," Liv states when I call her on my way home.

"That's because when Ben let me in the coffee shop, he locked the door behind me then asked if I wanted to grind his beans," I say with only a hint of the disbelief I felt in that moment.

"He didn't." She says, stifling a laugh.

"He did."

"Maybe he was being literal."

"Definitely not. He was taking his shirt off at the time."

Her laughter is getting harder to hide now. "What did you do?"

"I told him no. And then he asked why I said yes to dinner. Like I knew he was really asking me to have sex in the coffee shop."

"What did you tell him?" Liv's not bothering to hide her laughter now. I'm so glad she finds my dating life humorous.

Indignantly, I answer her exactly the same way I answered Ben. "That I thought we were going to have dinner. Talk and get to know each other."

"And?"

"And he said that's not usually how it goes and started taking off his pants!"

"Please tell me it was in the storeroom." I can barely understand her through her laughter and shake my head, finally starting to see the humor in the situation.

"NO! Right there in the front where people start their day! Can you imagine how gross it would be to walk in and see some unsuspecting person having coffee and a scone at the table your bare ass cheeks were sitting on the night before?"

Liv's infectious laughter fills my car and soon has me laughing too.

"Hopefully, he sanitizes the place after his... dates." She says when the laughter dies down.

"Hopefully, but I'm still finding a new coffee place."

"Ok, well, maybe you weren't so off in dating men with certain... career qualifications. You seem to have more in common with them." She concedes.

"I've been thinking the same thing," I admit. "My date with Peter..."

"That guy from work?"

"Yeah. It was better, we had things to talk about but..." I trail off because I know once I say the next words, there's no going back.

"But he wasn't Mitch." Liv finishes for me.

That determination to find someone else splinters inside me, leaving me feeling raw. "He wasn't Mitch. And none of the guys this week have even come close." I agree without enthusiasm.

"And you ready to talk to him?" The hope in her voice is endearing and I love that about her, but I can't tell her what she wants to hear. Liv probably knew these other dates were going to be a bust and hoped they would send me running back to Mitch, but they haven't. All this week has shown me is I have awful, horrible taste in men and the only one my heart wants is the one who has the power to rip it to pieces.

The rawness inside turns into a deep ache and I can't deny the pain I've been suppressing anymore. "Liv, I can't. Please stop asking." My voice breaks on the last word and I punch the button to hang up the phone.

Liv calls me right back, but I ignore the call and do it again when she calls a third time. We don't usually hang up on each other, preferring to talk through everything even when we disagree but I can't talk about this right now. The pain rushing through me is too much, I grip the steering wheel hard trying to fight it off.

When I get home, I drag myself inside and hide from the world for the rest of the weekend. Monday comes too quickly and after eight long hours at work, I'm back in my favorite chair, a blanket and the History Channel keeping me company until Liv calls again. I've ignored her calls all weekend, I know I can't avoid her any longer.

"Hello."

"Well, it's about damn time. Open the door." Liv commands.

Open the door? What does that... Oh, shit. She's here. I can't let her see the mess I've turned into.

Like a fugitive, I frantically look around for a hiding place. Maybe if I'm really quiet, she'll think I'm still at work.

"Dana. I know you're home. Open the damn door." Her voice is in stereo, coming from my phone and the front porch. "I'm pregnant. You can't leave a pregnant lady on the porch!"

"Fine!" I stomp across my glossy hardwood floors, my footsteps pounding out a bass line of irritation.

Flinging the door open, I glare at my best friend who's smiling like she didn't just coerce her way into my house.

"Hey. How was work?" She says like it's just any other day. Sidestepping me, she drops her purse and phone on the floor and makes herself at home in my chair.

Without waiting for my answer, she gets down to business. "When are you going to talk to Mitch?"

"I'm not," I say firmly, going to the kitchen to get us each a drink. "Water?"

"Sure," Liv calls back and I grab a bottle for each of us.

Maybe I can change the subject. "So, when's your next doctor's appointment?"

"Next week. Don't try to change the subject."

Damn. "You can't blame me for trying," I say and we share a smile as I hand her a water.

Curling up in the corner of my couch, I drape a knitted blue blanket over me and take a sip of my water. Liv is unusually quiet, letting me stall, watching me with those teacher eyes that see everything. Minutes go by, neither of us talking, and the sadness I've been feeling since Mitch hurled hateful insults at me two weeks ago, bubbles over the surface.

"I really thought he was it. The man I've always been looking for." I admit softly, unsuccessfully blinking the tears back.

"What makes you think he isn't?" Liv asks.

When I shake my head and sniff, she goes on. "Just because he messed up doesn't mean he isn't the one."

"But his work is always going to be the most important thing to him. Never me. I want someone who will put me first, not continually blow me off so he can work."

The ache in my chest cracks with each word and by the end, silent tears are streaming down my cheeks. This isn't like the angry tears I shed last week after our fight. This is the sad acceptance that the man I love more than anything doesn't feel the same way about me.

Liv lets me cry for a few minutes then reaches over and grabs my hand. "Dana. It's time for some tough love."

"I don't want it," I say but I don't pull my hand away. I need the comfort she's providing.

"Too bad. You gave it to me and now I'm giving it to you."

I already feel betrayed. I don't know what she's about to say but I know it's something I don't want to hear. Something that's going to sound a lot like she's taking Mitch's side on this. She's my best friend, she should be taking my side, not his.

My hackles rise instantly.

"You are my best friend and I love you." Not how I thought this was going to go. "But you can be stubborn..."

"Kettle." I snort.

"...and pigheaded."

"That means the same thing."

"You tried to date other guys, guys you never would have given a chance before, and it didn't turn out so well."

"It was only a few dates," I mumble in my defense.

"It didn't work out because we both know you want to be with Mitch. You're in love with him."

I refuse to comment, and Liv leans closer to me. "Mitch isn't Chris. You can't treat him like he is."

"Didn't we have this same conversation about Reed?"

"Yes, we did. Now it's my turn. Mitch's job is important to him, and he has to work a lot of long hours but that doesn't mean he doesn't care about you or want to be with you."

"Just that I'm not important enough for him to actually be with." The level of sarcasm I obtain on that impresses me.

"You said he's new to being in a relationship or caring about someone other than himself, putting them first. But he's trying. Something Chris never did."

Rolling my eyes, I cross my arms defensively. She may have a point, Chris never tried.

"As long as Mitch has this job, he will always have to work more than forty hours a week. My husband's job is the same. I don't see him as much as I would like to but I understand and we make it work. If you want to make a relationship work with Mitch, you'll both need to compromise. He cuts back some hours and you understand when emergencies require him to work unexpectedly. Him having to work doesn't mean he doesn't love you."

She's making sense and I kind of hate her for it.

"You need to decide if you love him enough to compromise. If you don't, that's fine. It's your relationship and your heart that are on the line and I will totally support you. Of course, Sunday dinners will be awkward."

Swinging the throw pillow, I bump it against her head. Not hard! She's pregnant.

She hits me back with another pillow then gives me a hug. Since her work here is done, Liv leaves me to think over what she said.

Do I love him enough to compromise on this?
I don't know.

Chapter Forty-Eight

MITCH

I stopped calling Dana a few days ago after losing track of how many calls and texts I'd sent her. All unanswered.

Every day, I've wanted to go over to her house and beg her to talk to me, even going as far as driving down her street. But the look on her face Saturday night when she uttered the single word, 'Don't', kept me from stopping and getting out. It was a look of hardness. I could practically see her mentally preparing for battle. I don't want to fight with her.

I just want to apologize.

In a perfect world, after I apologize, she gives me another chance, but this is real life. Second, or third chances in this case, don't happen as often and you think.

We're over before we really began.

And it's all my fault.

I stopped looking every time my cell rings, it's never her, so when it starts vibrating in my pocket, I consider it annoying and keep on working. It stops momentarily and I'm relieved until it starts back up again.

It's not Dana, I know it's not, but someone wants to talk to me this morning, so I give in and pull the phone out of my pocket.

Liv.

Great. I really expected an ass chewing from her earlier in the week, I'm surprised she made it to Thursday.

Accepting my fate, I answer. "Hi, Liv."

"Oh, good. You answered. I thought I was going to have to leave a voicemail and by the time you listened to it, I would be in my next class, and we'd play phone tag all day."

She almost seems happy, and that confuses me. "Well, you got me. What's up?" I ask perplexed.

"Ok. I'm mad at you."

So, it is an ass chewing.

"But I'm also rooting for you, so listen up."

This catches my attention and I sit up straight in my chair. "I'm listening."

"You need to go over to Dana's house and apologize in person."

Defeat slumps my shoulders. "I did."

"You did?" She sounds surprised.

"Dana didn't tell you I was there when she got home from the wedding?"

"No. She didn't want to talk about it, just said you two were done. What happened? What did you say?"

"I didn't say anything. She didn't give me the chance to speak. She just said 'don't' and then went inside and closed the door."

"You didn't leave, did you?" She asks appalled and I hesitate to answer.

"Yes..."

"NO! That was the totally wrong thing to do." Liv yells and I jerk the phone back from my ear.

"So, what? I was just supposed to sit outside her house until she decided to talk to me? I could be out there for days. I would still be out there!" If that's what women want, no wonder men don't live up to their expectations. This isn't a romance novel.

"No, of course not."

"Then what Liv? What was I supposed to do? I'm all ears."

"If Dana was angry and refused to listen, then yes, give her a few hours or even a day so she can calm down. When she's calm, she's actually very reasonable and will be ready to work it out."

"It's been almost a week and she's not ready to work it out." I point out to Liv, but she shushes me like I'm one of her students.

"But, when she's upset, if you leave her alone too long all her insecurities come out. She thinks she's not important to you and you not sticking around and fighting for her just tells her that she's right. Leaving her house so quickly and not going back just feeds those insecurities."

Fuck, that makes sense. I'm such a dumbass, thinking giving her space would help in my fight to prove she's the most important thing in the world to me.

"You have to stay there and show her you're not going anywhere. You're NOT going anywhere, are you? Mitch, tell me right now if you don't want to be with her."

I don't hesitate now. "I'm in this for the long haul. She's it for me."

"Good. Don't mess it up again." Through the warning, I hear the smile in her voice. "Now, you have to go to her today and show her you're not going anywhere. Even if Dana says she doesn't want you there, she does, trust me. If she's refusing to let you in or says there's nothing to talk about, she's lying, you and her both know it. Remember when I told you to give her space but make sure she knew you were still interested in her?"

"Best advice I've ever received."

"You're welcome. Don't do that now. Make her talk to you."

That doesn't sound like very good advice. Maybe she just got lucky last time.

"I don't want to push too hard, make her do something she doesn't want to do. I won't hurt her more." I tell Liv. Hurting Dana is the last thing I want to do.

"She wants to talk it out. I wouldn't tell you to do this if I didn't truly believe it."

I stir that around then decide she must be right, she is Dana's best friend. Liv knows her better than anyone.

"Ok. I'll go now."

"Now! That's perfect! You're leaving work for her! See, you don't even need me anymore." She boasts like a proud parent.

"I don't know about that." I chuckle, already preparing to leave.

"Go. What are you waiting for? And don't forget the flowers!"

Now, that sounds like good advice.

I'm walking through my office door when my phone rings again. I automatically answer without looking thinking it's either Liv again or Reed. I have no doubt she's already called and filled him in.

"Hello," I answer, locking my door behind me.

"Mitchell." Shit. I never called my dad back after hanging up on him when the pipe busted in my bathroom. That was... a month ago, maybe. Not that unusual for us but I try to check in a little more often than that.

"Dad. I'm just leaving the office and I'm in a hurry. Can I call you back later?"

"You're leaving the office in the middle of the day?" He asks, incredulously. "What could be so damn important?"

The truth comes out before I decide to say it. "I meet someone, and I screwed it up. I need to fix it."

A barely audible huff comes through the line followed by a curse word I've only heard my father say once before when he found out one of his partners was embezzling from the company.

"I just had this conversation with your brothers. You need to stop letting women distract you. Your focus should be on your career not chasing women."

He just had this conversation with Mike and Max? I need to check in with them too and find out what that's all about.

"Everyone is losing their heads. First Thomas..."

I cut him off before he can really start the lecture. "Look, Dad. I know you don't agree but this is something I have to do. I love her. I'll call you back later and tell you all about her. But right now, I really have to go. Bye."

I hang up before he responds and step into the waiting elevator. I haven't talked to my dad about a girl since I was in high school when he agreed I could ask out Bethany Levy. The conversation later is going to be awkward as hell but hopefully, I'll have good news when I call him back.

Chapter Forty-Nine

DANA

"You ou want to go to lunch with us today?" Allison asks me from her cubicle next to mine.

"No thanks. I brought something." I tell her and pretend not to notice her disappointment. She should be happy I said no. I'm not very good company right now.

My fingers fumble and drop my favorite pen, causing it to roll off my desk and fall to the floor. Leaning over to pick it up, I hear the door open, and several people enter the paralegal bullpen. This isn't unusual but my pulse quickens with the feeling something is about to happen and I freeze with my hand reaching out for the pen.

The footsteps come closer, but my eyes stay on the pen an inch from my fingers until two male feet stop directly in front of me. The usually loud space hushes and a floral aroma swirls around me.

Slowly my eyes travel up the long legs in navy slacks to a matching jacket and white shirt. When I get to the blue striped tie my heart gives a hard thump and my hands start to shake, my pen forgotten.

I don't have to look any further to know who's standing in front of me, I think I knew it was him the moment he walked in. I just didn't believe he would actually show up at my job.

The significance of him being here hits me with such force, I feel a little lightheaded.

He left work for me.

Mitch has the most serious look on his face, the face I love and have missed so much it hurts but his being here has to be a good thing, right? He's holding flowers. You don't bring flowers to tell someone you never want to see them again.

Behind him a security guard and one of the receptionists, Becky, are watching me over Mitch's shoulder. Becky looks ready to jump up and down along with all the paralegal faces peering at us over the tops of their cubicles. Even Mr. Security has a smile on his face.

I guess it isn't every day someone shows up here with flowers and wants to personally deliver them. An incredibly romantic gesture.

"Dana."

His voice melts me a little more, but I stiffen my shoulders. It's going to take a lot more than a surprise visit and flowers to fix us. A huge apology and some groveling to start.

Compromise, Liv's voice says in my head.

"I know I messed up. I hurt you. And I'm sorry, that wasn't my intention." He swallows audibly then continues. "I love you, and I did a terrible job of showing you that you are the most important thing in the world to me. I'm not trying to excuse what I did, I just want you to know I've never had a reason to not put work first in my life. Never cared about someone else's happiness, until I met you."

A round of awwwws ring out around the open office space and I'm pretty sure a few sniffles are in there too.

"I know I told you that before but I'm new to this whole loving someone thing and I screwed up. To be honest, I'm probably going to screw up again, but I love you, Dana. I want to make this work. Can you be patient with me while I figure out how to be the man you deserve?"

Definite sniffles this time, I know because they're coming from me.

I want to throw my arms around him and tell him everything's ok, but is it? I have heard this from him before and his past actions didn't line up with his words.

But he left work for you. Rational Dana says again.

Does that change the fact he has a job that's always going to require so much of him? One that will always come before me. Am I ok with being second place in his life?

I look away from Mitch and gather my strength. This isn't going to be easy.

"I don't think it's a good idea for us to be together."

A chorus of gasps hit me, and I feel them like a blow. They can't believe I would turn down this sweet, gorgeous man, but they don't have all the details. Yes, this is the most romantic thing anyone has ever done for me, but it doesn't matter if he's just going to toss me aside again.

"You've said that before," Mitch says with a smile. Taking a step closer to me, he lowers his voice. "You were wrong then. And you're wrong now."

God, I want to be wrong. I really do but I don't think I am. Not this time, even if pushing him away hurts.

The emotion keeps me from speaking, my voice drowning in the tears I'm forcing back. I can only shake my head no and hope he understands. This is over for good.

We stare at one another, surrounded by my co-workers, a receptionist, a security guard and now the breakroom's coffee vendor and of all people, Peter. After a full minute, Mitch seems to come to a determination and nods his head.

"I'm not going to take any more of your time at work but that doesn't mean I'm giving up. I may be leaving right now but I'm not going away. I'm a patient and persistent man when I want something, Dana. And I want you."

He holds the bouquet out to me until I'm forced to take it, then he turns and walks away, all of us watching him go. As soon as the door closes behind him, I'm rushed with paralegals all giving their input.

"He brought you flowers!"

"Who is that man? He's hot!"

"No man has ever brought me flowers."

"What did he do?"

"He loves you!"

"That was so romantic."

"He said he's not giving up on you."

"Why are you just standing there? Go after him."

Why am I just standing here? I should go after him.

"Dana, are you ok?" Allison asks, laying her hand on my shoulder and it knocks me out of my stupor.

Thrusting the flowers in her hand, I snap my eyes to hers. "I have to go after him."

Applause and cheers urge my feet to go and by the time I reach the door, I'm running. There are only a few people in the hall but none of them is the person I'm after. My heels thump on the industrial carpet as I fly past everyone and burst through another door, into the reception area.

My entrance shocks everyone. Becky and her co-receptionist jump and cover their hearts with their hands. Mr. Security crouches to a defensive position, ready to spring into action.

And the only other person in the room spins around with wide eyes.

Mitch barely has time to blink before I throw myself into his arms, knowing this is where I'm supposed to be. He's squeezing me tight, either from shock or relief, but I don't care. The only thing that matters is he's not letting go.

"Does this mean you'll give me another chance?" He whispers into my hair.

Tears are destroying my makeup, his jacket and my ability to speak. I can only nod vigorously against him, but he understands. Slowly, leaning back, he gasps my face in both of his hands and looks straight into my tearful eyes.

"I love you, Dana. More than anything." He says with complete sincerity, and I take in a ragged breath. My heart feels so full, I think it might burst. I didn't know I could ever love someone this much. Have them love me back the same way.

Taking another breath, I force my voice to cooperate. "I love you, too.

Mitch wipes his thumbs over my cheeks then gives me the sweetest kiss. One I will remember forever. I drop my head back to his shoulder and let myself enjoy his arms around me for a few more seconds until we both need to get back to work.

He presses a kiss to my temple and I'm so damn happy I almost miss what he whispers in my ear.

"By the way, the President apologizes for making me miss the wedding."

DANA

Saturday mornings are my favorite time of the week. No matter how busy the rest of the week is, the late nights, missed lunches or dinners, Mitch is always with me Saturday morning.

I used to run because I needed to get out my anger. Eventually, running just became something I did to help me relax, but now, running next to Mitch is when I most feel loved.

He's gotten better about his long hours, only working on the weekend if it really is necessary. Late nights at the office still happen but now he limits them to only a few times a week. More than making me a priority, Mitch is making himself one too. Before he worked all the time, not giving himself the chance to really enjoy life and his stress level was crazy high even if he won't admit it. I love this man way too much to let him work himself into an early grave.

The sunshine on my face feels perfect and I take a slow deep breath, drawing in the essence of a late summer morning.

"Thinking about our vacation?"

"I wasn't but I am now," I tell him with a smile only the thought of beaches, cocktails and Mitch can bring. We're flying out in the morning and spending seven days in an undisclosed location he's keeping a secret until we get to the airport.

"Me too," Mitch adds, his voice taking on a suggestive quality.

Tossing him a flirty look over my shoulder, I laugh when I see his eyes. Yes, the man still runs a step behind me so he can look at my ass. I pretend to be irked by it, but secretly, I love that he's always checking me out.

This man is good for my ego.

"What do you want to do first when we get there?" I ask, trying to pry a clue out of him.

Mitch does miss a beat. "Get you naked."

"You get me naked all the time." I deadpan.

"It's never enough. I hope you only packed a bikini. You're not going to need anything else." He tells me, sounding like he's five seconds away from ripping my clothes off now.

My blood warms, my skin going hot, but not from the summer sun.

We're closing in on the halfway point but finishing this run is suddenly not important to me. "Let's turn around," I say, stopping.

Mitch almost runs into me and sidesteps quickly so he doesn't take us both to the ground. I expect him to jump right on board with my idea, so his behavior is odd when he looks off at the trail ahead of us. I can see the wheels turning in his head, but I don't know why.

Sliding his arm around me, Mitch turns me forward again. "Let's walk. Really take it all in and enjoy the morning."

He wants to take a walk instead of sex?

Yep, he's acting weird, but I go with it. "I did pack a dress," I say, going back to our previous conversation.

"Hmmm?" He makes a noise, but I can't tell if he's confused or distracted.

"For vacation. You said I only needed a bikini, but I packed a dress in case we go out to dinner or something." I also packed some new lingerie since it was such a big hit last time but that's my surprise for him.

Nodding and still looking ahead, he just says ok. Definitely weird.

We walk a little further, me watching the ducks on the water and Mitch looking pensive until he pulls me to the side of the trail and I look around. "What's wrong?"

Mitch's fingers graze my neck, his thumb slowly guiding my chin up until I meet his eyes.

"Dana, do you recognize this spot?" He asks quietly.

I glance around us again before answering. "Yeah, we run past it every weekend."

He fights back a smile. "This is where I saw you the first time on this trail. You were stretching against this tree." He tells me and the Saturday morning he's talking about fills my mind.

"Actually, I saw you the week before at the beginning of the trail, but you had your headphones in and didn't hear me calling out to you." He says lovingly, still stroking his thumb along my chin.

"You've never told me that before."

This time he lets his smile out. "I like to think of this as the spot where you and I started."

"We met at the diner when Liv invited me to lunch with you and Reed. And then there's that Sunday night dinner." I remind him. How could he forget that?

"I know." He says indulgently. "But this is where I realized I would do whatever it took to be with you. I just made a few mistakes along the way."

We both smile at his admission, glad that we made it through those early relationship pains to get where we are now.

Mitch takes a step back letting his hand fall away from me and I lean toward him, missing his touch already but his next movement stops me in my tracks.

He's fully down on one knee when he speaks again.

"Dana. I didn't know what I was in for when you ran into my life, but I was smart enough to know I couldn't let you get away. You understand me in a way no woman ever has, and you challenge me to be a better person not just for you but for myself too. You like the nerdy parts of me I always kept hidden and you make me slow down and enjoy life outside of my job."

This is happening, this is really happening!

"I didn't know I could love someone this much, love being with someone so much that I would put work aside just to spend more time with them but this past year, I find myself doing it more and more. You've shown me there's more to life than my career and I'm so damn thankful for that every day."

Tears are pooling in my eyes from the depth of this man's love for me. His words convey that love so profoundly; I would feel it from a hundred miles away.

"But this is just the beginning. If you say yes, I want to enjoy the rest of my life with you. Take more vacations. Have a few kids. Maybe make some history of our own."

The tears are flowing in earnest now and I'm helpless to stop them.

Mitch grabs my left hand and I blink fiercely, so I don't miss a second of this. I want to see the look on his face when he asks me those words and slides that sparkling diamond ring on my finger. This moment is just as much about him as it is about me.

I swipe my right hand across my face impatiently then our eyes lock again.

"Dana."

He stops and I wonder if it's nerves, but the wateriness of his next words gives him away.

"Will you marry me?"

"YES!" I shout, my arm jerking but he holds on and slides the ring onto my finger.

Flinging myself at him, we topple over into the dirt laughing. I kiss him hard, trying to show him a fraction of the overwhelmingly joyful emotion bursting to get out of me.

Mitch's arms hold me tightly to him and our kiss turns heated, neither of us noticing or caring that people are running past us on the trail. Just before it becomes indecent, he pulls back.

"I'm so damn glad you said yes. Now I get to run behind this delectable ass forever." He says with a hard smack.

"Well, let's go," I say standing and dusting myself off. "And Mitch, it really is a beautiful morning. Try to enjoy the view." I tease and run off but not before I hear his reply.

"Gorgeous, there is no better view."

Looking over my shoulder, I see I'm right. He's checking out my ass.

THE END

ABOUT AMY LONG

Amy Long, an avid reader since she was old enough to carry her own books in the library, is the author of romantic fiction and the much-anticipated children's series *Rosie Can Be ANYTHING!*

Not long after turning 40, she realized her constant daydreams were just stories waiting to get out and began working on her first book. A year later her first romance and children's books were published and there was no looking back.

A native Texan, Amy now lives in Las Vegas with her husband and two kids. When she doesn't have her nose in a book, she's either thinking up her next story or relaxing in the sun listening to music.

She believes you're never too old to discover your dream and go for it. Anything is possible.

You can connect with Amy at:

Instagram: @amylong_author

@rosiecanbeanything

To get the latest news on Amy's books, sign up for her newsletter at amylongauthor.com or rosiecanbeanything.com